New

By Charlotte Hòlt

They will still bear fruit in old age, they will stay fresh and green, Psalms 92:14 (NIV)

Table of Contents

Dedication

I would like to dedicate this book to all those who have suffered the heartache of divorce, also, to those who have lost a close friend or loved one to the horrific disease of cancer. I've suffered both. The first tore my heart apart but helped me to come to the saving knowledge of Jesus Christ and the power of His Holy Spirit to overcome life's heartaches. I know God hates to see divorce happen. This was not his perfect design for the family, but he can restore what the locust ate from a life touched by this trauma.

Acknowledgements

I would like to acknowledge all those who helped me with this story. It has gone through the eyes of two critique groups. The first group: Janice Thompson, Sharen Watson, and Nancy Williams. The second: Henry McLaughlin, Carol McClain, Linda Randeau, JoAnn Swearingen, Tom Tarver, and Mary Urban. Another friend and writer, JoAnn Hillman, also helped with the editing. I would like to thank all of you. Each of you contributed to my writing journey. Bless you!

CHAPTER ONE

Working Late

"I won't be home for dinner tonight. I need to work late on a case. I have no idea how long it'll take, so don't wait up."

"But…but, I have dinner all prepared." Laura couldn't say anything else for the lump in her throat. She blinked and swallowed hard in order to hold back her tears of disappointment. Didn't he realize how much his not coming home again tonight would hurt her?

"Sorry, he continued. James and I will need to work through dinner. I'll grab something on the run. See you later." The phone clicked, and Laura heard only the dial tone buzzing in her ear. No goodbye. No I love you.

She eyed the two plates on the table. The Old Country Rose pattern she loved had lost its glitter. The fine china seemed to mock her as she returned one place setting to the hutch. What good did it do to have such treasures if they never used them? Might as well clear the table. When she picked up the coffee cups, she wanted to throw them across the room, but thought better of it. Frank had spoiled the surprise. The special meal no longer looked appetizing. Should she put the roast in a Corning ware dish or dump it in the trash? Maybe Betty and Jim could come eat with her. She glanced toward the grandfather clock. Seven. No. They would have eaten already.

Frank's all too familiar words made her hands tremble and a flush of heat filled her checks. She'd heard the "I won't be home for dinner" phrase numerous times over the years, but the frequency in the past few months let her know something wasn't quite right.

The ticking of the clock amplified by the quiet, empty room reminded her of the emptiness of her heart. Since her daughter left for Harvard and Frank stayed away from home more often, the big house rattled like a diamondback on a hot summer day.

The aroma of the roast curled around her nostrils and sent another wave of mixed emotions through her. The dish would soon be dried out and tough to swallow, kind of like her marriage.

She shuddered and stared at the phone, the instrument Frank used to upset her secure world. She hung her head, released a huge sigh, and slumped over the table. Her head rested on her folded arms. Their relationship might not recover this time. Still, she wouldn't admit defeat or think about divorce – a word and concept foreign to her very existence. Suddenly determined not to give up on Frank and their marriage, She lifted her head and straightened her shoulders. She'd win him back somehow.

In her heart, she knew he'd been unfaithful more than once over the past thirty-two years. But she never found proof. The late nights, excuses, lies, and phone calls gave her plenty of signs. This time she'd find out for sure.

Laura rose to her feet in the middle of the kitchen and gripped the handset so hard her knuckles looked white. Should she throw the receiver across the room or slam it back down on the charger?

Taking long slow breaths to release her pent up anger, Laura struggled to get a hold of her emotions. She pressed down hard on the end button. When she calmed, she reached over to put the phone back on its cradle with care. *Tomorrow is another day.*

Should I confront Frank? What about Christina? She adores him. Tears sprang to her eyes, and a chill tingled her spine at the thought of hurting their daughter. Family breakups caused too much pain. She'd seen the devastation left when some of her friends experienced the trauma.

I don't believe in divorce. Not one person in my family ever divorced. The Bible speaks against it. She paced the floor as she thought of all the reasons divorce couldn't happen to her.

Grabbing one of her everyday dishes from the cupboard, she plopped the plate on the kitchen table. She fell into the chair and sat still for a few moments, closed her eyes, and prayed. "Lord, let Frank come to his senses, or let me be wrong about my suspicions."

All those times he told her how he hated what his own father did to his mother when he walked out on her. Frank never forgave him. He described his father as always wanting his own way, having little regard for women, demanding, selfish…the list went on.

"I never want to be like my father," he often said.

In several ways he resembled what he deplored. *I feel sorry for him, not having a better example to follow.* Her emotions vacillated between sympathy and anger. The lump in her throat made her swallow hard. One minute, she choked up thinking of his sad relationship with his father. The next, her heart pounded, her checks flushed, and she clinched her fist in frustration. Why couldn't he see the truth?

The pungent smell of the roast made her aware of hunger pains in her stomach. The few steps to the oven to remove the hot bread seemed like a long journey. When she lowered the door, memories of the many times she'd done so captured her thoughts. She eyed the hot pad, the one she'd bought on vacation in Pennsylvania, on the kitchen island and carried the bread there.

The Amish design brought memories of the special time they shared together. Frank liked to watch the Amish plow their fields. They'd toured one of the model homes and gleaned information about the simple life of the people, and the reasons behind the way they lived. In some ways, she envied their lifestyle. Then, Frank had even looked at quilts with her and helped her choose one for the guestroom. The trip afforded them some quality time together. Something she missed of late. The sweet time together made her smile for a moment, but the reality of the situation wiped the merriment away.

Laura brought her plate over and scooped up a small portion of the roast, a few potatoes, and three baby carrots. On her way back to the table, she admired the appetizing presentation of her meal. With fork and knife she sliced off a piece of the roast and brought it to her mouth. As she chewed, the food tasted like sawdust rather than her usual succulent dish. She ate a few bites of the vegetables and then dumped the rest into the disposal. The smell of pot roast ordinarily made her hungry. But, not tonight.

Cleaning up the kitchen in a stupor, she mindlessly put the leftovers in the refrigerator in case Frank changed his mind, came home earlier than expected, and wanted something to eat when he arrived. *He can just starve*. She flushed at her own thoughts but found some satisfaction in wanting to hurt him as he had her. Then she lowered her head to pray. “Lord, help Frank to change and become less like his father. Help him come to his senses and not walk out on his family – on me.”

CHAPTER TWO

Fear of the Unknown

Tears clouded her eyes and loneliness set in as she thought again of Christina. The sheer misery nothing new, since Christina's departure from their home in Humble to attend law school in Massachusetts. With her daughter so far away, her life felt empty. The phone made her happy when they talked for hours, but not like having her daughter around. Her smile, her ambition, her drive, the two of them shopping together, especially antiquing – so many things Laura remembered.

I'll give her a call. Walking to her recliner, she sat down, and picked up the receiver on the end table beside her. Then, Laura remembered. *Christina goes to the library on Monday evenings.* The Grandfather clock chimed and bonged out the hour of eight. *She should be home by now.*

As she punched in the numbers, a wave of gladness washed over her. Talking with her daughter always made her heart lighter, but she couldn't let her problems come through in their conversation. She had to protect Christina at all cost.

When Christina came home for a visit, her presence filled the void that lay between Laura and Frank. In her absence, Laura rambled around the empty house with its vacant rattles. And for some time now, even when Frank came home, communication lagged, or was nonexistent. Christina gave them something in common. Without her, they lived in this huge five-bedroom house like complete strangers.

On the third ring, a voice not Christina's answered.

"Is Christina there?" Laura thought she had dialed a wrong number.

"No, she hasn't come back to her apartment.

"This is her mother, Laura."

"I've been waiting for her. I'm Jennifer. We were supposed to go to the library together this evening to work on a joint class assignment. She told me to come on in, but she's over two hours late."

"That doesn't sound like Christina." Laura never knew Christina to run two hours late.

"Maybe we got our wires crossed. She may have gone on to the library and is waiting for me." The hitch in Jennifer's voice heightened Laura's anxiety.

"Please have her call me once you locate her."

"Yes, I'll see if I can find her, and I'll tell her to call."

Laura hung up the phone. Anxious thoughts assaulted her mind. Her back tensed. Something bad could have happened. The rhythm of Laura's heart increased and several scenarios flashed before her. *I would die if something happened to my Christina.*

Laura drifted her images elsewhere, anything to keep from thinking about her offspring and husband. Placing the herbal teacup in the Keurig coffee pot, she surveyed the kitchen while it brewed. Looking around, she realized how much she loved the granite countertops, mid-island, and numerous cabinets to store almost anything. Most of the time, she took pride in organizing the insides, but lately things got piled in any old way. The green paint made her smile because she saw no chips or dirty spots. The cheerful paisley green and burgundy border still caught her eye.

Laura contemplated running next door to her neighbor's to chat, but held back. She didn't want to interrupt Betty and Jim on a whim. Jim didn't feel good in recent days, and Laura knew how much they liked their time together alone. The doctors hadn't yet given them a diagnosis, but Betty expected news tomorrow. And Laura didn't want to miss Christina's call.

She set her cup of herbal tea next to her recliner then sat down and turned on the television, but none of the programs interested her. She flipped through the channels stopping at numerous movies, all of which seemed familiar.

Pressing the power button on the remote, the television went black. Walking over to her desk, she took out her Bible study. The lesson for the week caught her interest. Soon, engrossed in the Word, she forgot her troubles and found comfort there. The Word of God affected her in this manner. The familiar passages she knew by heart, brought new insights and a sense of accomplishment washed over her.

The phone jingled, pulling her from the lesson. Laura quickly closed the book and grabbed the phone. *Was it Christina?* She pulled in a deep breath.

When Christina's voice rang across the line, Laura exhaled a huge sigh.

"Hi, Mom."

"Sweetheart, are you okay? What happened? Your friend Jennifer said you were two hours late." Laura sat on the edge of her recliner as she waited for her daughter's answer.

"Oh, we just had a mix up. I thought we were meeting at the library, and she thought my apartment."

"Whew, you sure gave me a start. I was worried about you."

"Mom, you worry too much. I'm a big girl now." Christina's warm laugh let Laura know she was okay, and her statement told her she could take care of herself. Yet, Laura suspected she felt a little pleased about her mother's concern.

Laura laid the Bible down and shifted into a comfortable position in her recliner, pleased by the sound of her daughter's voice.

"I'm just fine. How are you and Dad doing?"

"Well, your father's working late tonight, and I'm doing my Bible study. Wish you were here to help me eat this roast." Christina loved her pot roast, and Laura hated to stow the dish in the refrigerator only to throw out later.

"You could mail me some." Christina laughed.

Laura giggled at her remark and thought of how much she would like to see her daughter.

"I think I better stick to brownies or cookies in the mail." Laura shifted the phone to her other ear and pulled the lever on the side of her chair to lean back.

"Does Dad have a new client? Seems he's

working late a lot."

The tone of Christina's voice told Laura her Dad's constant late hours puzzled her, too. *Does she suspect something?* Laura wished she could confide in someone but knew her daughter shouldn't be that one. She didn't want her to worry. Nor, did she want to plant suspicion in her mind.

"He must have. Said he had to work late at the office on a case. Are you sure you want to be a lawyer?" Laura laughed and tried to keep her comments light and humorous.

"Well, it's a little late to back out now. I have just over a year to go. Anyway, Mom, I can't think of anything I want more. Guess it's just in my blood - like Dad."

"How are your classes going?" Laura changed the subject. She didn't want to disclose her fears, not to her daughter, or even think about them for that matter. The thought of Frank being unfaithful wrenched her insides into knots.

"Hey, I made a perfect score on my last test. My classes are great. I'm keeping my nose to the grind. I want to keep my 4.0 average."

"That's wonderful, honey. I'm so proud of you."

Laura took pride in her daughter's accomplishments, but wished Christina would find more time for a social life as well as her studies. She didn't think it too healthy to be interested in only her classes. She drove herself to stay on the task at hand. Maybe that was the situation with Frank. At least in his case, she hoped so.

Christina finally piped up, "Mom, I hate to go, but I've got to hit the books."

"Goodnight, sweetheart. I'll talk to you in a few days."

"Night, Mom."

Laura pushed the end button, slowly this time. Then, placed the receiver back on its cradle.

Her train of thought took her to other places rather than back to her study. She reminisced about some of her and Frank's earlier years when they first fell in love. The lump in her throat thickened and her eyes moistened as she compared then to now. She shook off the memories, walked to her bathroom, and ran water into her Jacuzzi. She relaxed in the tub and enjoyed the calming effect of the water over her body. As much as she tried to think on other things, her mind kept wandering back. Finally, she dried off and dressed for bed.

Between the lavender scented sheets of the bed

she shared with her husband…or used to, her mind wondered how long it had been since they crawled in together, giggling, shushing each other so as not to wake Christina. She clicked the switch on the bedside lamp and spent the next few minutes staring up at the painted ceiling. Frank let her chose the light blue color when they bought the house. Laura liked it because it reminded her of the sky on a summer's day. Frank couldn't understand her decision, calling her irresponsible and frivolous. The unusual color would make selling the house difficult when his job took off, and they could afford to move to a more affluent neighborhood. Did he prefer someone with taste more like his own? Had he found someone without her whimsical sentimentality? Had he found someone prettier or more attentive? Laura flipped onto her side and shoved her pillow up higher.

Was Frank really at the office working? She wondered why his workload increased so much lately. Why hadn't he made love to her for several months now? There surely must be someone else. Did she dare find out?

Laura wished he would talk to her. Lately when she tried to ask him anything about his work, or the office, he cut her off. He read the paper, watched the news or sports on television, got ready to leave, or headed out the door. He completely shut her out of his life.

Had she been too busy with work, ministry, and seeing to Christina's needs to take care of Frank's? She patted her bulging abdomen. The weight she gained made her feel unattractive. Were the girls at his office more appealing? She tried to be a good wife and mother. Where had she gone wrong? Laura struggled with the answers to her questions. She felt at fault if Frank had someone else – at least in part.

How long had it been since they attended church together? She tried to remember. For a time, Frank gave one excuse or another for not going. Usually it related to work, or the fact he needed to rest from working so hard. Finally, she quit inviting him. She dressed and went alone while he slept in. Choir practice didn't help the situation. She left early, so he opted to stay at home rather than come later. But she loved the choir, and didn't want to drop out on the chance he might attend church.

Tears pooled in the corner of Laura's eyes. She remembered how she would watch for him, but the past few months, she never expected him. Once in awhile, just to throw her off guard, and she supposed for appearances sake, he would walk in as if it were the most natural thing. As of late, even those rare visits stopped.

Soon people quit asking about him. No one looked for him anymore, at least not on a regular basis, and Laura felt secretly glad. She no longer felt obligated to make excuses for him.

Laura flopped from one side of the bed to the other. She tossed and turned as she thought on these things. Each time the clock gonged another hour, her eyes popped open and she stared at it, only to discover Frank's spot in the bed still empty. Finally, she drifted off, and after three she heard no more until morning.

Her eyes flew open, and she examined the other side of the bed. She could tell no one slept beside her the entire night. The sheets lay smooth, flat, but she did smell the aroma of coffee coming from the kitchen. So, he must have come home some time after three and spent the remainder of the sleeping hours in the extra bedroom.

Laura plodded to the bathroom, washed up, brushed her teeth and hair, and pulled on her robe. She walked to the kitchen and found Frank at the table reading the newspaper and drinking a cup of coffee. His empty cereal bowl sat in front of him. He didn't bother to look in her direction when she entered the room but continued to read the sports section. She felt invisible.

She stumbled to the coffeepot and poured herself a cup. Still, not a word.

"What time did you get home?" she asked, lifting the cup to take a sip of steaming coffee. She stood next to the pot and leaned against the counter.

Frank turned the page without missing a beat. "I'm not sure. It was late. Didn't want to disturb you, so I slept in the guestroom."

Laura stumbled to the table and sat down beside Frank and started again. "Well, how did you come out on your case? Did you get much work done?"

"Umm, oh yes, it's coming along just fine." He shuffled his newspaper, folding it back together and then stood to his feet. "I'm off. Have a busy day in court."

Frank picked up his dishes, placed them in the sink, grabbed his briefcase and car keys, and walked out the door.

He never even gave me a chance to tell him about Christina's call.

Laura sat at the kitchen table with tears streaming down her cheeks. *What type of life do we have? There isn't any 'we' anymore, only two strangers living under the same roof, at least drinking the same coffee…but not sharing our lives. What should I do?*

CHAPTER THREE

A Friend in Need

I've got to stop dwelling on this misery. Laura lowered her head and prayed. "Lord, please help and guide me." She sat at the table and ate her usual cereal, blueberries, and half a banana. The satisfying taste filled the hole in her stomach.

When she finished in the kitchen, she walked to her desk and picked up her daily devotional. She sat down at her desk and began to read. The message cheered her up. The Bible verses encouraged her. Her time with the Lord in prayer lifted her spirits. Then, she dressed, and made her way to help in the area ministry's donation store. Her mind cluttered with so many things. Today she would only work until noon and then join Jim and Betty at Luby's. There they would share the news – good or bad – of the test results they'd received from the doctors that morning. She slammed on the brakes. Her hands shook to think she'd almost gone through the red light without even noticing.

Laura prayed for Jim to get a good report, but she felt uneasy. *Sometimes, you just know when something's wrong. Jim hasn't looked well for some time now.* She paused several times during the morning to pray for both her friends.

For fifteen years they'd shared their lives, living right next door. Together they'd watched Humble grow from a small town to a thriving city in its own right. She remembered the few eating-places – The Palace, the Queen drive-in, and Princess House during earlier days. Now, on every corner, several food choices awaited them, and they no longer depended on going into Houston to eat out or shop.

Frank and Christina used to be included in their activities, but lately it became more of a threesome. Jim and Betty were by far Laura's best friends. She remembered a time when she counted Frank as her best friend. The muscles in her jaw clenched at she thought of him. Annoyed by the tension this brought, Laura fumbled through her handbag for her keys. She took a deep breath and climbed into her car to meet with her Jim and Betty.

She backed out of the parking lot and sped to the restaurant. Her coworker had not arrived on time, which made her run late. She hated to keep Jim and Betty waiting. Jim didn't need to be out and about any longer than necessary.

***

They waited in line about midway when she arrived. She waved. The cheery greeting she mustarded up made her feel better.

“Come on up here.” They motioned for her to join them.

She cut her eyes around at the other patrons in front of her. They invited her to move ahead. Relieved by their reactions, she walked forward to her friends’ side.

Jim and Betty smiled at her, but she could tell by the looks on their faces things weren’t good. Her instincts told her the report would not be favorable. She hugged each of them. They continued down serving line and made their choices for the meal. Betty and Jim ordered only soup, so she decided to eat light as well. *I sure need to watch my calories so soup sounds good to me*. She chose the soup of the day – vegetable, and set it on her tray alongside a diet coke.

“Let’s sit by the window,” Betty suggested. “We might see some of our friends pass by.”

“Okay.” Laura placed her plate opposite Betty.

Jim, not saying a word, set his tray next to his wife and unloaded his sparse picks. He appeared in deep thought.

"Sorry, I was late. Hope you didn't have to wait long. The next volunteer didn't make it on time, and I got tied up with a customer." Laura took their trays and placed them on the nearby stand.

"We just arrived ourselves. It took a little longer at the doctor's than we anticipated, but then it usually does." Betty made a sour face and laughed. Her usual humor didn't come across. Laura sensed something wrong. Betty's forced laughter and shaking hands gave Laura further indication of a problem.

Betty glanced her way and then bowed her head. "Would you bless our meal, Laura?"

Laura kept her prayer short, anxious to hear the report.

Jim took a taste of his soup, still without a word. Finally, he laid his spoon down beside his bowl. "Laura, Betty and I need to share the news with you. I wish I could say it's good."

"What…what is it?"

For once, Betty let Jim do the talking. For once, she seemed tongue-tied. For once, there were no words coming out of her mouth. But a few tears etched down her face.

"The doctors say I have terminal cancer.

Apparently, it started in my prostate and it's gone throughout my body."

He reached for Betty's hand, and her hand met his. Her shaking fingers intertwined with his, and both of them sat motionless for a time.

"If they'd caught it early, there might be something they could do, but it's in stage four. It's already in my lymph nodes." He paused and gave a resigned shrug.

Laura sat in total shock, her mouth wide open. She regained her composure and looked over at Betty. "You mean there are no treatments available?"

"No, they tell us it's too late." Betty shook her head for emphasis, and Laura noticed her tears flowed freely now.

"We'll get a second opinion and we'll pray," Laura offered.

"Oh, yes, we plan to do both." Betty wiped the tears away.

"We have an appointment to see the oncologist at M.D. Anderson on Thursday." Jim lifted his glass to take a sip of tea. His hands shook, and Laura knew his strength waned.

They ate while they talked intermittently.

However, the conversation lacked their usual chatter.

"You best get home for a rest. It's been a long day for the both of you." Laura looked from one to the other. She touched each of them gently on the hand. Concern overwhelmed her. She reached over and took the bill lying on the table. "Let me pick up the check and the two of you just run along." She knew if they stayed much longer, she would break down and cry right here in front of everyone. She needed to keep strong for their sake.

"No, I won't let you pay our bill." Jim stuck out his hand in an effort to take the paper from her. Betty nodded in agreement with Jim's statement. Laura held on tight and would not relinquish the tab.

"Pay me later then and go on along." Laura shooed them toward the door.

"Here take this twenty and just bring me the change." Jim handed her the money. She could tell he meant business. Rather than add to his troubles, she took the bill he offered.

Laura waited in line for several minutes after Jim and Betty left the cafeteria. Paying for a meal at peak lunchtime took just as long as ordering. She stood in a stunned stupor as the knowledge of what Jim and Betty told her sank in. She let a few tears fall but refused to completely lose control. She grabbed a Kleenex from her purse and wiped them away.

Laura paid the cashier, pushed her billfold inside her bag, and then walked toward the exit. With her peripheral vision she caught a glimpse of Frank and his secretary. They laughed and talked while they waited in line to be served. Her hands shook and her heart started to pound. She wanted to run, hide, and cry about everything. She couldn't bear the thought of a confrontation with anyone at this point. She exited the restaurant before they spotted her. *I don't think they're looking at anyone except each other.* Frank looked as though he could gobble up his secretary, and she appeared to think of him as her dessert. Their eyes glued on each other. They barely glanced at the food in front of them.

Laura stumbled to her car still in a daze, but anger started to rise. *How dare Frank publicly make such a fool of himself and me?* She climbed in and drove toward home. Her mind raced in several directions at once. She thought of the situation with her friends. Then her mind bounced back to her issues with Frank. W*hat's going on with him?* He never laughed or talked with her anymore. It had been months, maybe a year. Yet, there he stood having a grand time in the restaurant with his secretary, who looked half his age, and only a little older than their daughter. *I've heard of this happening to men in midlife, but Frank should be well past that by now.* She shifted in her seat and held the steering wheel tighter.

What should I do? Should I confront him? Should I have made a scene?

Laura pushed the thoughts aside. Frank would get angry and say, "it's only business. She supposed he and his secretary had to eat. She didn't notice the stoplight until the last second and screeched to a halt. She looked around to secure her surroundings. She put her flown belongings back on the passenger seat. Her worries distracted her, and she vowed to be more careful.

Why were they alone and no one else from the office with them? Their total absorption in each other clued her in to the real truth.

Just the same, she didn't want to believe the obvious. Sometimes her imagination worked overtime. Wasn't there a Scripture verse about vain imaginations … to cast them down? Besides, right now, Betty and Jim needed her.

CHAPTER FOUR

Does Life Go On?

Laura arrived at Jim and Betty's. Her fears and anxiety had abated to some degree, but her hands shook and her mind wandered. Jim slept. Betty waved her into the kitchen and they sat down at the table, their usual visiting place.

"How 'bout a cup of decaf?" Betty took two mugs out of the cabinet, showing she anticipated Laura's affirmative answer.

"I'd love a cup." Laura reached to take the steaming coffee from Betty's hand and sat it on the table in front of her.

"I baked cookies yesterday, would you like some for dessert?" Betty held the plate in front of Laura.

"I better pass. I know they're great. I love your cookies, but I'm trying to watch my waistline lately." Laura brought the cup to her lips and felt the heat of the piping hot coffee. She decided to let it cool a smidge, and set it back on the table.

"Then, I'll pass on the cookies too. Don't want to tempt you." Betty placed the cookies out of reach on the far side of the cabinet.

"Thanks. You're more than a friend to refrain for my sake." Laura touched Betty's hand, then placed hers on top and just held it for a few moments.

"What will I do without him?" Betty's question hung in the air between them.

At last, Laura swallowed the lump in her throat and managed a reply. "We'll call the prayer chain along with every Christian we know and ask them to pray. Let's keep the faith. We'll wait and see what the other doctors say. Would you like me to call the prayer partners now?" Laura pushed her chair back and rose to her feet. Before she could stand enough to move away, Betty waved her back down.

"Let's talk for a while and then you can call." Betty looked at Laura as if studying her. "Tell me what's bothering you besides my Jim." Now, Betty took her hand and held it tight. Then, she patted and rubbed it as if to sooth her.

Laura lowered her eyes to her coffee cup, squeezed Betty's hand, and then, looked back up at her. "I can't seem to hide anything from you."

"Nope, nothing at all. We've been friends too long. It's as if we read each other's mind. However, I think it's the Holy Spirit. People would think we're old married folk." Betty laughed, but Laura knew it was a hard laugh to come by.

"That's true." Laura sighed as she set her cup down on the newly refinished oak table. "It's the same old thing. Frank not coming in until the wee hours, saying he's working. We never talk. I try, but he avoids me. I saw him a few minutes ago at the restaurant, talking with his secretary. Laughing, having a good time." Laura's chin quivered as she fought back tears.

"Have you confronted him about any of this?" Betty lowered her cup from her lips and banged it on the table. She sloshed the coffee, almost spilling it when it hit the flat surface.

Laura jumped slightly when the cup hit in front of her. "I don't have proof anything is going on. What if I'm wrong? I'll feel like a fool."

"Well, you know something's wrong if he never talks to you, or makes love to you." Betty looked into Laura's eyes, and challenged her for an answer.

"I know." Laura hung her head. Her throat grew dry and she couldn't answer any further. The shame of rejection took hold of her insides, and she felt her cheeks grow warm and flushed. The butterflies in her stomach made her nauseous.

"Why don't you make a special dinner for him? Get him to commit first that he'll be there on a particular night. See if you can stir some of the old vibes again. It would be worth a try." Betty squeezed Laura's hand once more.

"I need to try something. I can't go on much longer. This is no kind of life for anyone." Laura studied her friend's tender face. *Here she's going through the most terrible time of her own life and there she sits trying to help me.*

Betty shook her head. "No, it isn't. So let's make a plan."

"What sort of plan?" Laura lifted her brows and tried to puzzle out what Betty had on her mind.

"What's Frank's favorite meal?" Betty looked in deep thought. Laura could almost see the wheels turning in her mind.

"Let me think…Cornish hens, wild rice, asparagus, and my broccoli romaine salad with strawberry shortcake for dessert. Why?" Laura spieled out his favorite menu without thinking twice. Unlike most men, he ate light. He watched his weight and avoided gaining an ounce.

"Okay, set a night with him when he can come home early for dinner. Don't take a maybe. Get a definite commitment. Make it soon. Like tomorrow or the day after. Then cook all his favorite food, like you've described. Use the good china, candles, the whole shebang – know what I mean?" Betty pointed her finger at Laura and held a smug look on her face. Then she added, "The way to a man's heart is through his stomach." She rubbed her own tummy for emphasis.

"Yes, I know. But what do I do with my left over roast from last night?" It seemed such a silly concern. Laura blushed with embarrassment. "Would you and Jim be interested?"

"You bet we would. We love your roast, and I haven't felt much like cooking lately. Those cookies were about all I could muster. With Jim so sick I can't get my mind on cooking. I know I shouldn't worry. I should just trust the Lord." Betty grabbed a napkin and dabbed at her eyes to stop the tears, but once again they coursed down her cheeks.

"I understand. It's hard to give our loved ones to the Lord, especially when we want to make everything right. You and I like to fix things, Betty, but we need to let Jesus fix our problems in whatever way He sees fit.

We must remember – He knows the whole picture. We only know in part." Laura came around the table and held Betty in her arms. She wanted to comfort and convince her friend of God's sovereignty, as well as herself.

"I know you're so right. I must let Jim go. You must do the same for Frank. However, we will try and do the part God has for us. For now, I must pray, take the best care I can of Jim, get him to the doctors, and remember God is sovereign." Betty looked determined to do all those things.

"And I must pray, try whatever I can to put my marriage back on the right track, fix my husband his favorite meal, and give him an enjoyable evening."

Betty nodded her head in agreement as Laura spoke her mind.

Encouraged by the idea, Laura gave Betty's shoulder a pat. "Whatever I can do to help, I'll be there for you."

"The same here. I will even get rid of your leftovers for you. I love helping you make your plans. Let me know if you need anything. Do you have plenty of candles?" Betty giggled and poured them another cup of coffee.

When they finished planning, Laura offered to

call the prayer chain. Betty gave her permission. Laura feared her friend might break down if she made the call in front of her. She walked into the den picked up the phone and dialed the number. A ball formed in her own throat as she told the prayer chain coordinator about Jim's diagnosis. She fought the forming tears and restrained herself from breaking down. She wanted Thelma to understand her message without blubbering.

"I hear Jim stirring." Betty walked toward the bedroom.

"While you're looking in on him, I'll run get the roast for your dinner tonight."

Laura started toward the door. "Okay. Thanks a million." Betty opened the bedroom door as Laura walked out the back.

Laura trudged to her house. The answering machine next to the refrigerator blinked as she entered. She punched the button to listen to the message before completing her other task. Frank's voice echoed from the device.

"Don't expect me for dinner tonight. I need to work on some last minute details for my court case tomorrow. Don't wait up. I'll just use the other bedroom." Click. Again. No "goodbye." Not even an "I love you."

Laura leaned against the counter. Tears burned her eyelids.

Oh, Frank we've had our rough times but we've never before had separate bedrooms. In the morning, I'll plan our special dinner and see if I can't rectify that situation tomorrow night, or the next.

She reached for a notepad and started a grocery list. Casey's received fresh produce every Tuesday. This would be a good evening to visit the store and pick up the things she needed for the dinner party.

She walked to the refrigerator, took out the roast, grabbed her list and made her way to Betty's. She tapped on the door and Betty yelled, "Come on in, Laura."

"You guys enjoy this." She handed Betty the roast, and watched her set it on the counter. "I'm on my way to the grocery store to get what I need for the special dinner. I think the sooner the better. Frank called and left a message he would be late again tonight."

"Good girl. Go for it, and don't forget the candles." Betty encouraged her with an enthusiastic thumbs-up.

"Okay. Bye now. See you later. Call me if you need me for anything."

Laura hurried to the store with Betty's words of encouragement drumming in her head.

"Life must go on." She repeated the words she'd heard many times as they rang in her ears and an invisible tape played over and over in her mind and spirit. *Must it?* She and Betty would do everything in their power to try and see that it did.

CHAPTER FIVE

The Meeting

Laura consulted her grocery list. Shopping carts and children crammed the cereal aisle. She skipped it and went to the frozen section to pick up a cartoon of Cool Whip. Halfway down, she spotted a gentleman, probably in his sixties, surveying the meat counter. Though they had never met, she noticed him in the store on several occasions. He was a regular. No one ever accompanied him. Was he a bachelor?

She looked at all the food in his basket. Not one frozen dinner, only meal ingredients. She would wager he knew how to maneuver around the kitchen. He represented a puzzle to her. A man who apparently did the cooking, or knew enough about it to do such major grocery shopping, intrigued her. She doubted Frank would know where to begin.

Laura couldn't remember even once during their marriage when he'd shopped for food. In fact, she couldn't remember when he went to the grocery store except to get a few items on special occasions. *Did I make things too easy for him?*

She shook her head to clear her mind, and tried to concentrate on her task at hand instead of John. She did know his first name. She remembered other folks in the store calling him that.

Laura shifted back to her mission. With careful examination of each bundle, she picked out the best bunch of asparagus in the produce section. She scanned through several cartons of strawberries before she found the perfect selection. She picked up a wilted broccoli stalk and threw it back down. Better to go with the crowns. The packaged romaine lettuce salad caught her eye. Why start from scratch with the head? *I can take a few shortcuts.*

Laura searched the shelves for wild rice. Diligently, she surveyed the variety of boxes and bags, but could not find her favorite kind. Her search grew more frantic. *Where is my brand of wild rice?* In her frenzied search, she pushed forward until she felt a sudden jolt. She turned and realized she had rammed head-on into John's cart.

"Excuse me. Hope I didn't hurt you." His voice sounded kind and apologetic.

Cheeks ablaze, she wanted to crawl under the shelf beside her. "Oh, no, it was my fault." Laura backed her cart away.

"I'm so sorry. I wasn't watching where I was going. I'm looking for some wild rice and can't seem to find what I usually buy." She scanned the shelf once more and then focused on John.

"Have you ever tried this one? I have good results with it." He picked up a package and handed it to her for examination.

Laura hesitated a moment before reaching out to take the box from his tanned fingers. "Okay, I'll try it, since I can't find mine. Thank you." She dropped the package into her basket.

"I don't think you'll be disappointed. By the way, I'm John Talbot. I live in the area. Retired school teacher," he held out his hand.

Laura extended her own, glad she kept her nails manicured. "I've seen you in the store a few times. Do you do all your own cooking, or do you just do the grocery shopping for your family?"

He laughed. "I live with my mother. Or, I should say, she lives with me. She became ill recently, and I take care of her. And yes, I do all the cooking. She taught me well."

"Excuse me for being so nosy. I'm not usually.

I've wondered – seeing you here often." Then, she remembered her failure to introduce herself. "Oh, please forgive me. I'm Laura Olson. I live close by and am putting together a special meal for my husband. All his favorites." She felt heat rush from the nape of her neck to the top of her head. Why had she blurted this out to a complete stranger?

"I'd say he's a lucky guy. It's nice to meet you, Laura."

"Nice meeting you too," she echoed back.

John walked away, and she thought about his comment. *I hope Frank feels that way when I get this meal cooked for him*. She finished her list and made her way to the checkout stand. Pushing her cart into line, she saw John leave the store. "He seems like such a nice man. I hope we'll like the rice he recommended." Realizing she'd spoken her thoughts out loud, she looked around to see if anyone heard her. Sure enough, a couple of ladies stood in the aisle with their heads turned toward her, a strange look on their faces.

Arriving home, she unloaded the groceries and hastened to check on Betty and Jim before they retired for the evening. She picked up the handset and punched in Betty's number. *I hope they're not already in bed.*

"Hi, Laura," Betty said when she answered the phone.

"How did you know it was me? Just because I call you all the time?"

"Oh, no. I had 'Caller ID' installed yesterday. It's pretty neat. You can see who's calling, and you don't have to answer or talk to them if you don't want. You can just let the answering machine pick it up. And if you don't like what they say, you can delete their message." Betty's chuckle came over the line. She laughed at her own joke.

Laura laughed at Betty's funny explanation as she always did. "Guess I'll have to try it sometime. I'd like to avoid some of those telemarketers. How's Jim feeling?"

"He's not doing any better. I'm afraid he's sicker than we want to believe." Laura heard Betty's voice crack with emotion.

Laura shifted her weight to her other foot and drew a long breath. "We must keep praying. We'll see what the doctor at M.D. Anderson has to say on Thursday. Remember we're putting Jim into God's hands."

"I know but sometimes it's harder to do than say." Betty sounded defeated.

"I know. I'm praying for you both." Laura glanced over at the groceries still sitting on the counter. She held the phone with her neck and shoulder as she unloaded and placed them in the cupboard and refrigerator. She stowed them away as they talked and shook her head at the jumbled up messy shelves. *Like the cabinets, the pantry and frig used to be organized.*

"Thanks." Betty changed the subject. "How was your shopping trip? Did you get everything you needed?"

"Yes, but I couldn't find the wild rice I normally use. A nice gentleman I ran into recommended another one, so I'll try it."

"You ran into someone?"

"Yes, I literally ran into him with my cart looking for the rice." She held up the box of rice as if Betty could see it, and laughed as she remembered the incident.

"Who was he?" Laura could tell Betty's curiosity stirred. She often called her curious nature her motivational gift.

"His name's John Talbot. Do you know him?" Laura figured Betty did.

"Oh, yes, the retired teacher."

"Do you know everyone in town?"

Laura thought of how easily Betty got acquainted with others. She drew them out and made each person feel important. With her fun-loving personality, Laura liked Betty from their first meeting. Not only did she remember others, they remembered her.

I wish I were a little more like her. She has the capacity to relate in a way I don't. She stopped herself. *It's best not to compare. I'm my own snowflake pattern.*

"Almost everyone." Betty laughed. "No, I'm sure there are many I don't know."

"Well, my dear friend, I will pray for you and Jim a good nights rest, and that you wake refreshed in the morning. Bye, now. Call if you need me."

"Okay, Laura, goodnight now."

Laura put the last of the groceries into the fridge and her growling stomach reminded her she hadn't eaten dinner. *Now, I'll have to call it supper since it will need to be a small amount. It's too late to eat much.* At any rate, she needed something. Remembering she gave the roast to Jim and Betty, she scrounged around in the icebox for something to eat. She spotted some eggs and decided to fix a breakfast taco when she saw tortillas and salsa. "I haven't had breakfast for supper in a long time." She said aloud as if someone stood in the room with her.

She poured a glass of milk to set off the meal. After eating, she felt revived. *Amazing what a little food will do.*

Her hopes soared when she thought of the fancy meal, and prayed things would turn around for her and Frank. Would her plan help revive her marriage? Could the special date create a turning point? She hoped so.

CHAPTER SIX

Dinner's Served

Laura jumped out of bed, hoping to find Frank still at home. She combed her hair, brushed her teeth, and put on her prettiest robe, trying to look her best without adding make-up. She hurried into the breakfast room determined to exhibit a cheery mood. Sure enough, he sat at the kitchen table just like he had the morning before. She beamed her best smile. "Good morning."

"Mornin."

Determined not to let his lack of enthusiasm throw her, she leapt right in. "Frank, I'm making us a special dinner one night this week. I'd really like to do it tonight if you can make it home on time. I know you've been busy, but I hope you can."

The paper rustled in his hands. "Well, I'll try."

"I need to know for sure. I don't want to prepare the food if you can't be with me to enjoy it. So, you just tell me which night you can *for sure* make it."

Frank's hands curled around the edges of the paper, but he neither moved nor looked up. "Okay, okay. I'll be here tonight at seven. Will that suit you?"

"That'll be great. I'll be ready and waiting for you." She smiled over at him as he peered around the paper's edge. "Would you like me to fix you some toast this morning?"

He returned to his paper. "No, no. I ate cereal already. I need to get to work if I'm going to finish and make it back by seven this evening." He folded the newspaper, gathered his folders and slid them into his brief case. Then he placed his bowl in the dishwasher without further conversation, grabbed his coat and keys, and started out the door.

"Oh, Frank."

"Yes?" He made a half turn and raised his eyebrows.

"I wanted to wish you a great day and kiss you goodbye." She moved to the door and put her arms around him. Oh, and Christina called night before last.

Frank's mouth dropped open in surprise, but he leaned over to accept her kiss. "I'll call Christina from work today around six or six-thirty before I come home for dinner. Thanks. You have a good day, too." He hesitated for a moment, but didn't say any more.

After he left, Laura smiled to herself. *Well, it started off pretty good. Thank you, Lord. Betty must be praying.*

She walked to her favorite place in the house – her desk. She wanted to spend time talking with her Heavenly Father. She started her prayer with thanksgiving. She mentioned Frank's and her relationship and asked the Lord to give them a good evening together. "Lord, let Frank enjoy the dinner, and help me prepare everything to his liking. Our marriage sure needs a boost. I could use your help."

Not wanting to be selfish, she brought Christina, Jim, Betty, and other friends before the throne. She thought of her pastor and the new altar that would be going into the church week after next, and asked God's blessing on the ceremony and the congregation. She petitioned for all the church leaders, the churches all over the world, and the leaders of the country, especially the President.

Her time with the Lord took longer than usual for much weighed heavy on her mind. She finished with a small prayer for herself. Guilt over asking so much washed over her. She ended with a rushed amen.

She cleaned the house from top to bottom and set the table with her Old Country Rose china, tablecloth with matching napkins, candle holders - the works. She wanted everything to be extra special. She surveyed the results and felt quite pleased with herself. She hoped all her efforts would put some romance back into her marriage.

She gave herself a facial, went to the beauty salon for a shampoo and set, and visited the nail shop for a manicure and pedicure. The blue cotton polyester dress seemed the right thing to wear, not too fancy, but attractive. *Frank will have a difficult time ignoring me tonight,* she vowed.

With so much to occupy her mind and her time, evening came like a silent visitor. By the time she finished everything, it was time to start dinner. She carefully seasoned the hens, humming as she worked. She wondered how many times she had prepared them for Frank. *Living with him for almost thirty-two years, I know exactly how he wants everything. Or at least, I thought I did. Lately, I'm not so sure.*

This line of thinking shook her confidence, and her hands trembled as she concentrated on fixing everything just right. Though she'd done this numerous times before, somehow this time seemed more important. And nerve racking.

Time slipped away, but everything fell into place.

When the grandfather clock struck seven, she looked out the window toward the empty driveway. *Where is Frank? He must have gotten tied up at the office again. He will be here soon. He promised me...*

Laura paced the floor. She kept the hens in the oven to stay warm and hoped they weren't overdone or dried out. She left the asparagus in the steamer so as not to get cold. The rice simmered in a pot on the stovetop with the burner turned down low. The prepared salad of broccoli romaine sat in the refrigerator. She would wait until the last minute to add the nuts, noodles, and dressing, to keep the taste fresh. The strawberries were cut and ready to add to the pound cake she'd baked.

Is he only late, or will he come at all? Laura felt like crying. She bit her lip to muster her courage. A few tears pooled in her eyes, but she held herself in check in order not to ruin her makeup job. *I looked forward to an evening alone with Frank to work on our relationship, and he doesn't even care enough to show up on time.* The clock struck eight. The gonging, louder to her than usual, made her heart pound in her chest. Her emotions skipped back and forth from pouts of anger to tears of disappointment. *How dare he promise me and then not show up? Can't he ever keep his word?* His sins of omission cascaded in her mind. With the memories, the tears flowed. Hurriedly, she wiped them with the back of her hand before they ruined her mascara.

Laura left the window and plodded back to the kitchen. She removed the hens from the oven, turned off the burner from under the rice, took the asparagus out of the steamer, and sat down at the table. Alone. She started to blow out the candles, now mere stubs. She heard Frank's car pull into the driveway. She looked out the window in time to see his black BMW sail into the garage. Then, she heard his brakes squeak to a halt.

Instead of yelling, she'd try to contain herself, not focus on his being over an hour late. She felt like yelling. She carefully sat everything back on the table, got the salad out of the refrigerator, and added the last ingredients. She was determined to spend a good evening with her husband. Betty must be praying for her. She stayed calm, at least on the outside, in spite of the rage that ate at her insides.

Frank came in through the kitchen door. "Something smells good." He inhaled deeply to get a good whiff.

"Sorry, I'm late. When I got off the phone with Christina, one of my partners came in and wanted to discuss a case on tomorrow morning's docket. I didn't think it would take long. First thing I knew it was after seven."

"Everything's still warm. Go ahead and wash up, and I'll have dinner on the table by the time you finish." Laura forced her voice to remain calm.

"Okay. I'll be right out." He didn't take long in the bathroom, and did return almost immediately, this time keeping his promise. Laura wondered if it were the smell of the good food, or if he wanted to make things better, too.

Laura poured the tea into the glasses and carried them to the table. Frank sat down and glanced around at the finery. He looked impressed, but a little off guard. Laura realized they hadn't eaten at the dining room table in some time, especially not with all the best china, candles, napkins, and the other niceties. *Frank must think I'm up to something. Well, he's right. I am.*

Laura bowed her head and gave the blessing. She stopped asking Frank long ago. He always grumbled, or asked her to bless the food. Out of habit, she thanked the Father for their food and asked His blessings upon it and them.

"And thank You for this special evening

together." She added as an afterthought.

Frank squirmed in his seat, but managed a wry smile. He smacked his lips as he ate. "Umm, this is delicious. I could stand a few more special dinners like this."

"If you can make it home on time, I'll be glad to prepare the dinner." The minute Laura made the statement she wanted to bite her tongue.

"Now, Laura, you don't have to bring that up again. You always nag me about my work. You know my hours aren't always nine to five." She could tell his patience wore thin, but he kept his anger under control. She suspected he wanted to finish the great meal. She reminded herself, *Betty is praying.*

She attempted to smooth the moment. "I didn't mean anything, Frank. I would like to have you home more for dinner so I can feed you good." She smiled, hoping she sounded convincing.

"Might be better I can't. I could get as big as a barn eating like this every night." He made an effort to laugh.

"I could prepare some of those low calorie meals. I do most of the time, but I wanted to fix your favorites tonight." She toyed with the food on her own plate, even though, her stomach growled from hunger. She hadn't taken time to eat lunch. That, combined with his tardiness, and the somewhat forced conversation, made her stomach churn. She could sense something gone from their marriage. *Can we ever get it back?*

"What's the special occasion, anyway?" He set his fork down with a clatter.

"Our having a quiet dinner at home together at a reasonable hour... It's been a long time, Frank." She hoped her voice didn't sound as sad as she felt. "I thought we might enjoy each other's company and have a fun evening together."

He looked at her with raised eyebrows. "What type of fun did you have in mind?"

"I thought we might have an early evening, go to bed together, and see what happens." She returned his look with a smile and hoped she had a twinkle in her eye.

Frank cleared his throat and tugged the edge of his collar. "Sounds good, but, uh, I'm going to have to take a rain check. After dinner, I need to go back to the office to pick up the briefs for tomorrow mornings court case, and meet with the partner again. We still have some work to do before court." He avoided her eyes as he spoke.

Laura sat with her mouth open. Stunned, she

couldn't believe her ears. *This is really nothing new. Why am I so surprised?* She fought to hold back the tears. She knew Frank hated for her to cry. She felt so humiliated. She swallowed hard, got up from the table, and cleared her dishes without saying a word. *Instead of Cornish hens, I feel like we had goose for dinner, and I'm the goose!*

Frank didn't seem to notice. They lived this way daily, ever since Christina left. Why did she think tonight would be any different? He finished eating, left the table, and went to shower and redress. What little conversation they engaged in, now terminated. He dressed in casual clothes, but looked pretty spiffy, as if he might be going out on the town. She noticed his cologne smelled extra strong.

"Thanks for the good dinner." His face took on a look of remorse. Or was it guilt. "Sorry, I have to go. Don't wait up for me. I might be late. No telling how long this preparation will take tonight." He patted her on the shoulder and turned toward the door. "See you later."

"Later." She mumbled.

The same old story – don't wait up for me... His car pulled out of the garage. The door closed automatically as she envisioned him pushing the opener.

Then the dam broke. Laura sobbed, and couldn't stop. She thought of calling her friend, but no one could make her feel better, and no one needed to hear this sob story. Besides, Betty had enough trials of her own right now.

Laura undressed, crawled into bed. Alone. The dam broke and she cried until there were no more tears. *God where are you? Where is my husband? What's happening to my marriage? Will I ever be happy again?*

She lay awake until the wee hours of the morning. She tossed and turned from one side of the bed to the other. The copious questions she asked the Lord amazed even her. She finally gave in, prayed, and asked His guidance. Then, she drifted off into a troubled sleep.

At dawn, she heard the door from the garage close in the kitchen. She listened as Frank tiptoed into the extra bedroom.

Even though she didn't want to think about it, she knew for her own peace of mind, she must find out why Frank stayed out late so often. Perhaps, work alone did not keep him away from her. *Is there anything left to save in our marriage?* She sighed. Her tired body wanted to give up, but the vow she took reminded her— a marriage should last forever.

CHAPTER SEVEN

What Does the Future Hold?

Laura avoided Frank the next morning. She didn't want him to see her puffy eyes. She lay in bed until he left so he wouldn't know she had cried all night. She couldn't face any further humiliation. Keeping those extra pounds off became more and more difficult, but her water aerobics class would have to wait for another day. Today, she didn't want anyone to see the way she looked, except maybe Betty. Laura needed her friend's love, compassion, and, most of all, her prayers.

She listened to Frank's car putter down the road, then got out of bed, dressed for the day, and gathered her usual small breakfast. Most she threw down the garbage disposal after a few bites. Her failing marriage loomed utmost in her thoughts. Her mind pictured a hundred different places Frank could have been last night, the arms of his secretary, the one most vivid. She tried to pray and reached for her Bible. Nothing registered.

Laura closed her Bible and headed out the door to Betty's. Her friend usually rose early, so perhaps she'd be awake. Laura walked to the back door and rang the doorbell. No answer. She rang again. No answer. After the fourth time, she looked through the window and grew more puzzled and upset by the moment. Surely, they were up by now. She walked back to her own place. When she walked in the door, the phone jingled.

When she answered, Betty's voice came from the other end of the receiver, her words barely coherent between sobs.

"Betty, what's wrong? Calm down. Tell me what's wrong. Everything will be okay …

"Laura, I'm at the hospital. It's Jim. He took a turn for the worse. He fell and hit his head. I had to bring him in through the emergency room." She managed to croak out the problem.

Laura's hand tightened on the handset. "I'll be right there."

"They have him in a room now. Room 420. He's having difficulty breathing. They're giving him oxygen."

"See you in a few minutes."

Thankful she applied make-up earlier; Laura grabbed her car keys and purse and ran out the door. She jumped into her car and sped toward the hospital. She punched down the accelerator and broke every speed limit. The usual trip took twenty minutes, but she arrived in ten. The work crowd had already thinned down, and traffic flowed easily today.

She considered calling Frank as she drove, but remembered he'd be in court. *I don't know if he would even care. He's so absorbed in himself and his work, and maybe someone else.* She felt ashamed of herself for thinking those things, but the anger and hurt from last evening still burned in her soul.

Instead, she dialed the church on her way and requested they activate the prayer chain for Jim and Betty. The receptionist assured her she would get right on it.

Laura found a parking place and ran into the hospital. Betty sat in the corner of Jim's room, her head resting in her hands. She looked up as Laura entered the room, rose to her feet, and the two rushed into each other's arms.

When they released each other, Betty spoke first, "Laura, he's really bad. They say he might not pull through. The cancer has metastasized to his liver, pancreas, and lungs. He's in such pain. They keep him sedated. She broke into tears.

"Oh, Betty, I'm so sorry." Laura wrapped her arms around Betty's sagging frame and hugged her again.

Then, she eased out of their embrace and took Betty's hands in her own. "Let's pray." Tears streamed down both their faces as they bowed to pray. The minute Laura finished praying, they turned and hugged each other again. Then, they sat in a stupor, waiting – just waiting.

Each time someone entered the room they jumped up to see if the doctor or nurse brought news. Time drug, the clock read only ten o'clock when the doctor appeared and asked to speak to Betty alone. She insisted Laura stay as she informed the doctor Jim had listed Laura on his permission form to share any news about his condition.

"We need to make a decision, Betty. Jim will not last much longer. Maybe a month, at the most, but I would say only a few weeks – maybe less. Could be a matter of days."

Betty broke into sobs.

Laura stood there stunned unable to say anything for the moment.

"We can keep him here a few days, or you can take him home with hospice care. I've already contacted hospice, and they have a nurse available. Either way, we can keep him comfortable for as long as necessary." The doctor's voice resonated with regret. "I'm so sorry,

Betty."

"If we can have hospice care, I would rather take him home in his own surroundings for the time he has left. Will he know me?"

"Probably part of the time, but he'll slowly drift away until he's gone. The nurse will keep him comfortable, so he doesn't have excruciating pain."

"When can we move him back home?" Betty looked in shock, but managed to ask the question.

"Let's get him stable and take him home later this afternoon." Dr. Thomas finished speaking, and then walked down the hallway, his head bent low.

They sat quietly for a time. Laura glanced at the clock. Half past noon. "Betty, did you have breakfast?"

"No, but I'm fine." Betty sat in the corner of the room in stunned silence.

"Let's go to the cafeteria and get something to eat. You have to keep up your strength. The nurse will call us if we're needed. I'll let her know where we're going."

Laura walked over to the nurse's station. A slim blonde-haired nurse with large, silver hoop earrings met her. "We'll be in the cafeteria getting something to eat. Please, please call us if Mr. Ivey wakes up or anything changes for him." Laura hoped her voice conveyed the sincerity of her request. “You can use the intercom or my cell phone.” Laura passed the nurse a paper with her number written down.

The nurse assured Laura she’d call if needed. Laura took Betty by the arm and led her toward the cafeteria. They walked to the elevator and waited to enter, the door opened to reveal their pastor. Tears welled up in Betty’s eyes, and Pastor Howard held her in his arms for a few moments.

“I’m so sorry, Betty. I wish you didn’t have to go through this.” He loosed his hold, looked into her eyes, and reached for his back pocket.

Betty took the handkerchief and wiped the dampness from her cheeks. “Thank you, Pastor. We are on our way to the cafeteria for a bite to eat. Would you like to join us?”

“How is Jim doing?” His gaze shifted from Laura to Betty.

“The reports are bad, but he’s resting and breathing easier.” Betty handed back his loan.

“At least that’s good.” Pastor Howard shook his head in agreement to his own statement.

“He’s still sleeping. They gave him some sedatives. The nurse assured us she would call us if anything changes. However, we must hurry. He might be afraid if he awakens and I'm not there." Betty walked into the elevator and pushed the button, barely giving Laura and the pastor time to enter. They both jumped in and all picked up the pace as they proceeded on their trip to the cafeteria.

The place overflowed with people. In the serving line, Betty took a small bowl of soup. Pastor Howard selected a hamburger, and Laura picked up a salad and placed it on her tray along with a diet soda. They placed their food on one of the tables, sat down, and bowed their heads as Pastor Howard prayed over their lunch and for Jim and Betty. Most of the talk consisted of the morning happenings and Jim's fall and turn for the worse. Some small talk entered into the conversation regarding church doings as well. Laura never mentioned her dinner with Frank. It all seemed too trivial at the moment.

"We better head back up to Jim's room." Betty fidgeted in her chair for a moment. She hopped up, cleared the table of the mess, and took her trash and dishes to the proper places. Pastor Howard and Laura followed suit. Once again they headed to the elevator and got in. Betty waited until they all entered before pushing the button this time.

"Is there anything I can get for you, or do for you, Betty?" Pastor Howard leaned against the back wall of the elevator.

"I can't think of anything right now, except your prayers. But I thank you for asking." Betty left the elevator with the Pastor and Laura trailing behind.

"Just let me know if there is anything—I do mean anything..." When he caught up to her, he took her hand in his and gave it a gentle pat.

Betty shook her head, tears brimming her eyes, and managed to choke out a few words. "Thanks, I will."

When they arrived back at the nurse's station, the blonde shook her head. Her large earrings jangled. "There's been no change. He's still sleeping."

They all gathered in the small room. Pastor Howard looked stunned to see Jim lying there. He had always been so active. "Why don't we pray?" He looked at Betty, and she took his and Laura's hand.

They bowed their heads and the pastor led them quietly to the throne. "Father, we lift Jim up to You. We thank You for his life. We ask You to keep him from pain. We believe You can heal him and ask that You do, whether it is in this life or the next. I pray Your peace will flood Betty's heart. Show her Your love and comfort at this time and the days ahead. Give the doctors wisdom and knowledge as to how to help and keep Jim comfortable. Be with Laura as she comforts Betty. Guide all of us to be Your servant. We pray in Jesus' Name. Amen."

After the prayer, Pastor Howard assured Betty he would be in touch the next day, pleaded with her to call if she needed him, and took his leave.

Betty turned to Laura. "Now, tell me about your dinner last evening. I take it things didn't go so well."

I didn't say a word. How did she know? "How could you tell?"

"Laura, we've been friends a long time. I know when something upsets you and when you hurt." Betty took Laura in her arms. The two of them embraced for a long time, tears flowed down each of their faces. Laura suspected they cried for each other, and their own situations as well.

"You're right. The dinner itself went pretty well, but Frank arrived over an hour late. When he did show up, I tried to make the best of the situation and served dinner."

"Good for you."

"He complimented me on the dinner, and we

enjoyed some pleasant conversation. Only a few times did things get a little sticky. Then, I suggested a quiet evening at home and mentioned going to bed." Laura looked away a bit embarrassed.

"Sounds like a good plan to me. So, what happened?"

"He told me he would take a rain check. Said he had to go back to the office to continue working on an impending case. I felt so humiliated." Laura lowered her head and the tears poured down her checks.

Betty stiffened, and her lips thinned into a slim white line. "That rat. I'd like to slug him. But, no, we'll just continue to pray. You keep being kind and maybe that will have an effect on him." Laura knew Betty found it difficult to show love toward Frank, but she did. *I think it's too late to change anything with him. But Betty hasn't given up.*

"I think things have gone too far and he no longer wants a relationship with me." Laura's fears came pouring out.

"I suppose time will tell. I don't know what to say, Laura. Just don't give up the faith. God is able. I hope Frank is willing."

"I spent the night crying, so I stayed in bed until

after he left this morning. I didn't want him to see my face." Laura continued to shed tears, but tried her best to wipe them away quickly.

Betty reached again to enfold Laura into her arms. Laura hugged her back. Neither said a word for several minutes as they comforted one another.

"I know God will work all things together for good. Sometimes we go through these rough spots in order to grow stronger in our faith."

"You and I must be gaining strength." Laura laughed through her tears. She dried them away, took a tissue from her purse and blew her nose, and decided to make the best of whatever came.

"I think I'll find the restroom and make a visit to the chapel. I'll be back shortly." Laura got up from her seat and walked toward the door.

"That's a great idea. Don't hurry. Spend the time you need with the Lord. We'll be right here." Betty smiled through her tears.

Alone in the chapel with her visions of the night before, she recognized the sweet presence of God calling her to pray, and knew the Spirit of the Lord abode with her. She prayed.

"Father, please guide me through these next days

with Betty. Help me assist her and Jim. I place You in charge of my marriage and my future. May Your will be done in all our lives. Help me endure whatever comes. I put my trust and confidence in You."

A peace enveloped her like never before, and she knew He would go with her through anything. She knew He wouldn't let her down, but could she hold up her end of the bargain? Could she help Betty, keep from falling apart, and try to salvage her marriage?

CHAPTER EIGHT

Welcome Home

Betty charged into the chapel where Laura sat collecting her thoughts and seeking answers in prayer. "Jim's awake and talking. He doesn't know where he is. Hurry, let's get back to him."

"Praise the Lord." Laura sprang to her feet and ran after Betty. They arrived back in Jim's room within seconds.

"Hi, Laura." Jim looked around the hospital room. He seemed to have difficulty focusing and understanding his surroundings. His hands shook, and he looked groggy, but he recognized her.

"Hi, Jim." She reached over to take his hand. "You gave us quite a scare. Glad you're back with us."

"Me, too." A faint smile crept over his lips.

"When can I go home?" He turned toward Betty for an answer.

"I think the doctor may let you go this evening. That is if you're a good boy." Betty laughed but added in a more serious tone, "However, if he does let you go, they want to send a nurse with us."

"You're the best and only nurse I need." Jim, with

a raspy voice and a trembling arm, smiled and reached for her hand.

Betty moved closer and squeezed his hand. Tears cursed down her cheeks. “Jim, I’m going to be really honest. I’ve never kept anything from you and I’m not going to start now. The doctor doesn’t offer much hope. The cancer has metastasized to your liver, pancreas, and lungs. He wants to send a hospice nurse to help make you comfortable.”

“I know, my darling. I know. It won’t be long. We better get things in order. I would like to spend the time at home with you. Whatever time we have...” His voice cracked and broke. Tears pooled in his eyes.

Laura stood watching the exchange between Jim and Betty. She observed the enormous love they shared.

“Excuse me.” She raced out of the room. She ran to the nearest restroom, sobbing as she went. She pulled herself together after a few minutes, and returned to the room where Jim lay, once again asleep.

“They gave him more Morphine. He’s in so much pain.” Betty rose from the corner where she sat with a blanket tucked around her slender body.

Laura sat down in the chair opposite Betty. “Have you heard whether or not they will allow him to go home today?"

"Yes, the nurses called the doctor to tell him Jim came out of the coma. He instructed them to fill out the release papers. He will come by to check Jim. And if he's stable enough, he'll probably release him around five."

Laura glanced at her watch. "That won't be long. It's four-thirty now. We could start getting things ready to go."

Betty held up the bag of Jim's clothes and personal effects. "Everything's packed. The sooner I get him home and situated the better."

"Is there anything else I can do?"

"Why don't you go on home, Laura? The techs will help me get Jim into the car."

"Okay. I'll go to your house, tidy up, and wait for you to bring Jim home." Laura looked over at Jim and then met Betty's eyes.

The frown on Betty's face lifted. "Okay, if you insist. Hopefully, we will be there before too long. You know how it goes with doctors and hospitals."

"I know what you mean. Promise me you'll call if you want me to do anything, or if you think of anything you need." Laura waited for Betty's answer.

"I promise. If we get detained, I'll call you.

Hopefully, you can go on home and start dinner for Frank."

"Oh, Frank! I haven't even called him to tell him about Jim. I'll do that on the way. He may be working late, as usual." Laura's face pushed up in a frown. Then she continued. "Besides, I'm still peeved and don't know if I want to cook for him," she looked away.

"I understand, but you must forgive, Laura. Why don't you try again? Surely, you will get through to him sooner or later."

Laura studied Betty thoughtfully. Her friend was right. But she couldn't seem to forget the pain Frank's late nights brought …nor could she shed her suspicions of indiscretion.

"First, I'll see what he says when I call, and then go from there. I'll pray on the way home, too." If only she could let go of her anger and sadness. The inward struggle felt like two dogs at war. P*erhaps, some of what I feel is woman's intuition.*

Betty waved her on when Laura hesitated. "Go on along now. I'll be fine."

Laura reached over and gave Betty a hug before she walked out the door. "See you in a few."

All the way down the hall, in the elevator, and

walking to her car, Laura thought about what she would say to Frank. *I'll try to keep my cool. I'll tell him about Jim and ask him if he will be home for dinner.*

She arrived at her Buick, fished in her purse for the keys, and unlocked the door. She had only just slipped into the seat when her cell phone rang. Her fingers shook as she scrambled to find the phone amidst her billfold, checkbook, lipsticks, and an odd assortment of bills she had meant to drop off at the post office. "Hello?"

Frank's voice came from the other end. "Laura! I tried to call home. Where have you been all day?"

"Oh. I haven't been there. I've been at the hospital with Jim and Betty." Laura bristled at his accusing manner and wondered if the hostility could be heard in her voice, too.

"Why, what happened?"

"Jim blacked out and went into a coma. You know he has cancer."

"No, I didn't. You never told me. How do you expect me to know what's going on when I can't even reach you? Am I supposed to read your mind?"

Laura winced. She could tell by the tone of his voice he was unhappy with her, and, as usual, he made her out to be the one at fault. He had a knack for shifting his own guilt to her. He always managed to make her feel as if she were the one to blame. *Is it to salve his conscience?*

Laura put the key in the ignition, then, rolled down the window to get some air. "Well, we haven't talked in awhile. With your late nights, we don't see much of each other." She swallowed hard and tried to deliver the news in a softer tone. "Anyway, Jim has terminal cancer, and the doctor only expects him to live a few more days."

The pause on the other end of the phone told Laura she could still count on Frank to show some compassion.

"I'll get by the hospital to see him tomorrow." He lowered his voice to a concerned whisper. "Did Betty say…is there anything we can do?"

"Actually, Jim will be coming home this evening. A hospice nurse will attend him there. He wants to be in his own room and his own bed with Betty by his side for the time he has left." Laura's eyes watered, but she didn't want to cry to Frank. If she started, she might not stop.

Frank cleared his throat. "Wow, that's tough. Maybe you could take them a meal or something, so

Betty won't have to cook. That reminds me of the reason I called."

Laura waited for the usual comments. *I won't be home for dinner. I have to work late. Don't wait up for me.*

He continued, almost verbatim. "I won't be home for dinner. Don't wait up for me. I'll probably be late. I'll sleep in the other room, so I won't disturb you."

The hair rose on the back of Laura's neck, and she gripped the steering wheel. Her jaw quivered as she spoke through clenched teeth. "Whatever you say, Frank. See you later."

She hung up the phone before he could even say goodbye. At least not having to fix dinner would be a blessing. She could spend whatever time needed helping Betty and keeping her company.

Her promise to Betty about praying on the way home nagged at her conscience. She finally took the time. She prayed fervently and soon felt God's peace envelop her again. When she arrived home, she walked inside, checked the answering machine, and sorted through her mail. The device stored a lone message from Christina thanking Laura for the brownies. If Frank had tried to call, he didn't bother to leave a message.

Laura strode back to her bathroom, took off her dress clothes, and climbed into a pair of jeans and tee shirt. She decided to sit down, try to relax, and collect her thoughts before going to Betty's. Knowing about hospital checkouts, it would be some time before Betty and Jim arrived. She sat down for a minute in her recliner to catch her breath and then dialed Christina's number.

I must call and let her know about Jim. I hope I can catch her. She will be even more upset with me than Frank if I don't let her know.

Christina answered on the third ring. "Hello?"

"Hi, honey. How are you today?"

"I'm doing fine, but feeling a little low. I miss you and Dad. I even miss Betty and Jim."

"I know honey. We miss you too. One reason I called is about Jim." Laura found it difficult to continue. A lump formed in her throat and she could hardly get anything out. Christina loved Jim. He had been like a second father to her.

"What's wrong, Mom?"

"Well, honey, the doctors have diagnosed Jim with cancer." Laura gripped the phone tighter in her hand.

"What? When did this happen? Is he going to take Chemo? What type of cancer?" Christina's questions tumbled out like spilled beans.

Laura took a deep breath and tackled each question one at a time. “Jim has prostate cancer, and now it has spread throughout his body. The cancer has metastasized into his liver, pancreas, and lungs. No, they won’t give him Chemo, because at this point the doctors feel it’s too late and it won’t help. Christina, he only has a short time to live. Maybe a month at the most.” Laura’s voice broke and she could hardly keep from breaking down.

“Oh, no, Mom!”

Christina’s sobs on the other end tore at Laura’s heart. “I’m so sorry to have to tell you like this, honey, but I knew you would want to know.” She waited until Christina quieted enough to hear the rest. “Honey, one thing we know - Jim is ready to meet his Lord.”

“Mom, what should I do? I want to see him before he goes, and I want to be there for the funeral, but I can’t take off too long from my classes. Things are critical right now.”

“Perhaps, when he has a good moment, I can call and let you talk with him on the phone and say your goodbyes. If you can’t say goodbye, at least you can tell him how much you love him.”

"Oh, Mom, I wish I could be there. How can I ever tell him over the phone how much he means to me, and how much I'll miss him?"

"Maybe you could come for the weekend. I'll talk to your father about it when I see him. He won't be home this evening, but hopefully I can catch him in the morning."

Christina fell silent. Across the telephone line, Laura heard Christina's chair scrape back. And Laura imagined her standing to her feet in either anger or concern. "Is he still working late all the time?"

"Most of the time, I'm afraid." Laura wished she'd left the topic of Frank's schedule alone. "One way or another I'll call you tomorrow night and let you know."

"Okay, Mom, thank you. I'll be waiting to hear from you."

"Sure honey. I better get off the phone now and go to Betty's house. I want to straighten things up and wait for her to bring Jim home from the hospital. A hospice nurse will help her with him, but I intend to help them both however I can. I'll talk to you tomorrow night, sweetheart."

They said their goodbyes, and Laura walked out

the front door almost immediately after hanging up the phone. When she crossed the lawn to Betty's house, the ambulance drove up bringing Jim home. Her failure to get things in order left her feeling bad, but she knew Betty would understand about her calling Christina.

She hurried to the house, unlocked the door, and waited for them to bring Jim inside. She waited at the backdoor entrance.

"It's good to be home. Thank you, Laura, for welcoming me." Betty pushed his wheel chair past the door. Laura moved further into the kitchen. Jim looked around. Laura knew he enjoyed the comforts of his home. And she wondered if he thought about his last few days there.

"I'm so glad I could be here. I always feel welcome in your home. As you know, there's nowhere else I would rather be than with you and Betty." The words came from Laura's heart. She smiled and held back the tears.

Jim reached over and gave her a hug. They huddled in an embrace as Betty came and put her arms around the two of them. The threesome held each other as if they never wanted to let go. Laura knew they each dreaded when the time would come.

CHAPTER NINE

Home Going

Laura and Betty got Jim situated in bed and tiptoed out of the room. Betty headed to the kitchen to brew a pot of coffee. Laura followed her and sat down at her usual place. They always did their best thinking and talking at the kitchen table over a cup of steaming decaf. Preferably hazelnut.

"I called Frank and Christina. Frank won't be home until late, but will come by to see Jim tomorrow evening." Laura watched for the coffee to perk. The rich aroma of the hazelnut flavor made her mouth water. The smell tantalized her and satisfied her senses as much as the taste of the full-bodied flavor in her mouth. She could hardly wait for the warm delicious liquid to fill up her senses and her stomach.

"So, he's working late again tonight?" Betty's question sounded more like a statement.

"Yes, he plans to work late and use the extra bedroom. I think he looks for any excuse to go there. We haven't made love in months. I suspect a mistress." Laura lowered her eyes. The reality of her statement stung her heart.

"Then why don't you confront him or do some checking on your own?" Betty poured the steaming coffee into their cups and set one in front of Laura. She sat down across from her and waited for an answer.

Laura ran her finger over the rim of the cup before she replied. "I suppose, up until now, I haven't wanted to know. I chose to ignore the signs in hopes they would go away." Raising her head she looked deep into Betty's eyes, as if she searched for her solution.

Betty set her coffee cup down with a thud. Some of the coffee splashed on the table. Laura grabbed a paper towel to wipe it up.

"I think it's time you stopped hiding, Laura. Either ask him or do some snooping. I hate to admit it, but I've suspected something amiss for some time." Betty lifted her cup for another sip.

"I think you're right. I'll keep my eyes open and find some solid evidence before I confront him." Laura looked down at her own cup, but didn't bring it to her lips. Nothing could get past the lump in her throat. She contemplated plans to confront Frank.

"How about Christina? What did she say?"

"I didn't tell her about Frank, but she cried and

her heart broke for you and Jim. She wants to come home for the weekend. I will talk to Frank tomorrow about sending her a ticket."

"I know Jim would love to see her. It may be the last…" Betty's voice trailed off before she finished. Laura nodded. She understood.

"Yes, Christina does need to come. She and Jim have always been close. I think she confides in him more than Frank. He has always made her feel so special." Memories trickled back. Laura envisioned some of the times Christina and Jim sat and talked together. Jim took her to driving lessons when Frank couldn't get away from the office. He watched her swim at meets when they both worked. Jim held a very special place in Christina's life, like that of a favorite uncle, or a second father.

Laura rose to her feet. "Let's make Jim some potato soup. That's what he likes to eat when he feels bad." Laura needed something to keep her busy. And forget her troubles, at least for a time.

"Sounds like a good idea." Betty stood up from the table to find the potatoes and a peeler.

"You point me to the pot, and I'll do the work. You sit and relax for a few moments." Laura took the potatoes and peeler from Betty and guided her back to her chair. Betty told her where to find the pan.

They continued their conversations as the potatoes boiled. But the topic changed to other happenings, such as the church's search for a new pastor.

When Jim awoke the soup sat ready and waiting. He tried to please the two of them and forced down a few bites. Then, they helped him to the bathroom, probably for the last time. He struggled to get there. He could barely put one foot in front of the other. Standing on his feet seemed painful. Laura and Betty could hardly support him as he wobbled from one side to the other. When Laura stepped outside the door to give him privacy, she could tell by his groaning the process was painful.

Laura let herself out, walked across the driveway, and entered her own empty house. She picked up the phone to call Frank about Christina's possible visit. She didn't like to disturb him at the office, but this was important. She dialed the number. On the tenth ring she finally hung up. No one answered the phone. He wasn't there. She made excuses for him. She thought he might have gone out for a quick bite with the partner, or perhaps, they worked from his home. Even while she surmised, she knew in her heart they most likely weren't the case.

She didn't pursue calling Frank any further. Tracking him down on his cell would prove nothing. She planned to talk with him the next morning at breakfast. Thoughts of Jim, Betty, Christina, and Frank continued to run though her mind. She decided to take time and pray for them. She brought her concerns before the Lord and knew in some way, somehow, He would watch over each one. She thought of one of her favorite Scriptures in Psalms about the Lord perfecting the things that concerned her and scrambled to find it in her worn leather Bible.

She started with the King James Version, but wanted to see how other versions read. She liked the one in the New Living Testament. *The LORD will work out his plans for my life- for your faithful love, O LORD, endures forever. Don't abandon me, for you made me.* Psalms 138:8 (NLT). Pleased and comforted by the Word, she laid the Bible down and made her way to bed. She soon drifted off to sleep.

When she awoke the next morning, Frank had either left for work or never came home. No sign of breakfast littered the kitchen, no coffee smell, and the bed remained made and untouched in the guestroom. She wondered where he spent the night.

She called him at the office. His secretary seemed a bit nervous when she answered. Laura noted hesitation in her voice when she asked to speak to Frank. "Uh, just a minute. I'll see if he's available."

After a few minutes, Frank came on the phone. "Yes, Laura, what can I do for you?" He sounded as impersonal as if he spoke to a client.

"Frank, I need to talk with you about Christina. She wants to come home this weekend to see Jim before it's too late." Laura blurted her words out before he could hang up. "And where were you last night?"

"I'll have my secretary get on line and find her a cheap ticket. I'm sure she wants to see Jim, and I'll be glad to see her."

"Yes, she definitely wants to come. Jim has been like a …

"Father?" Frank interjected before Laura could finish her sentence.

"Uncle was the word in my mind, but now that you mention it…"

"Laura, you're always nagging me about working so much, but I have always done it for the two of you." Even over the telephone, Laura felt his anger and impatience.

"I don't have time for this conversation."

"I know, Frank, you never have time to talk with me anymore." She fought to keep the bitterness out of her voice. "You didn't answer my other question."

Frank ignored her statement and her question. He always could evade an issue. *That's what makes him a good lawyer.*

"I'll plan the ticket for after six on Friday and returning on Sunday evening. That way she won't have to miss any of her classes."

"Fine. I'll call and let her know you will schedule everything, or your secretary will." Laura remembered the day she saw them together in the cafeteria. Almost instantly, she knew with whom he spent last night. Her heart sank, and she felt sick to her stomach.

"Okay. Bye." He hung up before she could reply.

Tears streamed down Laura's face. She felt like throwing things when she replaced the handset. But instead, she sat quietly and hung her head. Before long, deep sobs enveloped her, and she felt the pain from the very depths of her being. She knew in her heart it was only a matter of time before her marriage ended. In fact, she suspected so for quite some time, but didn't want to acknowledge the problem. When Christina left for law school things spiraled downhill. Just like losing Jim, this would be another death – maybe even worse. At least Betty would have good memories and no issues of rejection.

Laura hurried into the bedroom and flung herself on the bed. She lay there for some time. She pounded her pillow as if it were Frank, or maybe her own self for allowing this to happen. Somewhere along the line she lost control of her marriage and her life.

Laura drug herself from the bed to answer the phone when it jingled. Frank's voice came from the other end of the line. "I've called Christina and given her the particulars of her ticket. You'll need to pick her up at the airport." He proceeded to give Laura the information needed regarding Christina's arrival and departure. Then, he quickly said goodbye and hung up the phone. She suspected he didn't want to face any further confrontations.

The next few days Frank avoided her in every possible way. Before she could turn around, time came for her to drive to the airport and pick up Christina. When she spotted her coming down the jet way, Laura almost burst into tears, but she held back. She knew if she started, she might not stop. *I know I might be prejudiced, but she is beautiful. She has Frank's dark features with her brown eyes and dark brown hair.* Laura wondered where she got her petite figure. Her 5' 2" frame didn't match hers or Franks.

Laura rushed to her child and took her in her arms and held her for quite sometime, until Christina broke the embrace. Laura held her at arms length and surveyed her. "I'm so glad to see you honey. You've lost weight. Are you eating properly?"

"Yes, Mom, I've deliberately lost a few pounds. I feel great. I can now get into a size seven. You worry too much." Christina raised her hand as if to wave off the worry.

"You do look good. But wait until you have children. Then, we'll see who worries."

"That will be a long time, if ever. I want to make a go of my law career."

Laura cringed inwardly. She wanted grandchildren. She hoped Christina would change her mind, but knew the present wouldn't be a good time to pursue the conversation. So, she changed the subject to things more pressing.

"We best go for your luggage and get home. I

know Jim and Betty are anxious to see you."

"Yes, and I want to see them as soon as possible. I've been thinking about what to say. Mom, this is really hard." Christina's voice broke and tears pooled in her eyes.

Laura put her arm around her waist. "Yes, I know sweetheart. But I know you will have just the right words. We'll pray and God will give you His wisdom."

Christina didn't say anything in answer to Laura's statement. And Laura knew she struggled in her faith. So, instead, Laura offered up a silent prayer to her Father God.

The time Laura spent with Christina alone on the ride home brought a smile to her lips and a warming to her whole being, even with the heart wrenching circumstances. When they arrived at their next-door neighbors, Jim hugged Christina tight. Even though he was weak, pale, and slow of speech, he still recognized her. While she visited with him, he tried to stay awake, but often dozed off. The two of them spent precious, priceless moments together. During the weekend, she stayed with him as much as possible.

The hospice nurse put in a catheter. When she did, Jim became agitated. The shot of Morphine calmed him and apparently eased the pain, and then he slept again. His time grew short. Doubly glad Christina could visit; they'd made the right decision.

Frank visited Jim, but didn't stay long. He looked disturbed when he returned to the house. He left for work before Laura could even speak to him. However, he did stay home more during Christina's visit and even attended church with them on Sunday. Laura glanced over at him during the sermon. He read through the bulletin, fidgeted with his pen, and checked his cell phone for messages. He squirmed in his seat. He tapped his toes or fingers almost the entire time. For Christina's sake they acted civil and cordial to one another, but Laura watched as his unrest escalated. She sensed he wanted out. He never answered her question of where he spent the night.

Each night he slept in the guest bedroom after Christina retired and carefully folded the covers back each morning. Laura suspected he didn't want Christina to know about their marital problems just yet. Laura made every effort to be a loving wife, but he pushed her away and cut off communication more than ever. She didn't want Christina to suspect anything until she had confronted Frank alone. Not the appropriate time to converse about their troubles, conversations centered on and around Christina. Otherwise, they barely spoke to one another.

Even though he continued work and avoided Laura, Frank stayed at hand more than usual through Christina's visit and Jim's impending death. W*hat has happened to the Frank I knew? He's completely changed and become self- absorbed. At least, he does have the decency to not leave in the midst of this crisis.*

Two weeks after Christina went back to the East Coast, Jim passed away in his sleep early on a Sunday morning. Despite the pain of losing him, Laura thought his death a blessing. She and Betty had prayed his illness would not be prolonged. They released him to his Heavenly Father – at least as much as they could.

CHAPTER TEN

Lost Husbands

Laura watched the sun stream into the windows of the church. The day resembled spring. Not unusual for November in south Texas. Flowers bloomed, especially the roses. No rain, or even an overcast sky. A day Jim would have ordered.

Lord, I lift Your Name on High rose from the rafters as the congregation sang one of Jim's favorite songs. A time of praise and thanksgiving preceded the eulogy and message. Then, the pastor spoke of Jim's kindness, his heartwarming smile, willingness to help others in need, and his unfailing devotion to Betty. Hushed sobs filled the church.

Laura looked around and forced a smile as the pastor delivered a salvation message. She watched the congregation celebrate Jim's eternal home going. All around the room faces glowed with a peace beyond understanding. No one moved. The Spirit of God seemed to envelop the entire congregation. Laura imagined Jim walking on streets of gold. However, tears poured down her checks. The thought of his absence made them flow, and she cried for Betty.

Friends shared stories of precious moments spent with Jim from the pulpit. They addressed his wonderful qualities of kindness, gentleness, meekness, every fruit of the Spirit. Laura nodded her head in agreement.

"Jim served his brethren in love. He gave of himself freely to help those he encountered." Pastor Howard looked over the congregation as if he surveyed those Jim influenced. Laura reflected on how much he had given to her family. His love penetrated all of them, except Frank in recent days. But he tried.

Betty's sister left for the airport to fly home following the service. Laura imagined the pain Betty would endure staying in the house alone. Frank and Christina walked next door, but Laura hesitated to go. Then, Laura and Betty stood in an embrace and comforted one another in the middle of the kitchen. Tears poured down both of their cheeks. Laura hated to leave her friend alone, but knew she must get home to Frank and Christina. And her friend needed some private time to rest and grieve.

"Betty, I'm going home now, so you can get some rest. I'll be right next door, so you call if you need me for anything, anything at all."

"I believe I will lie down for a while. I'll be fine. Go on home to your family."

When Laura walked in the back door, Frank opened the door to the garage and headed toward his car. Before long, she heard the door open and the car chug down the driveway. She knew he headed for work or the waiting arms of his secretary. She shuddered to think about the second possibility.

Christina's packed bags set on her bed when Laura walked into her room. "Hi, Mom. Dad had to go to work. I thought I'd go ahead and pack. We'll need to leave for the airport soon. How is Betty?"

"She's going to rest for a while. I hope she can. She looks so tired."

"I know. I wish I could stay longer and help her, but I have to get back to my classes." Christina piled the last of her articles in her bag and zipped it shut.

The trip to the airport seemed long, yet short. They talked about Betty and the days ahead, but otherwise mother and daughter spoke fewer words than usual. Christina's mind seemed occupied with other things. *I wonder if she's thinking about Jim or her classes and upcoming tests?*

Preoccupied as well, Laura could not get her

friend or Frank off her mind. She didn't want to let Christina know a problem existed. In order not to hurt or worry her, Laura didn't tell her anything about her suspicions and Frank's staying out all night. Then, her daughter boarded the plane once more to fly away and leave her alone in her troubles.

Betty took Jim's death better than Laura expected, in light of a forty-year marriage and their inseparability. In the days after the funeral, Laura held her when she cried her heart out, but she also heard her say, "He won't have to suffer anymore. I will see him again, and next time not for just forty years, but forever."

"Betty, I want you to know, I will be here for you. When you're tired and weary, I want to hold you up just as others held up Moses' hands for him."

"Thank you, Laura. And I will do the same for you. I'm so glad God gave us each other. He knew what we would need before this happened. It's true. He knows the end from the beginning."

The vacant house continued to rattle as Laura sat at home alone night after night in the days following the funeral and Christina's departure. Frank seemed to find every occasion to pick fights with her when he came around. He stayed out all night regularly. She finally confronted him.

"Frank, are you having an affair?"

He looked at her stone faced. Then, he grew angry. "Laura, you're always accusing me of something. I might as well do what you say. You think I am anyway." Then, he headed for the door.

"Wait a minute, Frank. Don't just walk out on me, like you always do. You've never told me where you've been spending your nights."

"I'm not even going to dignify your accusations. Laura, you need to get some counseling." He continued on toward the door and jumped into his car and sped away.

Laura wanted to scream, but no one occupied the house for her to yell at. *That's just like Frank. He always tries to make me the culprit, or act like I'm the one with the problem. Now, he's implying I'm crazy.*

She sat down in her recliner and pounded her fists on the oversized arms. Her anger abated after a time, but she vowed she would find out what was going on, even if she had to follow Frank and do some snooping. She continued to pray Frank would come to his senses while she made her plans to find out the truth.

She decorated for Christmas and trimmed the tree.

She hoped to make their house a home. Frank didn't notice. When he came home from work, the house smelled like chocolate chip cookies. Sometimes he ate a few, but then dashed back out again.

Laura and Betty decided to rent a car on one such evening and follow Frank. *Will he go to the office or his secretary's apartment?*

The answer took only a short time. He drove straight to her apartment and stayed there for hours.

They sat in front of the complex until ten. Betty never once let go of her hand.

"Do you want to go inside and catch him being unfaithful, or drive on home now?"

"I would like to drive on home. I couldn't stand the thought of such a picture forever on my mind." Laura shifted in the seat and started up the engine.

"We'll take the car back to the rental agency, and then drive home."

"At least you know the truth now." Betty's voice held sadness, but relief.

"Now, what do I do with the truth? I asked Frank before if he's having an affair. He will probably just continue to lie. Unless, he's ready to leave."

Laura drove toward the airport to return the car.

All of a sudden she banged on the steering column. "I believe I'm ready for him to leave, but what do I tell our daughter? She loves her father so much. She'll probably think it's my fault."

"You've done everything you can to save your marriage. Even if she does blame you initially, she'll come around and see the truth. She's an intelligent young woman."

"Well, I'm tired of crying. I'll go on with my life. When the time comes and Frank leaves, I'll at least be prepared. I may just kick him out before then anyway. I won't live with a cheating, lying man any longer." Laura drove into the agency.

"That's my girl. I don't blame you. Get you a good lawyer and stick it to him. I'm so angry with him. I could give him a piece of my mind." Betty grew animated, ready to jump out of the car and charge into the office.

Laura placed her hand on Betty's arm. "Well, let's not take it out on the attendant here." Laura laughed to keep from crying or socking someone herself.

On the way home, the two of them devised many plans to get even with Frank. Then, they decided the best one would be for Laura to contact a good lawyer.

Someone Frank didn't know.

She made her plans the next morning and dialed the number of a divorce lawyer from the phone book, James and Associates, a firm located in Houston— not Humble. They might not know Frank. She made her appointment for Monday afternoon.

Then, on Sunday evening, when Laura arrived home from church, she found Frank in their bedroom packing his bag on their king sized bed.

"I didn't know you were going on a trip." Laura stood in the doorway and looked on.

"I'm not. I'm leaving. I want a divorce." His cold words ripped like hail.

"You - you want a divorce? I thought you might decide on one soon."

"We've both changed and have different interests. We've grown apart. That happens sometimes." Frank shrugged his shoulders, as if to say, "It's no big deal."

Laura raised her voice. "Frank, we've invested thirty-two years in this marriage. Isn't it worth saving?"

Even as she said the words, Laura wondered herself. She knew their marriage weighed in the balance for some time, but until the last few days she hadn't wanted to give up.

"Neither of us is happy, so I think it best we each go our own way." His response came as no surprise. She knew they had lived separate lives for years.

"Will you be moving in with your secretary?" She stood with her arms crossed in front of her.

He turned toward her, surprise written on his face. "I...I'll let you know. If you need to contact me, call the office or my cell phone." He piled a few more things into his suitcase and slammed the lid shut, like he closed their life together.

Anger boiled up in the pit of Laura's stomach. "So, you're ready to throw our marriage out the window? I suppose your secretary will be happy."

"As I said, we're not compatible anymore. I'll file the divorce. It will be easier and cheaper that way. I'll be fair with you, but you can contact your own lawyer, if you choose."

"Yes, I will hire my own lawyer."

Frank looked at her. He seemed amazed she sounded so confident in herself and wanted her own lawyer. "Suit yourself." He shrugged his shoulders.

"What about Christina? Who's going to tell her?" She raised her voice further. The thought of hurting their daughter seemed more than she could bear.

"I guess we'll each tell her our side of the story. That usually happens anyway. Everyone gives his or her own view." He swung the suitcase off the bed.

"Don't you think she should hear it from both of us? We could fly her home for a weekend and tell her together."

"I don't think that's necessary. I'll call and tell her and you do the same." He headed toward the door. Bag in hand. "I'll be in touch with the divorce papers."

"I'll have my lawyer contact you as well." She didn't want him to treat her like a doormat any longer. She would fight for herself if it were the last thing she did. *What a rat he's turned out to be. I can't believe I've put up with him for thirty-two years.*

Laura moved aside to let him pass. She held out her right hand and dipped her head as if to say, "be my guest." She wanted to say other things like, "don't let the door hit you on the way out." But she held her tongue. Her ire rose like never before. Yet, she managed some self-control.

He walked past her and out the side entrance into the garage, got into his car, and drove away.

Laura sank into her recliner and sat stunned for a long time as the tears rolled down her checks. Then she broke into uncontrollable sobs. She'd tried everything she knew to get Frank's attention and to turn his heart back to her. Her love for him diminished over the past few months as he grew more and more distant and cut her out of his life. She finally withdrew to her own world. In it she found peace, instead of the turmoil of trying to please him. She knew all this in her head, but the pain in her heart kept right on hurting. Not so much for any love left for Frank, but for a lost relationship, and the hurt it would cause her daughter.

In the dark room her emotions traveled the entire gamut. She felt dejected and rejected. The pain of the hurt, almost unbearable, caused her whole body to ache. Anger flashed through her when she thought of how nonchalant Frank acted about the whole thing. The way he cheated on her over the years. How she put up with his infidelity and became a doormat. How easy he closed their life together - like his suitcase. The way he wanted to just phone Christina tore at her soul. *How could he be so cruel to their daughter, to her?*

Christina deserved more than a phone call. She could not do that to her. Laura finally pulled herself together. She called her, but only to tell her she wanted to come to Massachusetts for a visit.

"How about this weekend or the next?" Laura didn't want to delay the inevitable. Nor, give Frank a chance to break the news by phone.

"This weekend wouldn't be good. I have a test on Monday, but the next weekend's cool. Oh, I can hardly wait. How come you decided to visit Massachusetts? You've never wanted to before."

"Just thought it would be a good thing to do, and I miss you so much." Laura hated not telling her the complete truth, but under the circumstances she couldn't tell her everything.

After they talked and made plans, Laura walked to Betty's to break the news. *Maybe Betty will come with me*. She thought it would be good for both of them to get away. They could have a good time together in spite of bringing bad news. Courage would come easier with Betty beside her.

She walked next door and viewed Betty through the window in the kitchen. She sat at her table alone, except for a cup of coffee, with tears streaming down her face. Laura pecked on the windowpane and Betty motioned for her to come in. Laura entered the back door and broke into fresh tears of her own.

"What's wrong Laura? You look as though

you've lost your best friend." Betty stood and hugged her, dabbing her eyes with a flower-printed napkin.

"Not my best friend, just my husband." She took a tissue from the multi-colored Christmas box on the counter and wiped her face. Her chin quivered.

"Oh, Laura, I'm so sorry." Betty held her at arms length and then put her arms around her again and held her tight. Laura returned the embrace. They stood there for some time comforting and holding each other. Laura felt as though her heart would fly into a million pieces. Her body, racked with sobs, trembled.

"Let's sit down here at the table. Tell me all about it and then we'll pray." Betty motioned her toward the chair and poured another cup of coffee.

Laura told Betty the details of how Frank left, what he said, their exchange of words, the call to Christina, and then asked her to come with her to the East coast.

"I'm proud of you for standing up to Frank. I'll pray about the trip. We've both lost our husbands in different ways. Let's pray." She took Laura's hands in hers and followed with a lengthy prayer. She prayed about every detail – comfort for Laura, Frank to wake up, how Christina would take the news, her going with Laura

- everything.

In turn, Laura prayed for Betty and her feeling of loss and loneliness. She prayed for God's comfort and guidance to make the right decisions in everything she did. Laura knew she struggled in the area of keeping the finances straight. Jim had been the decision-maker of the family. He attended to all the bills, made the arrangements, and balanced the checkbook His death now forced Betty to take over all of this.

"We might as well go to Massachusetts. Time away would be good." Betty picked up her coffee cup and held it in mid air as if contemplating their going.

"Good. I'll call Christina back and we'll make our reservations. Why don't we stay a few extra days?" Laura wanted something good to come from their trip, especially for Betty's sake. "We could take in the sights there." She grabbed Betty's hands and gave them a squeeze. "Thank you for always being there for me. I don't want to tell Christina alone. She's going to take this hard." Laura lifted her cup and took a slow sip of her own coffee.

The next day Laura made a call to Frank and asked him not to tell Christina until her visit.

"Okay, I'll wait. It probably would be better to tell

her in person. Don't make me sound like too much of the bad guy."

"Christina loves you so much. She probably wouldn't believe me if I did. Okay. I'll try not to if you won't tell her by phone until I've talked to her in person." Laura didn't know exactly what she would say, but she didn't want to turn Christina against her father – even if he were the bad guy. On second thought, maybe she hadn't been the perfect wife to him. *People say every story has two sides.*

Laura made reservations for her and Betty.

***

Laura looked out at the beautiful sunrise, a perfect day for travel. She heard the weather report, seventy degrees in Houston. She thought of the Internet's predictions for Massachusetts's temperatures. Cooler, but no rain or snow expected. They boarded the plane. They talked about their trip, and made plans. Then, Betty dropped off to sleep, so Laura tried to nap herself. But the anticipation of Christina's pain wouldn't let her rest.

Not wanting to prolong the agony, Laura prepared herself to tell Christina as soon as they arrived at her apartment.

She cupped her daughter's hands in hers and in a

soft voice and said, "Christina, let's leave the unpacking for after supper. There's something you and I need to discuss."

On cue, Betty pulled a chair up next to the sofa and motioned for Christina to sit down.

Laura plowed right in. "Honey, I don't know how to tell you. I wish I could make it easier. Your father has asked for a divorce."

"Mom, what did you do to drive Dad away?"

Laura's mouth flew open but no words came out for a few moments. To her surprise, Christina didn't blame her father at all. She jumped up from her chair knocking it over and glared at Laura, ripping her fingers away. "You shouldn't have nagged him about going to church or his working late. You know he enjoys his job."

"Christina, honey, I tried my best. I'm sorry if you think I failed."

Laura looked to her friend for support.

Betty looked surprised, but drew in her breath and defended Laura. "Christina, honey, I think your mother did all she could to keep the marriage together." She opened her mouth to say more, but Laura shook her head and held her finger to her lips.

Christina ran to her bedroom without another

word. Laura knew she went there to cry alone. Despite the longing to comfort her child, she gave Christina her privacy.

During the weekend, Laura noticed that Christina remained quiet and somber. She tried to be cordial and accommodate her guest, but Laura knew by her body language she struggled. Her puffy, red eyes revealed she must have cried.

On Monday, while Christina attended class, Laura and Betty took in some of the sights. They enjoyed each other's company and at times forgot their losses as they immersed themselves in the new surroundings.

The decision to stay longer than a weekend pleased Laura. It gave her time to make sure Christina would be okay. The day she and Betty left for home, Frank called to tell Christina his side of the story.

Laura listened to Christina's side of the conversation in silence. *Let her draw her own conclusions*. She knew her daughter's intelligence and wisdom would eventually help her put all the pieces together for herself. Even more than that, Laura expected God would be her defense.

Christina and her father possessed numerous common traits. They were both headstrong and wanted things their own way. Some of the traits, which made them both good lawyers, didn't work too well in personal relationships. They manipulated people and circumstances to their way of thinking. Kindness and love usually kept her daughter's motivation in check in most of her decisions, however. Laura knew Christina loved them both. She avoided putting her in a position to take sides. So, she left things unsaid that she knew the Lord would fill in for her and turned to walk down the hall – toward Betty and the suitcase in her hand.

CHAPTER ELEVEN

Moving On
Eight months later:

The rejection Laura felt consumed her, and cloistered her in a cocoon of her own making. She lunched with Betty, telephoned her daughter and close friends, worked at her ministry jobs, and attended church. But did little else. A friend informed her that Frank and his young secretary took up residence together in Kingwood, only a few miles away. The divorce finalized, but Laura remained in her own world. She wanted to guard against being hurt like this ever again.

Christina softened her attitude, but Laura could feel her hesitation to accept the divorce. Laura heard her refer to them as family whenever she talked to others. "Mom and Dad wants me to work in this area when I finish my law degree and pass the bar." Or things similar to make others think they united together.

Friends Laura and Frank once shared avoided her. Laura sensed they felt threatened by her new status as a divorced woman. The women seemed concerned that she might attract their husbands. Or they didn't want to be reminded the same thing could happen to them. Others didn't know what to say.

"Laura, it's time you got on with your life. It's been eight months since Frank left. He's moved on and so should you." Betty advised Laura, as they sat in the kitchen of her home drinking coffee and visiting about the upcoming church retreat.

Laura glanced around at Betty's newly painted walls. The odor still lingered from the paint. The oily smell of the baseboards mixed with what reminded her of fresh linen of the wall paint gave her a slight headache. She took in the sight of the pictures Betty used to decorate. The fancy plates displayed made the place look elegant, yet comfortable. "I really like what you've done with the kitchen. You've really brightened up the place. The light green paint made your oak cabinets stand out. Everything looks so neat and clean."

"Thank you. I'm glad you like my new look. But don't try to change the subject. You really do need to pull yourself together and go on with your life." Betty didn't let her get away with a thing.

Laura understood Betty's concern for her, and she too wanted to move on. What a scary thing to do. Her stomach churned just thinking about dating or going to social events. She didn't know if she could take any further pain in her life. Could she bear someone else pushing her away? Could she play the dating game and risk being hurt again?

"I know I should.... I don't know if I can play the dating game. I wouldn't know what to say or do. What do people talk about on a date this day and time?"

Betty laughed but sobered when Laura wrinkled her forehead into a frown. Betty looked concerned. She patted Laura's hand. "You will figure it out as you go. Besides the Lord will give you the words."

"Frank stopped talking to me long before our divorce. His work kept him too busy, and in hindsight, other things as well." Laura folded and unfolded her paper napkin, not really giving Betty her true feelings but hinting at them. Laura found it difficult to open up completely, even to her best friend. She couldn't risk rejection or betrayal from anyone ever again. She thought she could trust Frank, but look where that got her.

Where had the strength she showed during the divorce settlement gone? She stood up to Frank then, and made sure he didn't get off without treating her fairly. The law firm Laura hired to represent her in the divorce made sure Frank didn't leave her destitute. Mr. James, a fair but good lawyer, bartered for the house and a small stipend each month for her. Frank would continue to take care of Christina's education. Since then, after months of living alone, her wounded spirit found it difficult to summon the courage to move on as Betty suggested.

"You should accept the date offer from John. He's a nice guy. He never married. I understand he almost did once, but his fiancé wanted more than a schoolteacher's salary could offer, so she married a lawyer instead."

"Oh, how that must have hurt..." Laura looked down at the retreat map.

Betty didn't take a breath. "He took care of his mother for years, until she died recently. Between teaching school and his mother, I guess he never found time to marry."

Laura squirmed in her seat. But Betty continued her spiel. "Could be, he never found the right woman. I think he dated some, but nothing ever came of it. Maybe, he likes being a bachelor, but I can tell he's smitten by you." Betty pointed her finger at Laura and chuckled.

Laura listened to the spin her friend put on John until her last statement. Then she almost choked on a gulp of her coffee. She regained her composure and swallowed, but she hesitated before answering. "I guess I could go out to dinner with him. He's asked me several times, but I've always given him an excuse. He doesn't give up easily. He pops up everywhere I go." Laura waved her hands in the air to show Betty what she meant. "Maybe if I accept his invitation, he'll at least let up for a while…

"Great idea!" Betty fisted her hands and pumped them up and down several times.

"Now, I don't want to encourage him too much. I'll just let him know I'm not interested in a close relationship, just a friend and a companion for dinner once in a while." Betty nodded her head up and down to confirm Laura should accept the date.

"But that's all. I'm too old to even consider remarriage."

Betty almost spewed out her coffee. She gulped. "Are you kidding me? You're only fifty-five. I know people sixty and up, who are getting married. I know one couple in their eighties. You're just as old as you feel."

"Well, I feel pretty old right now. I feel like an old worn out shoe discarded for a newer style." Laura hung her head. She thought about how rejection hurt, and she didn't want to feel that way ever again. She remembered the first time she met John at Casey's. The time she ran into him searching for rice. He did seem nice.

"Now, Laura, life goes on. Frank didn't appreciate you." Betty patted Laura's hand again.

Laura looked up and made eye contact. "I guess we didn't appreciate each other enough."

"Frank wasn't worthy of you in the first place. I don't think he ever really knew the Lord, so you were unequally yoked. Even though he might have called himself a Christian, I never saw evidence in his life." Betty rolled her eyes with a smug look on her face.

"Now, Betty, we can't judge him."

"No, but we can be fruit inspectors." Betty crossed her arms and a smug look came on her face. "And I don't see much fruit in his life. This time we'll pray and ask the Lord to give you a Christian husband, who'll be the spiritual head of your household." She again shook her head in agreement as she talked.

Laura's forehead rose in a frown of disapproval regarding Betty's verbal evaluation. She felt the heavy crease in her brow. But Betty didn't seem to notice, so Laura gave a speech of her own.

"Hold on, Betty, you're getting way ahead of yourself. I've not even gone on a date yet. I don't know much about John, except he's a retired teacher, likes to cook, and lives on the next street. Besides what you've just told me, of course. He looks to be about sixty, and I'm not sure if he even goes to church." She stood up, reached for the coffeepot to refill their almost empty cups. The scent of the hazelnut made her mouth water. She carried the cups back to the table where Betty sat.

"Well, there's only one way for you to find out. Go out with him! You'll probably run into him at the bank, post office, or grocery store in the next few days, so tell him you'll go with him this Saturday night. You can tell me all about it on Sunday." Betty chuckled at her own cleverness, and then downed a large gulp of her full cup of coffee almost spilling it.

Laura's mouth flew open at her discourse. When she finally recovered, she challenged Betty. "I might do that! Mainly, to stop you from nagging me all the time." Laura reached over and playfully swatted at Betty. "Now let's change the subject and get back to planning for the church retreat. Do you want me to drive?"

"That would be great." Betty leaned across the table and looked at the brochure.

"Sure. I'll be glad to drive. I'm really looking forward to the time with the other ladies at church, and the Lord. It'll be great. I hear our speaker's dynamic!" Laura unfolded the brochure containing the information. They examined it together and excitement filled their voices as they continued the conversation. Laura's anticipation grew, and she suspected Betty looked forward to the time away with the others as much as she did. Laura hoped they could brave the September heat, but Lake Palestine should be a little cooler than Humble.

With their plans made, they parted. As they did, Betty reminded Laura once more. "Tell me all about it on Sunday."

"Okay, okay, enough already." Laura waved her hand to motion Betty to stop the conversation on this subject, and to say goodbye.

Laura realized she needed salad dressing from the store for dinner, and wanted to pick up a few other things as well. While traveling to the grocery, she secretly hoped she wouldn't run into John. She wanted to prolong making a decision. When she didn't see him, she breathed a sigh of relief. Then, she rounded the corner of aisle five and almost ran into him, literally. She stopped her cart just short of his.

"Laura, how in the world are you? I've been thinking about you."

Laura started to answer, but John kept on talking. “There’s a good movie showing this Saturday night and I wondered if you would like to see it with me? We could go to dinner before at *Steakout*. I’m not going to take ‘no’ for an answer this time.”

He stood there holding onto the cart handle. Dressed in shorts, a tee, and flip- flops, his face neatly shaven, and most of his brown hair in place, he reminded Laura of the things she liked in a man’s appearance. He took care of himself.

“Okay, that would be lovely. I haven’t seen a good movie in a while, and you chose my favorite place to eat. Your offer is too good to refuse. And I could use a friend right now.” Laura smiled as she held on to her own cart. Happy she had applied make-up before running out to the store, she wondered what he thought of her.

The stunned look on his face told her he felt shocked at her answer.

I want him to know I prefer to keep things on a friendship level, so he won’t get any ideas. She wasn’t ready for anything serious. She didn’t know if she would ever be again. She didn’t want to trust anyone with her heart.

Even though the past few years with Frank deemed difficult, she never expected him to walk out on her for someone else. She wondered if any woman ever did. Why couldn't things have stayed the same? Why couldn't she grow old with her husband of so many years? Oh, she knew divorce happened to other people, but not to her family, or to her personally. But, it did. Here she was - divorced! And accepting a dinner date with another man! She wondered what others might think of her. *Do they view me as an old discarded shoe?*

She couldn't continue to allow herself to think these negative thoughts. *What does it matter what others think? What really matters most is what the Lord thinks. I only want to please Him with my actions, thoughts, behaviors, and deeds.*

"Let others think what they will." She spoke to no one other than herself after she left John to continue shopping. Her thoughts kept her from concentrating on what she needed to buy. Good thing she brought a list. She used the paper to guide her as she gathered her groceries.

Boy, I had better be careful. Now, I'm talking to myself. I've always heard it's okay though as long as I don't start answering. She pushed her cart around the next aisle and giggled to herself when she realized she had.

Laura walked to the checkout stand and paid for her items, her mind still in a quandary. She handed a tip to the young sacker when he finished loading them into the car. For some reason, he made her think of Christina. What would she think of her mom going on a date? Laura drove home in deep thought.

I hate to do it but I guess I will call Betty and get her advice on what to wear or what to do tomorrow night. It's Friday already! Wow, look at my hands. She turned them over and viewed their dry, wrinkled appearance, and her uneven, unpolished, and unkempt nails. *I didn't realize I'd let them get in such bad shape. I haven't gotten a manicure since Frank left. Maybe I'll just call the nail shop and see if I can get in to have them done. I don't want to go out in public or on a date looking this bad. What am I thinking? This is just a friendship date. However, I guess even for friends you should look your best.*

When she walked into the house and unloaded her groceries, she almost put the lettuce in the pantry and the bananas in the refrigerator.

Who do I call first Betty or the shop? Guess I better call the shop and see what time I can get in. She still questioned herself, even as she dialed the number.

"Beautiful Nails, may I help you?" The voice on the other end chirped.

Laura scheduled her appointment for eleven the next morning.

Maybe I should see if I could get my hair done at nine. It's been a long time since I've gone to the beauty shop.

She dialed the number and found she could get in at the desired time the next day. Breathing a sign of relief, she felt blessed to find an opening on Saturday on such short notice. *Well, at least my hair and nails will look good for Sunday. I guess it's time I started looking like my old self again. I need to come out of the haze I've lived in for the past several months.* She couldn't be hurt there. But, Betty was right. She did need to move on.

She picked up the phone once more, and dialed Betty this time.

"Hello, Laura."

Whenever she called, Betty answered by calling her name. She had finally gotten over the initial shock and grew accustomed to this Caller ID.

"Are you sitting down? I have some news that may floor you."

"What are you up to, Laura?" Betty giggled.

"Well, I finally did what you've been harassing me to do. I accepted a date with John." Laura let out a nervous laugh.

"Way to go. That's more like it. I'm so proud of you!" Betty sounded like a cheerleader.

"Whoa, don't get so carried away. It's just a friendship thing. I let him know that right away. We're only going out to dinner and a movie." Laura sat down in her recliner to get her breath. Sometimes, Betty could take it away with her enthusiasm. "Now, I need to know what I should wear, and what do I do?"

Laura could hear the giggle in Betty's voice as she went on to tell her what to wear and advise her. "I'll come over and help you pick something out this evening. We'll talk about what you should do. My best advice - be yourself and act natural. Like the old song says, 'all you gotta do is act naturally.'"

CHAPTER TWELVE

Preparation

Laura popped a frozen Chicken Alfredo dinner into the microwave. Tomorrow night, she would dine on a good meal at Steak Out. Her mouth watered at the thought of one of their steaks, or coconut shrimp. Though, she wasn't sure how the meal would digest because of the butterflies already forming in her stomach.

She sat down at the table and a jumble of thoughts invaded her mind. *I'm not sure about this idea. But, it's the only way to get Betty off my back about moving on with my life*. She didn't want to admit the excitement she felt about making a new friend.

Before she finished her entree, Laura heard a knock on the front door. *Betty must've eaten fast in order to get here this quick.* Laura grabbed her plastic tray, dumped it in the trash, and inserted her dishes in the dishwasher. Clean up didn't take long for one person.

Laura answered the door and motioned Betty in through the foyer to the kitchen.

"Would you like a cup of coffee and a piece of pie?"

"No, I'm full from dinner. If it's okay with you let's have our treat later. Right now, I just want to help you pick out what you'll wear tomorrow night."

"Betty, you're more excited than I am about this date. Maybe *you* should go out with John."

"Don't think I haven't thought about it." Betty's eyes twinkled mischievously, then, she grimaced and continued. "He doesn't even notice me. His interest lies only in you. I see the way he looks at you and watches your every move."

"Stop teasing me. You're making me more nervous by the minute. I may back out yet."

Betty's mouth flew open, and she gaped at Laura

"No, I wouldn't do that." Laura shook her head back and forth. "It'd be rude at this late date. So, I'm committed, but there might not be a next time."

Betty gave a sigh of relief. "You'll probably enjoy yourself so much you'll want to keep going out with him. Who knows, maybe the two of you were made for each other." Betty chuckled as she stood waiting in the middle of the den. They bantered back and forth, laughing, enjoying their time together, even though, Laura felt awkward about the whole dating situation.

Laura shot her friend a warning look and started for the bedroom door. “You’re getting carried away again. Let’s get this done. Help me find something presentable to wear. I don’t want to look like a frump. I do have my dignity to keep, you know.” She looked back over her shoulder and smiled. “Also, I wouldn’t want to embarrass John. He does seem like a nice man.”

In Laura’s bedroom they headed for the closet. As they did, Laura passed the dresser mirror and caught sight of her reflection. *Good thing I’m getting my hair done tomorrow. I didn’t realize how bad it looked until now. I haven’t taken care of myself since Frank left.* Her hair, practically all gray and brown, looked like a skunk with blond only on the ends now. No sign of a perm or any type of curl. The scraggly mess stuck flat to her head. She lifted a strand with her fingers and frowned.

Thoughts of Frank made her realize what a peaceful, pleasant life she now enjoyed, even though, she sometimes felt lonely. In the past few years, they either argued or didn’t speak at all. *Why such grief at his loss?* She surmised that no one liked to feel rejected, even when things turn out for the best. She determined not to grieve and to conquer her feelings of rejection.

Laura reached the closet and opened the door to survey the contents. Betty stood beside her and conducted her own wardrobe inspection. She pulled out a dress, soft blue polyester and cotton, and held it up in front of Laura. “Let’s see how this looks.”

“You mean you want me to try it on?”

“Oh, yes. Let’s have a fashion show. It will be fun. Besides what else do we have to do? Unless you prefer reruns on television.” Betty giggled. “I do watch them over again at times. I don’t remember if I‘ve seen them or not, until they’re at least half over. By then, I want to see the rest, because more often than not, I don’t recollect the ending.”

“I know what you mean. I sometimes sit almost all the way through before I realize I’ve already seen the show.” Laura released another giggle of her own. *We sound like a couple of teenagers. Except they would have better memories!*

“So, I’ll bring you the dresses and you put them on. Then, we’ll decide what you should wear tomorrow night.”

Laura hesitated. “Sometimes, I don’t know what to do with you. But you do make me laugh.” She hugged

Betty close. "You're the best friend I've ever had. Thanks for being there for me."

"It works both ways. You're always there for me, too. Especially, when I get myself in a jam. You manage to pull me out. We make a good team. Anyway, let's start the show before we get too mushy and start crying." Betty had a knack for giving instructions.

"I'll try this blue one on first. While I'm doing that, you pick out something else and have it ready. Maybe we can save some time that way." Laura took the dress, laid it on the bed, and pulled off her outer garments.

"Let's savor the moment. Our agenda for the evening consist of modeling. No gin rummy tonight. And no reruns." Betty barked out her orders like a general.

Laura put on one thing after another with accessories to match, even down to the shoes and jewelry as Betty lined up the outfits. She pulled out garment after garment, looked through jewelry to match the dress, pantsuit, or skirt and blouse. Together they unboxed shoes, and Laura slipped on one pair after another with each outfit. When all was said and done and almost everything in the closet suitable to wear for the next night's date tried on, the dress of choice emerged - the soft blue polyester and cotton Betty picked out in the beginning.

At the end of the session, Laura ushered Betty toward the kitchen. "Let's have some chocolate chip cookies and hazelnut coffee."

"Sounds good to me." Betty sat down with a thud and pushed out a huge sigh. "Whew. That was a lot of work, but, so much fun."

"Yes, I'm exhausted. My jaws ache from laughing so much. I've never tried on so many frocks in one evening. I had forgotten about some of those old shoes. I don't even remember buying some of the jewelry and purses."

"You do have a lot to choose from." Betty stuffed down several cookies. "Whew, I must have worked up an appetite."

Laura ate right along with her and laughed. "Me, too."

When they had eaten their fill, Betty let out a big yawn. "I'm off to find my bed." She rose and headed toward the door.

"Thank you for a fun-filled evening and helping me find something to wear." Betty nodded and turned to give Laura a big hug when she reached the doorway. Laura hugged her back.

Laura switched on the porch light. "I'll watch while you walk home. I'll wait until you turn on the light before I find my own bed."

Laura watched her friend head across the yard through the darkness to her back door. *What a wonderful friend.*

She turned out the porch light and walked to her bedroom once more. She changed her clothes quickly and lay down. Once again, before she drifted off to sleep, she reflected upon shoes. M*aybe I'll trade in some of my old outdated shoes for new ones.* She would check them out more closely tomorrow. With a big day ahead of her, she pondered why she expended so much effort and energy just to go out to dinner and a movie with a friend.

CHAPTER THIRTEEN

First Date

The day of the big date sped by like a whirlwind running through a small town with a population of fifty. Laura barely turned around before the time came for her to get ready for her evening with John. She spent the day in constant preparation. The visit to the nail shop and the beauty parlor proved productive. The difference in her appearance gave her new confidence.

The thought of trading old shoes for new lingered on her mind from the night before. She stood in the department store and surveyed the racks and displays. She walked over and picked up a pair that looked like her blue dress. Sure enough, the color was identical. She didn't bring the dress, but she knew they would match exactly.

"What a great pair of slides." The saleslady took her money and commented about them.

"I'm certain they will match a dress I plan to wear tonight."

"You know, I believe I saw a purse this color on the sale rack." The clerk handed her the package along with her receipt.

"Thanks for your help. I'll check for the matching bag."

Laura quickly walked toward the purse aisle. Right away, she spotted the blue bag on top of the rack. When she picked up the find, she opened the box, took out a shoe, and held them side-by-side. *A perfect match!* She made her purchase and smiled about the great find. Right across the way the jewelry counter caught her attention. Silver earrings, a necklace, and bracelet lured her in the direction. She knew the ensemble would add the finishing touch to her outfit for the evening. The price tag fit her budget, so she couldn't resist buying them. Her attire for the evening suited her. God surely must be in this. *Perhaps, He wants me to move on with my life. I suspect Betty is praying for me.*

When she arrived home with all her purchases, time had slipped away. She hurried to bathe, put on her best perfume, the dress of choice, and the new acquisitions. She barely popped the clasp on her new bracelet when the doorbell rang. She jumped at the sound. Her jitters compared to her first date in high school.

What's wrong with me? I'm a fifty-five year old woman, not a sixteen-year-old teenager. Calmed by her self-talk, she managed to open the door without shaking out of her new shoes. She greeted John with a big smile.

***

John stifled a gasp when he saw her. He realized her beauty long before this time, but what a knock out tonight. He took in the pleasant sight of her as he looked her up and down.

"My you look ravishing tonight." He retained his wit and wondered about the adjective he chose. He didn't want to offend her on their first date. His hands shook as he stood in the doorway wondering how he landed a date with such a beautiful lady. Sticking his thumbs through his belt loops, he hoped she wouldn't notice.

The town bachelor, he dated a few women over the course of the years, but not many interested him. This one caught his attention. Her outward beauty exceeded most. And something about her struck him as different. His curiosity peaked and he wanted to get to know her. He hoped she would afford him the opportunity.

***

"You look nice yourself." She assessed his coordinated attire of black casual sports pants, a colorful casual shirt with a hint of black, and polished black loafers. His coordination of clothes outshined most men she knew. She always matched things for Frank. Happy with her and Betty's choices, she felt ready for the evening – at least to some extent.

"Would you like to come in for a few minutes while I get my purse?" She looked at him for an answer.

"I'll wait here. We must be on our way soon. I made our reservations for seven fifteen, and it's seven now." He checked his wristwatch.

"It'll only take me a moment." She noted his punctuality, something that impressed her about a man, or any person. He passed that test. He could make her a good friend. She had a few guy friends, but not any she could really confide in. A man's opinion came in handy for certain things. She picked up her purse and hurried back to the door. She didn't want to keep him waiting, or be late for their reservation. Like John, she, too, liked to be on time.

They arrived at the restaurant and found it buzzing with people. The hostess ushered them to a table near the back.

"I'm glad I called ahead. Quite a mob here tonight." John pulled back her chair and waited.

He's even a gentleman. In this part of the restaurant the noise didn't keep them from talking or hearing each other. They didn't have to shout like in some places.

Intent on menu selection, conversation dropped. Earlier she thought about what she would like to order when the time came. *Would it be steak or coconut shrimp*? She asked John what he liked before she decided.

"I like their coconut shrimp here. But their steak is great too. I switch from one to the other depending on how I feel."

"That's always my dilemma when I eat here. I love both of them. That's so funny." She laughed and felt a blush rise to her cheeks at the same time.

"I could order one and you the other and we could do some trading." He peered over the top of his reading glasses to search her face. She could tell he was serious.

Laura relaxed. They laughed together.

"I think that's a great idea!" Her own enthusiasm surprised her. She found the laughter and excitement exhilarating. Frank never encouraged her to show emotion. He squelched any attempts she made at showing them. *I'm not going to think about him tonight. I'm going to enjoy the evening.*

When the waitress arrived, John ordered one coconut shrimp and one steak, the special. They both chose Ranch salad dressing and steamed vegetables. *Most men like potatoes. I wonder if he's watching his weight or just going along with me.*

They engaged in light conversation while they waited for the food to arrive. Laura looked across the table at him.

"How many years did you teach before you retired?"

"Thirty. I taught history right here in town for the whole time. Some people like to move around, but I like roots." Laura heard the pride in his voice regarding his decision.

"I've lived here all my life. I wonder why we never got to know each other." Laura shifted in her seat to take a more comfortable position.

"I guess we never traveled in the same circles. Otherwise, I would have remembered you. I met you for the first time when you ran into me at the grocery store." John's eyes twinkled when he made the statement, or did Laura imagine the sparkle.

"I still can't believe I ran smack into you at the store that evening." She didn't really want to remember the circumstances of why she went to the store in the first place, but she did recall their meeting. The combination brought more heat to her cheeks.

Laura pondered his first line of thinking for a short time. She and Frank traveled in the attorney group. Maybe John avoided it since his first love married a lawyer instead of him. John didn't seem the type to hold a grudge that long. *Why am I going there anyway? We just didn't know the same people or go to the same church.* She hated to ask him right off what church he attended. *What if he doesn't go*?

When their food arrived, Laura recalled not having eaten since breakfast. Her stomach growled. She hoped he didn't hear the noise.

"Why don't we split this steak and coconut shrimp right down the middle?" John picked up his knife.

"Sounds good to me. I'm starving. I haven't eaten since breakfast, so I can do my part." She admitted. She couldn't believe her boldness. *He's so easy to be with. I no longer feel nervous.*

Laura enjoyed the leisure talk as they devoured their meal.

"Tell me a little about yourself." John sat down his fork and looked over at her.

"I sing in the choir, have a grown daughter away in college, like movies, reading, playing cards, and fishing."

"I can't believe you like to fish. I'll keep that in mind and take you sometimes." He lifted his tea glass and pushed it toward her as if pleased.

"I like to cook, read, play board games and cards, watch sports on television, fish, and enjoy movies." He never mentioned a church.

The conversation kept up steadily while they enjoyed their shared entrees. Laura saw John check his watch and frown. "I'm so sorry. We're not going to make our movie on time."

"Oh, that's okay. I've had a great time." Laura folded her napkin and placed it on the table. She left only one morsel of fat cut from the steak on her plate. She glanced over at John's and he had cleaned the dish.

"I promised you a movie. I'm sorry, and yet, I'm not sorry. I'm glad for the chance to know you a little better. However, I do want to keep my word. Will you go with me next Saturday? We can eat hotdogs at the movie, so we don't miss it. Or, I can cook us some burgers for lunch, and we can catch the afternoon matinee and eat popcorn for dessert."

"The latter sounds good to me. Since you tell me you enjoy cooking, I would love it! I also love movie popcorn." *I bet his food taste better than even Steakout, judging from the shopping I saw him do at the store.* Laura wiggled in her seat just thinking of his cooking for her.

"Now that's settled. We might as well stay for dessert and more conversation." John didn't seem to want the evening to end.

"I really shouldn't, since I ate so much already." Laura rubbed her full stomach under the table.

"Me, either, but it sure sounds good." John motioned for the waitress.

"How about we split one?" Laura knew the restaurant's dessert tasted as good as their entrees, maybe better. She couldn't resist his offer. She moaned as she shook her head in agreement.

"Okay. Let's do it." John gave her a wink.

"The triple chocolate tower is my favorite. Laura couldn't believe her continued boldness.

"I like that one best of all myself, so it's decided. " John gave the waitress their order.

Laura savored each bite of the delicious dessert. And she also enjoyed the company and conversation.

"Do you keep in touch with any of your students?" Laura wanted to know more about John and his teaching career.

"I can't seem to get rid of some of them." John laughed. "I don't really want to. Several contact me often to ask my advice, or when they want someone to listen to their troubles." John took another bite of the rich dessert.

Observing his listening qualities first hand, she could understand why they kept in touch.

John stood and helped Laura from her chair when they finished their dessert, and then they exited the restaurant. He continued his manners by opening the car door for her. She felt like a queen out with Prince Charming.

John got her home at a decent hour – ten o'clock. He walked her to the door. "I sure enjoyed the evening. Good food, but the conversation and company I enjoyed even more."

"My sentiments exactly." Laura fumbled with the key in the lock. "Thank you for a lovely evening. It doesn't matter that we missed the movie."

"We still have one to look forward to." He lingered in the doorway.

Once more she felt a bit nervous about his next move. "Oh, yes. I look forward to your cooking."

He pecked her cheek, then, waited for her to open the door and turn on the light inside before he turned to leave.

"Goodnight."

"Goodnight." She watched him amble down the sidewalk from the window. She floated to her bedroom and wondered about his walk to his car.

Laura undressed and got ready for bed. She looked down. *I am so glad I traded the old shoes for new!*

Before she went to sleep, she recognized the Lord wanted her to trade some other old things for new – her fear of rejection, her anxiety, and her lack of trust in others. She hoped they would be as easy as the shoes.

CHAPTER FOURTEEN

The Early Bird

Laura woke early on Sunday morning. She dressed for choir practice faster than usual. But before she headed out, the doorbell rang. A breathless Betty stood there when she opened the door.

Betty stepped into the entryway in one motion when Laura answered. “Well, how was it?”

“You’re sure out early this morning.” Laura raised one eyebrow and looked at Betty as she entered.

“Don’t be coy with me. Your date. Did you like him? What did you talk about? Do you want to see him again? Tell me all about it!” Betty stood in the hallway with her arms folded, tapping her foot.

“Come on in the kitchen, Betty. We have a few minutes before we leave for choir practice. The coffee’s still hot, so let’s have a cup. It’s hazelnut.” Laura walked toward the kitchen with Betty trailing.

“Oh, yes. I’d love some.” Betty sat at the kitchen table, their usual serious talking place.

Laura filled their cups, brought them to the table, and took the chair across from Betty. “There isn’t much to tell. We had a lovely time. He's very much a gentleman. We talked too long at the restaurant and didn't make it to the movie, so we plan to go next Saturday."

"Oh, you mean you already have another date scheduled? And you told me you couldn't play the dating game!" Betty laughed and rolled her eyes as she lifted the steaming cup to her lips.

Laura giggled. Laughing felt good, something she hadn't done much of in the past few months. She struggled to keep up appearances and continue with the charity and ministry work, for depression dogged her every step. The emotional upheaval of the divorce sapped her energy and left her listless and lethargic. Hopefully, this dark time in her life had come to an end and the light would come peeking through. She could feel Betty's happiness for her. Her friend liked seeing others enjoy themselves. She seldom thought of herself and her own needs.

Laura glanced at the clock and realized the time. "Wow, where did the extra minutes go? We're going to be late."

They scurried around, picked up their coffee cups, rinsed them in the sink, and then, literally ran out the door to their respective cars. In her haste, Laura wasn't sure she locked the door. She walked back, turned the inside lock, and pulled the door shut one more time.

On the ten-minute drive to the church, Betty must have remembered to refresh her lipstick. Laura saw her pull down her mirror, and apply some, so she reached into her own purse, found her lipstick, and traced her own lips as well. After these many years, she didn't need a mirror to get it straight. Her fingers knew the shape of her lips.

Upon arrival, they hurried into the choir room, yanked on their robes, and then, took their places in the assembly. Never late for practice before, others looked at them with a puzzled look, as if to say, "What's going on?"

Laura sighed, smiled, and winked at her friend. Betty returned her wink.

Laura sang with more gusto than usual, but on occasion her mind drifted off into another world. The world of dating, shoes, John, and what lay ahead.

The choir sang several upbeat songs and the preacher's sermon about the prodigal son, one of the best Laura ever heard, seemed to catch most everyone's attention. Laura loved how he compared the prodigal son's homecoming to one of a sinner coming into relationship with the Lord. She hoped parents, waiting for their own prodigal to return home, were encouraged.

The crowded foyer after the service revealed everyone's need for fellowship before they hurried off to the local restaurants and cafeterias. One thing about this church, the people loved to visit as well as eat. Laura and Betty invited other women in their same situations: widowed, divorced, or single, to join them at the cafeteria. Six of them gathered to share lunch together today. Dutch treat— a group policy.

Some of the younger women didn't know what *Dutch* meant, until Laura explained that each person paid for their own.

Seated at the restaurant, Myrtle Robbins, the oldest member of the group, took Laura off guard when she asked, "How was your date with John?"

"I guess the news was bound to get out." Laura smiled. She knew everyone in town probably knew by now. So Laura did take some ribbing and fielded some questions.

"John could call on me anytime." One of the other women voiced her admiration.

Laura understood. He was nice to look at, friendly, and a perfect gentleman. However, she planned to take it easy. She didn't want to run ahead of the Lord or go outside His will for her life. Besides, she thought herself too old to remarry, even though Betty told her otherwise.

Near the end of the luncheon, Betty piped up after a long yawn. "I'm ready for my Sunday afternoon nap."

"Me too. Sunday's my day of rest. We better hurry if we want to make it back to church for evening service." Laura chimed in after she found the yawn contagious.

Laura ended the yawn with a start. She looked across the dining hall and spotted Frank and his *live in* sitting down for lunch. After all these months, she still hurt to think he threw her away for a younger model, especially when she sat face to face, or at least across the restaurant, to the reminder. Her heart raced and her hands trembled a bit.

Laura's demeanor changed. Betty followed her gaze across the room. When she saw the reason, she took Laura by the hand and helped her from the booth. "Let's go." She spoke softly. "Don't let him bother you. Just act as if you don't notice him."

The young woman looked her way, but Laura avoided eye contact and followed Betty out as if she didn't see them, even though, her knees nearly buckled beneath her.

With shaking hands, Laura turned the key in the ignition and then drove away. She thought she would have to fight to keep her eyes open on the drive home from the cafeteria, but, after the encounter, she found herself wide awake. Even after arriving to the safety of her bed, her eyes stood open and she couldn't sleep. She no longer loved Frank, but after years of marriage, she couldn't pretend the incident didn't disturb her. The sting of rejection still hurt.

Then, she thought about the evening before, and the comments the others made at lunch. Yes, she welcomed the diversion. But, she didn't want to get serious. She never wanted these awful feelings of rejection again. *I will guard my heart and be careful.* The thought stilled her beating heart and brought peace. Within minutes, she drifted off to sleep.

When Laura awakened, she dressed and walked over to Betty's. This particular evening Betty invited

Laura to ride with her to the service. Laura fielded more questions from Betty as they talked on the way to church.

"Well, does he go to church? Is he a Christian?" Betty turned inquisitive eyes to her when they stopped for the red light. She reached over and turned the radio off.

"I don't know. We didn't broach the subject. I didn't want to turn him off, or chase him to the hills. I think maybe he has known the Lord. He acts like a Christian. I thought I would just go slow and build a bridge."

"Sounds like a good idea to me." Betty turned her eyes back to the road and concentrated on her driving.

"I thought of bringing up the subject, but I didn't feel comfortable with asking him. Seriously, I don't think I need to bombard him, just yet." Laura shook her head, wondering if she thought clearly.

Betty stepped on the gas as soon as the light turned green. Laura knew why. Before someone in the long line of traffic behind them started honking.

Once she sped through the light, Betty turned again in Laura's direction. "Then you were right to hold steady. At times, the Spirit leads us to keep silent. Some people need to be won by our quiet and gentle spirit instead of our talk. Sometimes they have heard too much talk and not seen enough walk."

"That's exactly what I discerned. I think there's a definite reason I didn't say anything about church or religion."

"When it's time, you'll know." Betty shook her head up and down, then glanced over at Laura.

"I think you're right." Laura crossed her arms and squirmed in the seat, ready for this conversation to end.

"I noticed how upset you were when we saw Frank today." Betty turned empathic eyes toward her.

"I know I'll run into him from time to time, but I've got to get over these feelings of rejection and hurt. Please pray for me." Laura looked over at Betty and felt the tears well up in her eyes.

"You know I continue to pray for you. And I will definitely pray about the rejection issue. I can't even imagine your pain." Betty stopped the car. They had arrived. She reached over, took Laura in her arms, and gave her a hug.

Laura hugged back then wiped away the tears. She sat up in her chair, straightened up her lipstick, and, then, opened the door. Betty followed her lead.

The opening song chorused to them at the door as they walked into church. They slid into a center pew and entered into the song of praise from their hearts. Laura enjoyed the praise team that led the music on Sunday night. When the worship time ended, the pastor stepped forward for the sermon. Laura especially liked Sunday nights. She relaxed with the slower pace. She looked around and sighed, grieved that not many attended. Still, the pastor brought an anointed message. Her own spirit fed, she would draw strength from his words during the week.

On their way home, Betty pulled into IHOP. Laura felt relieved when Betty spoke of things besides John, and Frank. All the talk about the date made her feel self-conscious, and the hurt of her dead marriage didn't liven her spirits either.

They sat in the booth drinking coffee. Laura decided not to indulge in a meal this late. Betty ordered a senior breakfast of eggs, bacon, and pancakes. She delved into her food, not laying her fork down once. Laura had never seen her eat so fast. She acted as if she hadn't eaten all day.

"You know I have the ladies canasta group at my house this week. Want to help me plan for the refreshments?" Laura hoped her friend would be a part of the preparation.

"Sure. I'll help. Why don't you come over in the morning for coffee around ten and we'll discuss the menu. I'm ready to go back to bed now." Betty yawned.

Laura wondered why Betty was still sleepy, since she slept most of the afternoon. But she let it pass.

Laura walked across Betty's driveway, unlocked the door, and dressed for bed. She picked up a Christian romance novel someone loaned her and started to read. Since she napped in the afternoon, sleep eluded her. The book intrigued her, and she didn't want to put it down. Around midnight, she fell asleep with the book still in her hands. When she felt something hit her chest, she put the romance story on the nightstand and turned over. Her friend, the early bird, might wake her up in the morning. Every day she grew more thankful for their relationship.

Laura wondered what the next day might bring. Lately, every day seemed new and exciting. And some filled with surprises – both good and bad. God had ushered the sunshine back into her life, and the old feeling that everything was going to be okay returned. Would it last? She hoped so.

CHAPTER FIFTEEN

Show Time

"We better decide what to serve for the canasta group tomorrow. I sure enjoy the ladies." Laura sat at Betty's kitchen table sipping coffee and eating homemade chocolate chip cookies.

"It doesn't really matter what we serve. Those ladies will eat just about anything. However, we need something diet. You know everyone counts calories, at least they say they do." Betty laughed and bit off another bite of cookie.

"Yes, everyone watches their figure. Except us, right now." Laura held up her cookie and groaned. "But these are wonderful."

"Thanks. A couple won't hurt us." Betty took another one from the tray.

"Do you suppose everyone will show up? I hope we don't have to call someone else at the last minute." Laura looked over at Betty and frowned.

"You always worry too much." Betty took another sip of her coffee to wash down the cookie.

"I'm glad we joined the *Hi Neighbor* group. I hope our influence leads some of the ladies to Christ." Laura turned to Betty. "You always lift everyone's spirits. You're the life of the party."

"Well, you will outshine everyone this week. You look great. The new hairdo and manicure lifted your spirits and made you look even more beautiful. Your date with John brought a new bounce to your step." Betty leaned back in her chair and grinned.

"Maybe the new clothes and shoes helped my appearance." Laura flushed with embarrassment at Betty's teasing.

"I do believe you're blushing." Betty squinted her eyes and looked more closely at her friend.

Laura shook her head and swiftly changed the subject. "Come on. Let's make the plans for the refreshments. You said you wanted to help."

"Well, let's make a fruit plate, serve nuts, drinks, a vegetable plate, and a low calorie pie for dessert. Maybe we better make a couple of those." Betty held up two fingers.

"I think you're right. We don't want to forget about the dieters." Laura laughed and then stuck another bite of cookie into her mouth.

"I'll make the pies, and you fix the drinks, fruit, and vegetable plate. I'll pick up some nuts at the store." Betty picked up a pen and wrote nuts on her shopping list lying on the table beside her.

"Thanks Betty, I knew I could count on you to help me decide. What a relief to have all the plans made." Laura signed and settled back in her chair.

Betty leaned back, stretched, and yawned. "I'm exhausted. All this planning wore me out. Think I'll crawl back into bed when you leave." She did look tired. Her face appeared drawn, and she had lost weight. Dark circles appeared under her eyes. Some of the usual dancing light had disappeared.

"Are you feeling okay?" Laura scrutinized her carefully.

"Yes, I'm fine. Just a little tired. You've kept me pretty busy lately."

"I'm sorry." Laura stood, walked to the sink, washed out her coffee cup, and headed toward the door.

"Oh, don't think a thing of it. I was only kidding. I'll see you in the morning." She walked Laura to the door.

Laura wanted a nap herself when she arrived home, but finished up the last minute details around the house. She needed to run her errands and prepare her part of the refreshments. *I hope no one teases me about John tomorrow.*

Later in the afternoon she phoned Betty to check on her. She sounded better, but Laura still heard a hint of weariness in her voice. Exhausted from the busy day, Laura fell asleep before she said her prayers.

The next day everyone showed up, and on time.

Sue Jones, the lady in charge of the group, tilted her head back like a lawyer drilling a witness. "Laura, didn't I see you and John Talbot at *Steakout* last Saturday night?"

"Well, yes…"

Sue looked up over her reading glasses. Her short dark hair cropped close to her head. All 5'2" inquiring. "We were across the room, but I never got a chance to come and talk with you. You appeared to be in deep conversation, and I hated to interrupt."

"We're just friends. You should have come over to visit." Laura squirmed in her chair. "Whose turn is it?" She wanted to change the subject and resume the card game.

Betty must have sensed Laura's discomfort and came to her rescue. "Mary, how is your new grandbaby doing?"

Mary popped out her newest pictures for all to see. Laura previously thought Mary got her flaming red hair from a bottle, but seeing the child let her know differently. The same curly red hair blazed from the photo. Laura felt relieved and grateful to Betty.

Grandchildren took the conversation in a whole new direction. Several ladies pulled out pictures, and told stories about their offspring's smart children. Laura breathed a silent sigh of relief, and Betty gave her a wink.

"Thanks." Laura mouthed, and Betty nodded in acknowledgment.

Concentrating on the game proved difficult. Her mind drifted to John and their upcoming movie date. She wondered what he would choose. She didn't attend R rated movies anymore. *Would he pick one?* If he did, she would object. He might think her a prude, but she made a pact with the Lord not to view any beyond a rating of PG13 after she fell under conviction a few years ago, and some of those were iffy. She and Frank had disagreed about this, but she stood her ground on this issue, one of very few. He almost always got the last say about most things.

Laura partnered with Janice at one point in the game. Janice talked very little and seemed quite shy. She failed to drag out any pictures. Most of the conversation centered on children and grandchildren. She speculated Janice as a single lady, even though she looked to be in her forties. Laura sensed something troubled her, but found no opportunity to talk or become better acquainted with her. She kept to herself and didn't volunteer any information. Her red hair looked quite natural. They went with the freckles on her face. Laura wished she had such a petite figure.

When the game ended, they tabulated the scores and Betty scored the highest. The ladies each put in a dollar to play, and the two highest scores split the pot. The lowest score received her dollar back from the second highest player. When Laura first came to the group, she thought the money went for the snacks. Not until the end of the game, did she realize its purpose.

Frank had teased her about gambling when she told him the story. She didn't view the game as such. She thought of playing cards as a fun time with the ladies. Even though, some of the conversations today made her feel a bit uncomfortable, she still enjoyed herself. She received her dollar back as the low score for the day.

Laura worked on Wednesday at her job as a volunteer for the area ministry, assisting in the donation store, one of her favorite things. This ministry helped hundreds of people. She smiled and felt a sense of pride when one of the usual customers came in and greeted her by name.

"Mrs. Laura, you sure are looking fine today. You look happier than I've seen you in months."

"Thank you, Mary, I'm feeling great today. I'm blessed. And how are you doing?"

"Well, Mrs. Laura, to tell you the truth, I'm doin' fine myself. The good Lord's done blessed me too."

More conversations of this nature ensued as the day progressed. Laura relished the fact that others wanted and needed her here at the store. She loved the feeling of acceptance and appreciation it afforded her. *I am truly blessed.*

Before she realized the time, the day came to an end. She picked up Betty for choir practice. Afterwards, Laura and Betty could hardly wait to turn in for the night, so they didn't linger or stop off for coffee or dessert on the way home like usual. Laura needed a good nights rest. She fell into bed almost immediately upon arriving home.

After breakfast, she headed to the local Christian radio station to help fill in for the receptionist.

"My, you're looking lovely today." One of the deejays complimented her when she walked in the door.

"Thank you." The heat rose in her cheeks. *What is it with all these people? I look the same as always.* However, she conceded. *I have fixed myself up some*. She surmised the visits to the beauty salon and nail shop paid off, or perhaps the new shoes she wore made a difference.

She packed everyday with activity. She went early to water aerobics class three mornings that week. She wanted to go back to sleep but persevered. *I have to keep up my exercise program. I feel so much better when I do.* She skipped her walking exercise on Thursday. She couldn't manage to pull herself out of bed soon enough before heading to the radio station. R*etirement is busier than when I worked, or have I just slowed down*? *How did I ever find time to work? My nurse's schedule kept me busy, but nothing compared to this.* She had saved toward retirement, but times came when money proved a bit tight. Frank did all right by her in the divorce settlement. Thanks to her lawyer.

At any rate, the week flew by.

***

John met with a group of retired teachers for a luncheon on Monday. Senator Clark spoke on current events. A former history teacher, he enjoyed listening to history in the making.

Who knows maybe this senator will be the next president? John decided he would certainly vote for him since they shared the same views on what was happening in the world.

On Tuesday while he did his own housework, he sang one of his favorite hymns. He often sang around the house, especially when he made up different dishes. An even happier melody carried in his voice today. *I'm so glad I learned to cook. I suppose living with mother and her being ill taught me a lot of things*. He contemplated what he would prepare for Laura.

A knock sounded at the door. John wiped his hands on the towel looped over his belt and went to answer. A fresh-faced youth stood on his doorstep.

"Hello. My name is Bob Swanson. I'm raising money for a mission trip to Mexico." Bob pulled a brochure from his pocket and handed it to John. "We're doing vacation Bible schools at several impoverished villages."

John glanced through the pamphlet, impressed by the scores of faces that shone from the pages. "Bible schools you say?" He reached for his wallet before the youth finished his spiel. "Sounds like a good cause." He reached for his back pocket, took two twenties from his billfold, and pressed the money into the young man's hand. "Good for you, son."

He ignored the tax receipt the young man offered, waved away his thanks, and went back to the kitchen glad he had accomplished his good deed for the day. He wouldn't need to think about doing one again for at least another twenty-four hours.

Since retirement, John managed to keep busy. Besides going to the meeting that week, he went fishing. This time he took his friend, James, out in his boat instead of fishing from the bank. James eyed him from the front of the boat. "Say John, you're looking happier than usual. What's going on in your life?"

"Well, to tell you the truth, James, I've met a wonderful lady. She makes me smile. Don't know what will come of it, but for now I'm happy she's going out with me."

"John, that's great! Maybe this one will catch you." James smiled and gave him a wink.

Feeling a bit embarrassed, John bent to retrieve his hook from the tackle box. "Speaking of catching, we had better get busy catching some fish." He didn't want to say too much for fear the town gossips would get hold of it and make more out of the situation than they should.

Time slipped away as they baited their hooks and caught fish, but spent no more time discussing John's new girlfriend.

John enjoyed advising young people when he could. He met with Donna, a former student, one day for lunch. "Mr. Taylor, I don't know what to do. My mom's sick, I'm supposed to leave for college next week, but I can't leave her and just go off."

"Doesn't her sister live next door?" John knew the family history.

"Yes, but I think it's my place to look after her." Tears pooled in Donna's eyes.

"I'm sure your father will help as much as he can." John looked across the table at her. His bright blue eyes conveying empathy. "I know for a fact he wants you to return to college."

"I suppose …" Donna looked out of the window, and John gave her a moment to collect her thoughts.

He sat and listened as she voiced her problems and objections and asked just enough questions for her to come to her own decision. She would return to school.

"You can call every day and check on your mother's health. I'll let you know if a problem exist. I'll keep tabs with your dad." John hugged Donna gently as they parted.

John walked into the lodge for a board game or a hand of cards. Effram Middletown slapped him on the back as if he had just made a touchdown. "Hey, didn't I see you out with Laura Olson the other night?"

Well, it looks like the gossip has already started. "Yeah, we went out to dinner." John didn't want to make too big a deal, so he gave him a short answer and acted as though nothing out of the ordinary had occurred. Someone won the game about that time and the conversation shifted. John smiled, happy the kidding stopped.

John loved to read, so he grabbed a few minutes with a new book during the week. And, he watched the Rockets play, and even win for a change.

The doctor recommended he exercise more, so he went to the local health club and worked out on the machines and treadmill during the week almost every morning, except for the day he went fishing.

Saturday arrived, but not too soon. He surveyed everything. The last minute preparations would make everything perfect for Laura. The burgers lay on a platter ready to be cooked, the trimmings for them sliced, potato salad for a side dish in the refrigerator. Chocolate Mousse sat alongside the others. He passed a critical eye over the house, and smiled at the spic and span rooms that winked back. At noon, he left to pick up his date. Just as they left her residence, the clouds opened and the rain came down in torrents. *Now, how do we cook the burgers*? *What a bummer!*

***

Laura couldn't believe such a downpour. "I didn't even bring my umbrella." She didn't want to get her hair wet. Her beautician worked extra hard today on her. Laura hadn't told her about the date. But she liked the outcome and the confidence the style gave her.

Luckily, John carried two umbrellas in his car, so he took them from the back seat pockets and handed one to her. "Here, you go."

They laughed together as they opened them and jumped from the car to dash through the rain. They ran inside for cover. Laura's damp, slick shoe hit the polished floor and she skidded across the entryway. She went down with a bang as she slipped and fell on John's freshly shined tile. She took a pretty good bump on her backside.

Laura laughed even though tears formed behind her eyes. *How embarrassing, besides, it hurt.* "I can't believe I fell into your house. How clumsy of me."

They both laughed, but John kept repeating, "I'm so sorry. Are you okay?" He helped her off the floor. His laugh turned to a frown.

"You'd better sit down over here, and let's make sure you're okay." He guided her to the sofa.

He is really a nice guy.

After a few minutes of examining and discussing her injuries, they decided she would be okay.

"I'm so glad you're all right. The water must have made the floor slick." John looked at her, relief showing on his face.

She noticed the glistening tile when she fell. "Yes, well, I can't fault you for taking such good care of your home." Laura pointed at the gleaming entry. "Mine don't look like that. You'll have to teach me how you get them so spotless and shiny."

"Next time." John promised. "Right now, we have a slight problem." He glanced out the window.

"I know what you mean. How are we going to cook the burgers?"

"Exactly. How did you know what I was thinking?" John looked at her and laughed heartily.

"I have a George Foreman grill at my house. Would you like to go back and get it? We could cook them on it."

"You know, I received one of those for Christmas, but I've never used it. I'll bring it out, and you can show me how." He ushered her into the kitchen area and drug the machine out of the pantry. "I'd forgotten about it."

"It only takes five minutes to cook burgers on it. We should get the other things ready first."

"They're all ready. All we have to do is get them out. I think the grill even has a bun warmer on it. Hey, this may be more convenient after all. However, I do like to cook on the outside grill. We'll do that some other time."

He sounds as though I'm a permanent fixture. I hope he knows we're just friends. I'm sure he does...

"You get out the rest of the fixin's and I'll heat the grill and make the burgers. I have the easiest part. However, I may let you clean the grill, since that's the worst part." She plugged in the grill.

They chatted as they worked together and fixed lunch in no time. Laura observed John's culinary skills. He really knew his way around a kitchen.

When they sat down to eat, Laura hesitated and John looked at her. He nodded to her. "Would you like to say a blessing?"

She flushed and squirmed a little in her seat, but bowed her head and said a prayer. "Father, we thank You for the food we are about to receive, and thank You for the hands that prepared it. In Jesus Name. Amen.

Laura bit into her burger. The moist tender meat delighted her taste buds and the warm bun accentuated the patty. "Wow, these burgers taste great. Better than Fuddrucker's." She considered Fuddrucker's as having the best burgers around. "What's your secret?" Laura bit into her burger again and moaned with pleasure.

"They would taste better cooked outside, but I guess George did okay."

Laura ate more than usual. *This meal taste better than any I've had in a long time. This guy can really cook.*

"What did you do to these burgers? And that potato salad is to die for." She observed the vegetables were fresh and the buns some of the best she had ever eaten. She would buy this brand next time.

"They're both family secrets. I don't usually share them with anyone, but maybe I will someday."

"I sure hope you will. They're great, and I'm stuffed." She rubbed her hand across her stomach.

"We haven't had dessert yet? Chocolate Mousse chills in the refrigerator." John motioned toward the corner of the kitchen where it stood.

"Maybe later. Right now, I can't eat another bite. My daughter, Christina, should be here. Chocolate Mousse is her favorite dessert."

"I'm pretty full myself. Food tastes better when you have someone to share it with." He looked over at her tenderly, and she felt the heat rise to her face.

"Let me tell you how to clean this grill." Laura wanted to move on past the moment.

The table cleared, John stood ready. "I don't want you to mess up your nice manicure."

How thoughtful. Not every man would even notice. She gave him verbal instructions.

After lunch and clean up, John took Laura on a tour of his home. The furnishings surprised her.

"Most of the antiques you saw belonged to my mother. I couldn't part with them. They meant so much to her." John held out a chair again at the breakfast table.

"I love antiques. I don't have any of my own, but I go to the antique shops to look at them frequently. I've never seen a table and chair exactly like this. And the bedroom furniture in the guest room, the intricate carving surpasses any I've ever seen. I liked your traditional bedroom set with all the drawers and cabinets, also." The set in his room met her expectations for an organized man like John. Everything fit in place. The huge den just off the kitchen held a big screen television, a traditional sofa, a stereo, and a large recliner along with end tables and lamps. The guest bedrooms, the dining room, formal living room, and breakfast room all had antique furniture. Laura figured John's mother brought in the furniture for those rooms, and John contributed those for his bedroom and the den

The rain continued to pour. They turned on the weather channel and found flood warnings were issued throughout the area. They debated whether they should go to the movie or not.

"How about staying here and watching a video for now?"

"Sounds good to me. I certainly don't want to get flooded, or stranded, somewhere."

"Okay, let's choose a movie from these DVDs. I have several choices. Some I bought yesterday." John held out the DVDs for her to pick one. "It's show time!"

Laura glanced at the stack wondering what she might find. Would she have to turn them down due to their rating, or did he choose to her liking?

CHAPTER SIXTEEN

The Retreat

Laura pushed down the accelerator and drove up Highway 59 to Highway 287, then into the beautiful countryside of Palestine for the women's retreat. She and Betty planned for weeks and looked forward to a special time with all the other ladies, and the Lord. Laura elected to do the driving this time, since she owned a late model, Buick LaSabre and kept it in shape. Betty needed new tires and some work done on her air conditioning, something the ladies didn't want to be without in Texas. The day, hot and humid, resembled so many in the Lone Star state, but the view took their breath away.

"What awesome scenery! The Lord's handiwork amazes me." Betty stared out the window at the wooded areas. "Peace floods over me when I look at the trees, flowers, and green grass. I picture Heaven like this. Look at all the clusters of flowers. And the grass reminds me of carpet, even fuller than the Astroturf at Minute Maid Park."

Laura noted the tall pines dwarfed some of the other native trees. The dense vines and shrubs added to the beauty of everything. A few flowers bloomed on the bushes. She didn't recognize them enough to call them by name. Silence prevailed for a time as they admired everything along the roadside. Finally, Betty broke the spell.

"You've really seen me through some hard times. I don't know what I would have done without you during the time of Jim's sickness and death. I know my sweetheart left me for a better home in Heaven, but I sure miss him. For the forty years of our marriage, we hardly left each other's side." Betty sounded melancholy and tears etched down her checks.

"I know the two of you were inseparable, content, and compatible. Something I always wanted for Frank and me. I almost envied you. Instead, I chose to be happy for you. Still there were times the comparison hit a nerve" Laura looked over at Betty and smiled.

"Frank didn't appreciate you the way he should have. Besides, he had a roving eye, something my Jim never had." Betty crossed her arms and set her jaw.

"That's because you made him feel so loved. I could never satisfy Frank. I guess he finally found his happiness somewhere else."

“I wouldn’t be too sure of that. Men like Frank don’t find happiness, or what they seek, until they find the Lord. That’s what’s missing.”

“I know in my heart you’re right, but sometimes I feel as though I failed.” Laura glanced over at Betty as she drove. A large Magnolia tree caught her attention and she turned for a better look in the opposite direction. She couldn’t remember ever seeing one so tall. “Oh, look, Betty, have you ever seen a Magnolia tree that huge?”

“No, the one in my yard isn’t near that size, and I thought it was big. But I do hate picking up the leaves in the springtime. They look like large pieces of paper spread over the lawn.”

“I know I’ve watched you and Jim gather them. They do make a mess, but the blossoms smell so sweet.” Laura recalled Betty picking up the leaves almost daily when they fell in the early spring.

The girls admired the tree and then fell back into their conversation as if they hadn’t missed a beat. “You didn’t fail. You tried everything you could from what I saw. Frank wants to be in charge, and so he won’t let the Lord have control of his life.”

“Yes, he’s manipulative and domineering. I never want to be another man’s doormat again. He got worse the more I tried to keep peace in the family. Most of the time, I just gave him his way."

"I know, Laura." Betty patted her shoulder. "You did the best you knew how, but no, I don't think you'll ever allow another person to manipulate you. At least, I hope not. Sometimes, we have to go through these trials to grow in our faith and stronger in our resolve. God has a way of turning bad things for our good."

Has she found the good in her own situation?

"Thanks for being there for me through the tough times. God knows what each of us needs, and I definitely needed you in my life." Laura reached over and patted Betty as she spoke.

Laura concentrated on her driving and Betty grew silent again as she observed the view. With her peripheral vision Laura watched Betty, and suspected she reflected on times gone by just as she did. Her heart warmed and she felt grateful for such a friend in her times of desperation, and knew Betty felt the same. Yes, God met their every need.

Betty broke the silence. "I'm fortunate. At least, I will someday be together with Jim again, forever. He left loving me. Frank's rejection must have really hurt. I reiterate. He never deserved you." She shook her head back and forth for emphasis.

Laura reminisced and Betty listened. "I'll never forget that Sunday evening when I came home from church, and he told me he wanted a divorce as he packed his bag to leave. 'I just don't love you anymore. We've both changed and we have different interests. We've grown apart. That happens sometimes.'" Laura tried to mimic Frank.

"I stood in the doorway of the bedroom in a state of shock, and tried to persuade him to go for counseling and not give up on our marriage. He packed while I cried, and even begged a little. Things had been on the rocks for some time. Finally, I asked, 'where are you moving to?'"

Laura took a breath. "Why am I telling this again? I've told you before. You went through the whole thing with me."

"Yes, Laura. But I wanted to let you tell your story one last time. After this weekend, you won't need to ever again, except for God's glory, for He will take away those hurts and heal the pain." Betty spoke with confidence, as if she knew the Lord's intention for Laura.

"Let's talk about something more pleasant now." Laura wanted to get away from the subject of Frank. The sting of rejection, hurt, and desertion still plagued her. She felt Frank had thrown her away.

Betty must have sensed the pain Laura endured for she changed the subject. “Do you remember the time we went shopping separately, came home with the exact same dress, and held them up simultaneously for the other to see? I thought Jim would never stop laughing.” Betty laughed as she told the story.

“I would like to have a picture of the look on your face. You know we never did wear them at the same time.” Laura spoke as the realization hit her. She remembered the light blue dress with swirls of multi-colors throughout the dress, the scooped neckline, and the three quarter length sleeves. She loved the dress and wore it often.

“No, we never did.” Betty started laughing, and kept on until tears streamed down her face. She couldn’t stop long enough to say a thing.

Finally, Laura reached over and shook her. “Why are you laughing so hard?”

When Betty regained her composure, she let Laura in on her secret. “Well, the reason we never wore them at the same time was because I took mine back to the store for a refund. I never told you. I couldn’t have you showing me up in the same dress. It looked better on you."

"Betty, you're a hoot. I never knew. I still never know what you will do next. Now, I realize why I never saw you wear it." They both laughed long and hard.

"Do you remember the choir program we did when two of the ladies showed up in the same costume?" Betty rolled her eyes.

"Oh, yes. After the first time, I never saw those costumes again. Talk about being vain. Guess they both made new ones or hired someone else to sew them another."

Laughing together felt good, but after a while Betty stopped and looked over at Laura with a serious look on her face.

"Laura, let's talk seriously for a moment. I'm glad you're dating John. Don't let him get away. I think he might be the Lord's choice for you."

"Sweet friend, I appreciate your love and concern. But I'm not ready to marry again, and may never be. So keep me in your prayers. I don't want anyone to get hurt, me or John."

"So, how was the movie? Is John a good cook? Did you find out about his church?" Betty asked one question after another before Laura could even answer the first one.

“We never made it to the movie. We decided to stay at his house and watch a DVD.”

“You didn’t make it to the movie?”

“If you remember, it rained cats and dogs that day. We cooked the burgers on the George Foreman grill. It was too wet to cook them on the outside grill.”

“Oh, yes, it did rain last Saturday.” Betty’s brow went up in a puzzled look. “I need to get me one of those grills.”

“No, I didn’t find out about his church, or if he has one. But, none of the DVD’s were rated R.” Remembering her pleasant surprise, Laura smiled.

“Well, that’s good they weren’t rated R.”

Laura laughed. “Betty, you should see his house. It’s immaculate. Talk about a good cook. I think we easily had one of the best meals I’ve ever tasted. Oh, and he asked if I wanted to bless the food.”

“You could use a husband like that. You might not ever have to cook again.” Betty chuckled.

“You’re getting ahead of yourself Betty…. Have you picked out my wedding dress too?”

Betty chuckled.

"I'm so glad to see you getting your life back on the right track, to see you laugh again, taking care of yourself, getting your hair and nails done, and moving on with your life." Betty looked over at Laura with no sign of jest on her face any longer.

"Thank you, my dear friend, for encouraging me. You've been the biggest help to me with all of this. I would still be wandering around with no direction if it weren't for you." Laura stopped the car at the retreat grounds and gave Betty a big hug.

When Laura released her, Betty remarked, "Wow, if numbers are any indication, this should be a great weekend."

Ladies streamed from every direction. They watched the steady flow of women unloading their suitcases and walking to the office to check in. Then, they jumped out of the car and opened the trunk for their own bags.

Once the meetings began, the speaker proved to be as good as Laura anticipated and the Spirit moved in every service. One night as she walked the aisle for prayer, sure enough, a work began in her heart, and she felt a release from the pain and hurt of the divorce. The Lord set her free as she wept before the altar. She laughed and cried at the same time and forgave Frank as she let go of her fear of rejection.

However, she knew the battle might continue when the enemy brought the pain back to her remembrance. But she knew God would see her through whenever she drew close to him and resisted the enemy's ploys. She wondered why things couldn't always be settled once and for all. She liked to have things wrapped up in a neat package, never to deal with them again. She concluded that as long as the Devil dominated the earth, the packages would continue to come unraveled to a degree. She would work toward overcoming these feelings of rejection, and maybe, just maybe, one day she would be completely free.

Betty joined her, held her in her arms, and Laura recognized Betty's earlier statement as a prophecy, or word of knowledge. She no longer needed to tell the story or feel the pain. *God you're so good.*

She looked at her friend through teary eyes. "God did what you said He would." They held each other for the longest time, and then returned to their seats. The shining faces in the auditorium held a peaceful joy. All too soon the retreat came to an end.

On the way home, Laura elaborated on the awesome time together with the Lord and the other women. "We made a lot of acquaintances, and I enjoyed all of them, but I found no better friend on earth than you, Betty."

"The feeling is mutual." Betty shook her head in agreement.

Silence followed as Laura reflected on the retreat. She suspected Betty did the same. Then, Laura glanced over at Betty after traveling a few miles down the road. "What do you think about Pastor Howard leaving?"

"Well, the church will go through a transition time. The search committee is already looking for our next pastor, but they plan to wait on a decision until right before he leaves. I hate to see him go, but he wants to retire and spend some time with his grown children and small grandchildren in Arizona. Goodbyes aren't something I like, but God has the future in His hands. And He is still in control."

Laura admired Betty's wisdom, faith, and foresight. "Your good attitude amazes me. Some people dread the changes and complain."

"No need to get upset. God will take care of everything. Whether everyone believes it or not, He knows what He's doing." Betty folded her arms as if to say, "That settles it."

Laura laughed. Betty could make a joke out of anything. She thought of how Betty's humor kept depression away from her many times. "I'm so glad He's in charge of my life again, and He took away the pain. I feel like a bird let out of a cage. I'm ready to get my dancing shoes on and dance before the Lord." Laura pounded on the steering wheel. Her voice rose an octave and bubbled with joy.

Her life as a doormat ended at the altar. Jesus would be the only Lord of her life from now on. She looked forward to what the days, months, and years ahead would bring. *Will John be a part of my future, or does He have someone else in mind? Or, will I spend the rest of my days alone.*

No matter what lay ahead for her, she rejoiced to have Him and her best friend, Betty, in her life. With their help, she could survive in victory. Time to put on those walking shoes and continue to wherever he took her. *Sure wish I knew the direction. Help me to do what You would have me do, go where You would have me go, say what You would have me say, and be what You would have me be. I want to walk in Your will and Your way.* She breathed these thoughts as a silent prayer.

Laura looked over at her friend to tell of her decisions, but she turned to find Betty fast asleep, contentment shining on her face. However, Laura's concern for her friend's lack of energy, continued weariness, and sleeping habits as of late gave her an uneasy feeling. *I hope she's okay.*

CHAPTER SEVENTEEN

An Old Flame

The morning after the retreat, Laura woke to thoughts of John. They hadn't talked about the Lord, or church. So, she still didn't know where he stood on the issue. *Why haven't I asked? Maybe I'm not ready for the answer, or maybe he's not ready for me to ask.* She turned her face toward the pillow, certain they would see each other again. He had mentioned going to a movie.

Her daydreaming ended abruptly when she gazed at her bedside clock. She jumped out of bed, bathed, and ate her breakfast within a few minutes. She pulled on her favorite magenta top and black skirt. Betty expected her in less than an hour.

The phone jingled. "Laura, I'm not feeling well today. I'm going to beg off of choir practice and church." Betty's raspy voice came across the phone line barely above a whisper.

"Are you okay? What's wrong? Is there anything I can do for you?"

"No. Nothing... I think I'm just tired. I'll let you know if I should need anything. I believe I'll be fine."

Laura's thoughts drifted to her friend during choir practice and service. *I sure hope she's okay.* The minute church ended, she headed to her car and sped toward Betty's house. She dialed the number on her cell phone. When Betty answered, Laura informed her of her plan. "I'll stop at the drive through and pick up something to eat. What would you like?"

"Just get me a small bowl of chicken soup. My throat's sore, but maybe I can swallow something warm and smooth." Betty's voice cracked.

"You got it. I'll be there as soon as I can."

"You don't have to hurry. I'll still be here." Betty whispered.

Laura snapped the phone shut, picked up speed, drove faster than usual, and almost missed the entrance for the drive up window, even though Betty cautioned her not to hurry.

Laura ordered the food. When it came, she hastily drove the rest of the way. Rather than disturb her sick friend and make her trudge to the door, she used the spare key and let herself in. Laura called softly, not wanting to frighten Betty.

"Come on in." Betty's whisper sounded strained and barely audible.

Laura tiptoed into the bedroom where Betty, propped against the pillows, laid wide-awake, but not her perky self.

"You look terrible."

"Thanks a lot! That really cheers me up and makes me feel better."

Laura chuckled, and Betty smiled and held back her own giggle.

Betty pressed her palm to her forehead. "Please don't make me laugh. It hurts."

"I'm sorry. What can I do for you?" Laura walked over and stood by her bedside, ready to do whatever Betty commanded.

"Just bring me the food, sit down, and tell me about church service." Betty lifted her hand and motioned to the chair beside her bed.

Laura described the service and shared her heart. "Everyone missed you in the choir. No one can take your place. You liven up the group. Pastor preached a good sermon. I brought you the tape. I sure hate to see him leave in a few months."

"Maybe the Lord will send in a better one, if that's possible. Of course, we know all things are possible with Him. He does all things well." Betty's faith and attitude always remained constant and positive.

"Have you heard from John since we got home? He wasn't at church by chance this morning, was he?"

"No. Betty, I think you're fixated on John." Laura busied herself opening their lunch and setting things up for Betty.

Betty stifled a laugh, but managed to get out a light chuckle. "So, we still don't know where he stands with the Lord?"

Laura shook her head. "I'm afraid not. Guess that'll have to wait for another day. I'm convinced the Lord has a reason for the hold up."

"I'm sure you're right. When will you see him again?"

"I don't know. He talked about seeing a movie. We didn't set a date. But, enough of that! The main concern is to get you well. You need to see the doctor tomorrow. I can drive you. Would you like me to call and make an appointment for you?" Laura tasted her soup.

"Don't bother. I'll call first thing in the morning and let you know what time. You can drive me, if you don't mind." Betty's eyebrows rose, waiting for Laura's answer. She handed her half empty bowl to Laura.

Laura leaned close for a quick hug. "You know I don't mind. I'll clean up and let myself out. You get some rest. If you need anything, please don't hesitate to call and I'll be right over. For sure, call me in the morning when you know your appointment time."

"Okay." Betty's eyes drifted closed. Laura concluded she needed her rest.

By the time Laura finished the few chores for her friend, Betty slept soundly. She let herself out and walked the few steps home to take a nap of her own. Sunday afternoon naps seemed almost a must anymore.

The phone jangled in her ear and startled her awake. *Betty must need me! Or is it just a salesman?* She wished for Caller ID.

"Hello?"

"Hello, is this Laura Olson?"

"Yes, how can I help you?" She hoped it wasn't a telemarketer.

"Laura, this is Tom Lockhart from high school. Do you remember me?"

Wow, I sure do remember him. He was the best looking boy in my class. Wonder what he looks like now. Wonder how he got my number.

"Of course, I remember you Tom. Every girl in the class would remember you. You were the star quarterback!"

His low chuckle rumbled in her ear. "You're too kind. I don't think they all would."

"Goodness, Tom, how in the world are you? It's been a long time."

"I'm doing okay, Laura. What about you?"

"I'm okay, too." She could seriously say this now.

"Listen, dear, I've had you on my mind lately. Are you sure you're okay? I heard you and Frank got a divorce. I never thought he was good enough for you in the first place. With the way things turned out, you and I should have married each other." Tom chuckled.

Some of the old feelings for Tom surfaced. In high school she had quite a crush on him. *Maybe I should have married him, but he married Ellen.*

"What about Ellen?"

"We got divorced a few months ago too."

"I'm sorry."

"It's okay. I'm doing alright now."

"I'll be in Humble next Wednesday and would love to see you. I thought maybe we could have lunch together." Tom sounded a little unsure of himself. Not like the old Tom she knew.

"That sounds great. Will you be here on business?"

"I'm a salesman for a pharmaceutical company. I plan to make some calls while I'm over there. I travel a lot, but I'll be in town for a while. Actually, I live in The Woodlands.

"Oh, I didn't know that. It's good to hear from you after all this time."

With the way things turned out for the two of us, maybe we should have been together. I can't even think that, for then there would be no Christina.

"I look forward to seeing the prettiest lady in my high school."

She blushed. Happy he couldn't see her. "Oh, Tom, you were always a kidder. I'll be glad to see you. Shall we meet for lunch at Luby's in the mall?"

"That'd be fantastic." His voice rose and flowed like a strong breeze.

"See you then. I'll meet you there. I'll probably be out and about anyway." With him working, she didn't want him to waste time picking her up.

"Okay, I'm looking forward to it." His voice took on more confidence. I've got to run. I'm late for an appointment."

"Bye, Tom."

"Bye, Laura. Until Wednesday..."

She replaced the handset, and pictured Tom as the star quarterback. *He's probably bald and fat by now.* All the same, excitement stirred within her. They dated a few times in school. Tom's popularity and sports kept him busy. All the girls swooned over him. Then, Frank came along and swept her off her feet.

Laura finished getting ready for church. She stopped in to check on Betty. Still asleep. Laura hated to leave her. Laura's couldn't keep her mind on the pastor's sermon. Thoughts invaded her mind. During the service time, she prayed for Betty. Her curiosity peeked regarding Tom, and she didn't know what to think about John. *What's happening, Lord? My life, all of a sudden, is moving on.*

On Monday morning Betty phoned a little after nine and informed Laura of the doctor's appointment at eleven.

Laura held the phone between her shoulder and ear and scribbled the time on a piece of paper. "I'll pick you up at ten-thirty. Is there anything I can do for you? Do you need help getting dressed? Can I fix you some breakfast?"

"No, to all the above, except for picking me up. I'll see you then." Betty's voice lowered and Laura pictured her speaking through gritted teeth. From the tone of her voice, Laura suspected she didn't want to be coddled.

Laura dressed and then scurried around to straighten the house. She wanted to be on time for her appointment with Betty, so she left the bed unmade, something unusual for her. She liked to keep up appearances. Someone might come by, even though she knew they seldom did, but just in case.

Betty looked no better than the night before. Her face looked drawn, circles still underlined her eyes, and she appeared as though she might collapse at any minute. However, this time Laura didn't tell her. She'd learned her lesson. After she helped her to the car and started toward the doctor's office, she told her about Tom's call.

"Wow, all of a sudden, you're getting so popular with the guys. Frank doesn't know what he lost. It'll be some lucky fellow's gain." Betty's sense of humor prevailed, as always.

"You're so funny." Laura giggled. *I sound like a schoolgirl.*

The doctor diagnosed Betty with a flu bug or virus, but wanted to make sure, so he took an x-ray of her swollen throat and her chest. He promised to call her by Wednesday afternoon with the results.

Laura kept her usual routine during the week. She walked on the treadmill and worked at the donation store on Tuesday.

Wednesday at noon, Laura drove to the mall and parked, her heart pounded and her hands shook. She dropped her keys when she took them from the ignition. *I'm as nervous as a teenager meeting her first boyfriend. We're no longer in high school. I'm a grown woman. I may not even recognize him. It has been several years since we last saw each other.*

The self-talk helped her regain composure as she walked across the parking lot. She took out her pink lipstick from her purse and traced her lips. When she opened the door of the cafeteria, Tom stood there waiting for her. A huge smile covered his face.

"Laura, you haven't changed a bit. You're just as beautiful as ever. No, even more so..." He rushed up to hug her, but not too tightly.

Taken aback by his hug, she almost lost her balance, but she welcomed his greeting and hugged him back. “You look pretty good yourself. You haven’t changed much. Maybe a little more mature and filled out, but as handsome as ever, and as big a flatterer as always.” They laughed together.

She relished seeing an old friend. Laura knew there were no coincidences with God – just God instances. *Lord, why have you brought Tom back into my life?*

CHAPTER EIGHTEEN

Bad Report

The doctor insisted Betty come to his office the next morning for the tests results. This didn't sound like good news to Laura. But she tried to encourage Betty as much as possible and lift her own spirits at the same time.

"He probably wants to explain the treatment to you in person." Laura drove Betty for her appointment.

"I hope you're right and there's nothing seriously wrong." Laura took her eyes off the road for a second and looked over at her friend. Betty's worried frown melted as she continued. "Still, it'd be good to see my sweetheart again."

Laura wrinkled her forehead to show her concern. "Don't even talk like that. I need you around to help me keep my love life straight. I couldn't do without you. You're a great strength to me. Besides, the Lord's not finished with you yet."

Laura gripped the steering wheel as she talked. She couldn't even think about life without Betty. She pasted a smile on her face and tried to keep things light, so her friend wouldn't worry. However, she fought to keep her tears from bursting from her eyes.

"All I know is, God knows best. Either way, I feel like Paul must have felt when he said to die is gain and to live is gain. Whichever the Lord has for me, I trust Him." Betty's faith remained strong, and Laura knew she meant every word she spoke.

"Let's wait and see what the doctor says. I know you're going to be fine." Laura attempted to convince herself as well as Betty. She didn't want her friend to worry, but she couldn't help but do so herself.

When they arrived, a nurse ushered them in to see the doctor.

"This is unusual." Betty remarked as Laura saw her glance around at the other patients as they walked back toward the doctor's office.

"I'll have to agree with you. Dr. Thomas must not be busy today." The minute the words escaped her mouth, she knew how dumb it sounded. Laura kept up her optimistic chatter for Betty's sake, but the office full of people pressed upon her senses.

The doctor sat behind his desk, concern clearly etched on his face. His usual smile replaced with a frown and his jaws clenched tight told Laura not to expect good news. He stood, walked around to the front of his desk, and sat on the edge.

"Have a seat, ladies. How're you feeling today, Betty?"

They took the chairs facing him as Betty answered his question.

"To tell the truth, I don't feel much better than when I saw you on Monday. I feel so tired and worn out all the time. I want to sleep constantly. And my throat's very sore." She touched her fingers to her neck and gave a slight cough.

Dr. Thomas rose, pulled up a third chair, stared at the signed release with Laura's name listed, and sat down next to Betty. He took one of her hands in his own and offered a weak smile.

"What I must tell you I find very difficult." His voice broke, but he continued. "Something I hate to tell any patient, especially one as special as you. Betty, I'm very sorry. The tests show stage-four throat cancer."

Betty sat perfectly still for several moments. Only the ticking of the wall clock next to his medical diploma filled the silence.

"Exactly what does that mean? Will I need treatments?"

"We can try treatments, but I'm afraid you're beyond that."

He let go of her hand and searched her face. His expression held such tenderness. Laura thought he might cry at any moment.

Laura caught her breath. When she finally exhaled, she could feel her heart drumming in her ears and pounding in her throat.

"So, you're saying her condition is terminal?" Laura couldn't believe her ears or take in what the doctor conveyed to them. She wanted to deny his diagnosis. But from her experience with Jim, she knew what stage four meant, or could mean.

"The cancer has already spread and I'm afraid there isn't much we can do. The test looks as though the esophagus is involved. However, we won't give up just yet. I want you to see the Oncologist." The doctor turned from one to the other.

"How long do I have?" Betty asked in a calm voice. She stared at the doctor, who now stood by her side.

"Probably a few months would be my guess, if the treatments aren't effective. But the Oncologist can tell us more and maybe he can give more hope. We want to conduct some other tests to make sure I'm right. We suspect the cancer's spread to other parts of the body. That will give us more indication about how long you have, and any possible treatment." Dr. Thomas walked back to the edge of his desk.

Anger rose within Laura. "I think we need another opinion?"

"You're welcome to get one. I even encourage it. But, let's do the other tests in the meantime. I think we need to pray and keep her comfortable. I wish I could offer more." He lowered his head and appeared defeated.

"I trust your opinion and findings. What else should I do now, Dr. Thomas?" Betty remained strong and showed confidence in her doctor.

"I'd advise you to get all of your affairs in order. I'm so sorry…" His voice trailed into a whisper. Tears glistened in his eyes.

Betty sat quietly for a moment. She didn't appear too shaken.

"Well, Laura, I may get to see my sweetheart sooner than we thought."

Laura resisted the urge to scream from her own pain, shout a loud, "No!" to the world. Instead, she leaned over and took Betty's hand. *I must stay strong for Betty's sake.*

"I can't believe it. I refuse to accept it. We will bombard Heaven on your behalf. I won't let you go."

For one of the few times in her life, Betty fell silent.

"Prayer is the only thing that can change things at this point, and I certainly believe in the power of prayer. However, it doesn't look good from a medical standpoint." Dr. Thomas's compassion evident in his face, he struggled to comfort all of them. "We can pray, but God's sovereign. I'm only his servant. He does the healing."

Betty didn't say anything more other than to thank the doctor and ask Laura to take her home.

"I need some rest and some time to absorb all of this." Laura watched Betty mumble. She tried to hear but soon realized her friend wasn't talking to her, only to herself.

They stumbled out of the office and made their way to the car. For once in their lives together, total silence prevailed.

Laura reached over and took Betty's hand and held it from time to time while waiting for stoplights to change. Laura wanted to cry, but she kept her tears inside and refused to break down. When they reached home, Laura helped Betty into bed and waited until she fell asleep. She sat Betty's African violets in the sink to give them a drink of water, swept the floors, cleaned the bathrooms, and put away some magazines.

Laura waited until she walked out the door before the dam broke. She sobbed until she had no more tears. At home, she called the prayer chain and their pastor. With the chain activated, she felt her confidence return knowing the saints would pray.

The next day the doctor's office called to schedule further testing. Laura, checking on Betty at the time, answered the phone. Betty looked worse than yesterday. Laura wondered if it were the illness or the stress of hearing the doctor's report.

"Betty, this is Jill from Dr. Thomas's office."

"No. This is her friend Laura. May I give her your message?"

"We've scheduled her for further testing tomorrow at nine. Can she come at that time?"

"Yes, I'll bring her myself." Laura picked up a pen and note pad lying by the phone and jotted down the time.

"Tell her not to eat after eight this evening, or drink anything after midnight. She needs to fast for these test." The nurse continued her instructions.

"Okay. Anything else I need to mention to her?" Laura wanted to get everything down on paper, so she didn't forget anything.

"No. That's all. We'll see you and Betty in the morning."

Laura placed the handset back on the stand and looked at the waiting Betty. She repeated the nurse's instructions.

"We should leave here by 7:30. You know how bad the traffic is that time of day. We'll face the work crew." Laura started making the plans for the next day.

"I hate to get you up so early, but I suppose we need to do this." Betty smiled an apology.

"Don't worry about me. We're going to take care of you." Laura choked back her tears.

Even when ill, Betty tried to make things comfortable for those around her. *What will I ever do without my friend if it comes to that?*

Laura wanted to spend time with Betty. She fluffed her pillows, fixed her lunch, and talked with her until she grew drowsy.

"I'll bring supper over later." Laura walked toward the door.

"You're going to fatten me up. Besides, I don't want you to wait on me. I'll tell you what; I'll buy supper if you'll pick us up hamburgers from Fuddruckers."

"That sounds good to me. I love their burgers. Do you want fries or onion rings? Maybe a milkshake?" Laura wanted to get as much food down her friend as possible. She thought somehow it might make her well.

"Yeah, go ahead and get me a chocolate milk shake and a third-pounder–medium well. Don't forget to tell them senior rate. They give seniors a ten percent discount, you know. But, you have to ask." Betty laughed and continued. "Sometimes, it pays to be old."

Laura chuckled along with her friend. "No, I won't forget. I like receiving a discount too, even if it is for being old." She headed out the door, talking all the way. "Now you sleep and work up an appetite. I'll be back soon."

She walked down the sidewalk to her own house. She thought about Betty's lack of appetite lately and her continued loss of weight. Laura wished she could fatten Betty up. Hopefully, the treatments would help. She planned to make her friend dishes she would enjoy, given the chance. *I will spoil her as much as I can.*

On the drive to pick up their meal, Laura wanted to have another good cry, but held back the tears. She couldn't have Betty see her with tearstained makeup, or red eyes, and know why she cried. She would keep up a good front. Somehow, she felt tears might weaken Betty's faith and make her give up the fight. Laura refused to cave in. So, instead, she used the time to talk with her Heavenly Father about the situation.

"Please Lord, don't let Betty die. I need her here with me. I don't know if I could make it without her. Whatever your plans are Lord, give us your peace." When her prayer ended, she felt God's peace wash over her like a river.

Refreshed after her talk with the Lord and her spirits lifted, she felt better than she had since she heard the news regarding Betty's illness. She placed the order and waited for the hand buzzer to go off. Then, she loaded the food into the car and drove back to Betty's. She sang a song of thanksgiving to her Father on the way. *Nothing or no one, except the Lord, can bring this peace that passes all understanding.* She faced Betty with a calm not present earlier.

Laura watched as Betty choked down her first bite of the burger. She could tell the solid food brought pain, for Betty winched and tears came to her eyes. She washed it down with some of the chocolate shake. When she saw Betty couldn't eat anymore, Laura cleaned up. She looked at Betty's plate. Only a couple of bites gone. The rest remained. But, the shake, only a few drops from empty.

"Would you like me to wrap this up for later in case you get hungry?" Laura held the burger out for Betty to make a decision.

"No, just go ahead and throw it out. To tell you the truth, I think I'll stick to something softer for now."

"Do you feel like playing some gin rummy?"

"Yeah. The chocolate in the shake revved me up. I might even beat you." Betty resembled her old self again, but Laura wondered if she faked the extra energy.

Maybe God's peace energized Betty as it did me.

The ladies played only one game and Betty won. Laura put the cards away because she knew seven-thirty would come early the next morning.

Laura sprinted home, read her Bible, and changed into her pajamas. Thankful for a good evening, she hoped for many more with her special friend. She prayed

Betty's tests would result in a good report. Whatever the outcome, Laura would believe the report of the Lord, continue to ask for Betty's healing, and not give up. With that thought in mind, Laura climbed into bed and fell asleep as soon as her head hit the pillow.

The next morning, Laura drove the car to Betty's driveway to save her a walk next door. Instead of honking as usual, she climbed the steps and rang the bell. Betty met her at the door with her purse in one hand and her jacket in the other. Laura took her arm to help her to the car. Betty backed away with a stern frown.

"Laura, I'm not an invalid yet. I can maneuver on my own."

For a moment, Laura forgot Betty's independent nature. She didn't want to make a fuss, so she released her arm and kept silent. She let her open her own car door for fear of further wrath. Laura felt glad Betty still had fight in her. Perhaps, it would help her overcome this awful disease.

On the drive to the hospital, their usual chatter subsided. Betty fell asleep before they reached the freeway. The cancer seemed to take a toll on Betty already, and a few tears slipped down Laura's checks as she drove. Grabbing a Kleenex, she brushed them away.

CHAPTER NINETEEN

To Live or Die is Gain

Laura paced the waiting room while Betty took tests. Laura thumbed through magazines but couldn't keep her mind engaged. *What's taking so long? Lord, please let everything turn out all right and let this be just a bad dream. I'm not ready for my friend to leave me.* Laura begged the Lord again to keep her friend earthbound, and then realized her selfishness. She wanted Betty here for her own sake.

"Lord, not my will, but Yours." She finally conceded.

Determined to keep a happy countenance around Betty, Laura plastered a smile back on her face. When Betty returned from the testing room, Laura tried to cheer her up.

"Let's do lunch. We'll go wherever you want today, and I'm buying. No argument." Laura walked beside Betty on the way to the car, careful not to lend her a hand.

Betty kept up a jovial attitude, even though Laura knew how she must hurt, especially emotionally. *It must be a difficult thing to find out you are dying of cancer.* They stopped in at S*teak and Ale*, a quiet place where they could talk. The lunch went well under the circumstances.

"When will you get the results of these tests?" Laura questioned Betty as they made their way to the salad bar.

"They will send my results to Dr. Thomas in a few days, and he will notify me." Betty chose the potato and macaroni salad.

"Well, I'll pray for a good report."

"I've thought and prayed a considerable amount myself. I believe I understand how Paul felt in Philippians 1:21: *For to me, to live is Christ, and to die is gain."* Betty shook her head up and down. "I'm ready to concede my will to the Lord and whatever He has in mind. I can witness for Christ and live for Him here on earth, but I also know, if I die, I will gain heaven and eternity with Him. Either way I win."

"That's true, Betty. But …"

Betty pressed the salad tongs into Laura's hand.

"No more buts about it. Don't you know that the 'buts' separate the sheep from the goats? We are the sheep of His pasture – not goats. We continue on with His perfect plan. And remain happy about it."

They finished loading their plates and made their way back to the table.

"Let's eat and enjoy ourselves. You know what they say, 'eat drink and be merry, for tomorrow you may die.'"

"Betty, you're something else. I can't believe you just said that."

"We're going to enjoy ourselves and talk about this thing. You and I have never hid our feelings from one another in the past. At least, I haven't. I don't want to start now, or in the future – whatever is left."

That being said, Betty looked at Laura.

"Do you want to say the blessing or shall I?"

Since Laura didn't know what to say, or how to keep from crying, she motioned to Betty.

Betty's eyes glistened as she thanked the Lord for the food and for her special friend. Her words also brought tears to Laura's eyes. They enjoyed their lunch. Almost. Laura noticed Betty wasn't able to eat much of her food.

They talked about other things – past, present and future – just like always. Almost.

When they finished lunch, Betty reached to get out her billfold. Laura covered Betty's hand with her own.

"Remember, I told you, lunch is on me."

Betty tried to argue, but Laura insisted. She didn't win too many arguments with Betty. Usually Betty won, or she kept silent. *I sure hope I get to have her around for a long time to disagree with me.*

The next few days, an uneasy knot lodged in Laura's stomach as she waited on pins and needles until the tests results came back. Finally, Dr. Thomas's office called and made an appointment to see Betty on Thursday at two o'clock. She felt better and informed Laura she could drive herself, but Laura insisted on taking her.

This time they weren't hurried into the doctor's office. They waited their turn like everyone else. Tension rose, but Laura distracted herself with a magazine. Betty brought a book along and read while they waited. Another lady sat across the aisle from them, alone. When Laura spoke to her, she poured out her story.

"I've been taking chemo treatments and lost all my hair. That's why I'm wearing a scarf around my head. My husband wants me to buy a wig, but I haven't yet." She squirmed in her chair. "He couldn't come with me today because he needed to work. He's missed too much lately."

After listening to her talk for a while, Laura and Betty assured her they would pray for her. Tears clouded her eyes as she thanked them.

"I can use all the prayers I can get." She shook Laura and Betty's hands and wished Betty the best.

The nurse called for Betty. Laura, determined to go with her this time, stood and followed her. Dr. Thomas remained seated behind his desk and sat as he motioned for them to sit in the seats opposite him. A slight smile bent his lips.

"Betty, I have a bit of good news. We can try some treatments. Lymphangiogram showed the cancer has not spread to your lymph nodes." He pulled a calendar from his desk drawer. "We can start treatments on Monday."

"Chemo treatments?" Betty looked him in the eyes.

"Yes, I think we can try a series of ten treatments and see how you do. Then, evaluate and go from there. We will do them every weekday if your body can tolerate them that often. So it will take approximately two weeks." He spoke with authority as if everything was settled.

"Wait a minute. I have a few questions to ask." Betty continued to show her spunk.

Laura's head jerked up in surprise. *What questions could she have? Surely she intends to follow her doctor's advice.*

"Okay." Dr. Thomas rose from his desk, crossed his arms over his chest, and stood facing them.

"Will it cure the cancer, or just prolong the inevitable?"

"Betty, I really can't answer that. Stage four cancer is considered incurable. But, we would like to try and shrink the tumor, or at least put you into remission. We hope to prolong your life indefinitely, but, as I said, we will re-evaluate when the treatments are done."

"Will I lose all my hair like the lady in the waiting room?" Betty patted her hair, then, ran her fingers gentle over her head as if she couldn't bear to part with it.

"Usually with the drug you will be taking there is minimal hair loss. If we have to add other agents to your regime, then that might be an issue."

Laura could tell he spoke honestly and didn't sugar coat anything. She watched him as he went to sit back in his chair behind his desk.

"You will need someone to bring you for the treatments. Just in case you get sick. Some of the side effects you can expect are nausea, mouth sores, and flu like symptoms. But, we will give you medication that will help you cope with the discomfort. "

"I'll be glad to bring her." Laura spoke up. Her gaze shifted from the doctor back to Betty.

"I figured that would probably be the case. Betty, you're blessed to have such a good friend." The doctor smiled.

"What time should we be here on Monday?" Laura asked a question of her own.

"Wait just a minute," Betty's voice held an alarm. "I haven't decided yet if I want to go through with it."

"Betty, I have to tell you, without the treatments, you stand no chance." The doctor shook his head and leaned back in his chair. He interlocked his fingers and stared at her.

"I don't want to lose my hair. I don't want to be sick. It would be easier to go on and be with my sweetheart and with my Lord." Her pent up sobs finally broke through. The first time Laura had seen her break down.

Laura held her in her arms and cried with her. The doctor came around the desk and laid his hands on both their shoulders. A few tears flitted in his eyes. Before long Betty took out a Kleenex and sat back in her chair. The doctor let go and sat on the desk edge. Laura fished for her own Kleenex.

An awkward silence fell, until finally, Betty spoke.

"Okay, Dr. Thomas. I'll give it a try."

Laura took her hand.

"That a girl! I knew you couldn't give up. I'll help you. The Lord will see us both through."

Dr. Thomas smiled and wiped a tear from his own face.

"Have the receptionist make your appointments. I'm glad you're not going to give up the fight, Betty."

CHAPTER TWENTY

Looking Good

Word spread quickly throughout the community. Wherever Laura went, people asked about Betty's illness.

"We're praying for Betty." Laura heard often.

On Monday, Betty started Chemo. Laura stayed close by in case she needed anything. Her new cell phone tucked inside her purse comforted her, for Betty could call anytime. When Laura ran errands, worked at the ministry, or radio station, she made sure the phone was on and completely charged.

Laura kept up her volunteer work for the area ministry and the radio station, but at times, she asked them to get someone else. She rearranged her schedule to take Betty for her appointments. Each session lasted only a few minutes, but the time traveling to and from the infusion clinic took most of the morning. Sometimes they stopped for lunch when Betty felt like doing so. The chemo took its toll, and at times she grew too exhausted. On those days, Laura picked them up something from the drive through. Most of the time, Betty only wanted soup, a frosty, or a milkshake. Often times, she couldn't eat at all. Betty finally gave in and took Phenergan for the nausea.

The two weeks finally came to an end. Dr. Thomas checked Betty over and ran more tests upon the conclusion of the treatments. A couple of weeks after the ordeal, Betty went downhill physically. Dr. Thomas explained this happens after chemo. Not only did she experience nausea, diarrhea, but mouth sores plagued her as well.

Magic mouthwash took care of the mouth sores and the diarrhea finally dissipated. The cancer appeared to be in remission. Betty got stronger, and the two ladies planned a trip to the Hill Country. The blue bonnets were in full bloom.

Then one morning, Betty called Laura in a panic.

"Laura, could you come over right away?"

Laura slammed down the portable phone and ran to Betty's.

"Are you okay?" She drew short breaths when Betty met her at the door.

"Yes and no. Come in, and I'll tell you about it."

Betty sounded mysterious and upset, but not really sick. She motioned for Laura to follow her toward the bathroom. When they arrived, she pointed to the sink. "Look. My hair is falling out by the handfuls."

Laura didn't know whether to laugh or cry. Relieved, it wasn't tragic. She almost chuckled, but realized Betty's heartbreak. She knew her friend dreaded the possibility of losing her hair. Quickly, Laura regained her composure and avoided both laughter and tears.

"We'll go shopping and find you the greatest wig ever."

"Can you imagine me with a wig?" Betty let out her own chuckle.

"Sure. I think you'll look fabulous. I might pick one out for myself, too." Laura wanted to support her friend. She reached over and hugged her. "It might save me from going to the beauty salon so often."

"Well, I suppose a wig beats wearing a scarf like the lady we saw at the doctor's office a few weeks ago. I wonder how she's doing."

Betty got a far away look in her eyes. Laura wondered if Betty thought the woman had died, since they hadn't seen her anymore.

"Let's just stop right now and pray for her."

Laura led her friend back into the living room. When they concluded their prayer, Laura turned to Betty before she headed out the door.

"Now, get dressed. We're going wig shopping. I won't take *no* for an answer. I'll pick you up in thirty minutes."

***

Laura put the last finishes on her make up, picked up the keys, and walked to her car. She checked her watch to make sure Betty would have enough time. Her watch showed the thirty minutes had lapsed. Her timing was right on the money. She started the car and drove into Betty's driveway. She almost honked, but thought better of it. She headed for the door.

She reached to ring the doorbell. Betty appeared at the door. "I'm ready to go." She pushed the lock button and pulled the door shut. Excitement filled their chatter as they walked to the car.

"Now, I don't want anything outlandish. It must match my hair. I certainly don't want anyone to know I'm wearing a wig."

Laura listened to Betty as they drove toward the wig shop.

"I might get something totally different for a change, so I can go incognito whenever I want." Laura laughed at her own joke.

Betty stared at her. "Whew. I'm glad you're only teasing. For a minute there, I thought you'd flipped out on me."

"Yeah, I'm kidding. I, too, want something natural looking."

Laura drove her Buick beside the shop and wondered about its status. Only one car parked nearby. She assumed the Mercury Marquis belonged to the owner of the place. When she tried the door, she found it unlocked.

"Looks as though we're the only ones wig shopping this morning."

"I'm glad. I hoped we wouldn't run into anyone we knew. Even better the shop is empty."

Betty walked toward a wig the color of her hair.

The owner popped up from behind the counter. "May I help you ladies?"

"We're looking for wigs to match our hair color for occasions when we don't feel like fixing ours." Laura pointed to her head.

"I believe I can help you." The owner brought out several styles similar to their hair shades.

They spent the rest of the morning examining and trying on wigs. Betty slipped one on her head. "It's perfect for me."

Laura could hardly believe Betty finally decided on one. Laura examined the light brown wig closely and agreed with Betty's decision.

"Yes, it's perfect, and looks great on you. I can't tell the difference in the wig and your own hair."

"Great. I'll take it." She turned over the price tag and caught her breath. "I had planned to spend less, but what the heck. You only go around once."

Laura chose one a little less expensive. She knew she wouldn't wear it often. She mostly wanted to encourage Betty.

"I think I'll take this one. What do you think?" She held the blond piece of hair up for Betty to see.

"Looks good to me." Betty examined the wig a little closer. "Yes, it's very close to your color and style. No one will ever know the difference."

Laura looked at Betty as they paid for their purchases. She was fading fast. "Shall we stop for lunch, or do you want to go on home now?"

“Home would be my choice. There’s sliced ham and the fixings in my refrigerator, so we can make a sandwich for lunch. As you know, a friend went to the store for me yesterday,” Betty gave Laura a knowing wink.

“Sounds good to me. *Your friend* will fix them since you’re supplying the ingredients.” Laura grinned and linked arms with Betty as they walked to the car–new hair in hand.

CHAPTER TWENTY-ONE

Making Plans

Monday morning Laura rose early and went to her water aerobics class. She showered at the club then drove home to eat breakfast and finish dressing. At nine thirty, she knocked on Betty's door.

"We're planning our trip today." Laura stood on the doorstep.

"What trip?" Betty's eyes narrowed into a bewildered stare.

Laura held up a map of the Hill Country. Betty opened her eyes wide and a smile covered her face.

"Oh, you mean to see the bluebonnets. Let's do make our plans. Come in." Betty swung the door wide open to welcome Laura and her map.

As usual, they went straight for the kitchen. Betty set about making coffee and flipped the switch while Laura spread out the map to plot their route.

"Why don't we stay in Johnson City and visit the Johnson ranch? Then, we can drive back through Wimberley and shop at all the neat shops on our way home. If you like, we can spend a night there as well. If you feel up to it…." Laura hesitated as she waited for Betty's answer.

"Sounds great to me. I'm feeling fine. Carrying around this extra weight might tire me. You've fattened me up lately." Betty smiled as she set two cups down on the table.

Laura couldn't tell she'd gained an ounce. Matter of fact, she probably lost, but Laura humored her.

"Well, let's decide on exactly when to go. Then, I'll call and make the hotel reservations." Laura filled the mugs with steaming hot coffee.

"How about this weekend?" Betty lifted the edge of the cup to her lips.

"Great! Yes. Let's leave on Thursday afternoon. We could spend the night in Wimberley on Friday evening and tour the shops on Saturday. Then, drive back on Saturday night, so we don't miss church on Sunday." Laura looked at Betty from across the table.

Betty shook her head up and down as if the plan soaked in and she agreed. "I'll be ready." Betty grinned from ear to ear.

Laura smiled back. I*s she really up to all this? I hope I'm not pushing her too hard.*

"Hey, we can take our new wigs along, and then we won't have to fix our hair." Laura suggested, and they both laughed.

Laura enjoyed watching her friend laugh again. Their time in the Hill Country would be special. Laura pushed aside any concern about Betty's health. She hoped the trip would prove good medicine for her.

"I better make reservations. I told the donation center I'd work this afternoon. I begged off this morning. I wanted to plan our trip."

Laura headed to the sink, rinsed out her coffee cup, and placed it in the dishwasher.

"You go ahead. I'll pick things up." Betty urged.

Laura gave her friend a quick hug and then started to the door.

Betty followed. Laura turned abruptly almost running into her. She remembered one of the reasons she came. In the excitement of the trip planning, she almost forgot.

"Before I go, let's pray together. I want to pray everyday for your healing and for God to do His will in both our lives."

"You are full of great ideas today." Tears pooled in Betty's eyes, but her smile never faded.

They stepped into the den and sat down on the couch, held hands, and prayed for one another. Almost everyone's name they knew got mentioned before the throne – even the lady from the doctor's office.

When their prayer time ended, Laura rushed home. She called a host of hotels and then dashed out to the donation store. Her busy day continued in the same fashion it started.

In the middle of the afternoon, Laura took a few moments to call and check on Betty. She informed her their reservations had been made and confirmed. Their plans worked out perfect.

"What shall we eat for dinner?" Laura asked out of her recent habit.

"I'm planning to eat a frozen pizza for dinner. You don't need to take care of me all the time. You're welcome to share it with me, if you like." Betty's old spunk showed up.

Laura knew it was time to give her a little space and take care of some of her own affairs.

"I think I'll pass on the pizza. I'll stay home this evening, take care of some bills, call Christina, and eat my own frozen dinner. I'll see you tomorrow. But you call if you need anything."

The minute the words slipped out of her mouth, she knew Betty's scolding would follow. "I'm just fine. You need to stop fussing over me so much."

"Okay, okay." Laura backed off. "I'll see you later. Got to get back to work."

When the store closed, Laura headed home. She undressed, took a shower, and got into her robe and slippers. She popped a frozen chicken enchilada dinner into the oven. She planned to call Christina while her dinner heated. She dialed the number. No answer. Where could she be? She looked at the clock. *Already six-thirty*? She remembered. Christina went to the library on Monday nights to study. She would give her some time and call again later.

She found the bills and placed them in the middle of her desk. They would be ready when she finished eating. The buzzer on the oven sounded. She fixed a small salad to accompany her entree and poured herself a glass of decaffeinated iced tea. She scooped the food from the foil tray and placed each part of the entrée onto one of her everyday plates. Even eating alone, she liked for her food to look appealing.

When she finished her meal, she cleaned the table and put things away. Just as she finished the phone rang.

Again, she wished for caller ID. When she picked up, John's voice came from the other end.

"How are you doing Laura?"

"I'm fine." She sat in her recliner to settle in for some small talk. "And how are you?"

"Everything's fine with me. What about your friend, Betty?" The concern in his voice filtered through the phone line and comforted her.

"She's much better. The doctor seems optimistic. She and I planned a trip to the Hill Country this weekend."

"That should be good for both of you. Where are you staying?"

She detailed the travel plans. Their conversation continued for some time as they chatted about the weather, what each had been doing, and even the high prices at the grocery store.

"I hope we can get together sometime soon. I miss seeing you." He sounded a little lonely.

Laura didn't know exactly what to say. She felt a little embarrassed, but managed a shy, "Thank you."

"I'll call you again when you get back from the weekend. Maybe we can see that movie."

"Maybe so." Laura didn't want to commit to anything with Betty's recent history.

They said their goodbyes and she pushed the end button on the phone. She missed him as well. The house seemed mighty empty tonight.

CHAPTER TWENTY-TWO

Bluebonnet Times

Laura loaded the last suitcase into the car and shut the lid on the trunk. Betty handed her a thermal of coffee. "It's hazelnut."

"Great. The chocolate chip cookies I brought will go down even better with our favorite coffee."

Betty shook her head in agreement, rubbed her tummy, and licked her lips. "Umm," her only word.

"I can't believe the week is already over and we're on our way." Laura started the car. "Here we come Hill Country." A giggle escaped from Betty's lips. They traveled on highway 290 toward Johnson City.

After a couple of hours they stopped for a bathroom break. Betty climbed out of the car and stretched. "Maybe we can spend a few minutes browsing this shop."

Laura agreed. "We do need to walk around for a while. We might even find something we like."

Betty found a picture frame she liked, and Laura came away with a souvenir of her own. After about thirty minutes, they crawled back into the car and continued their journey.

"The flowers are more beautiful and abundant this year." Betty snapped a picture alongside the highway from the window as they rode. The Indian Paint Brushes stood tall and vibrant orange. "You know, I love the brilliance of the Paint Brushes as much as the bluebonnets. They make a lovely contrast."

"The bluebonnets seem fuller and more robust. You're right. They seem to be more plentiful. Thicker than ever. Probably because of all the rain this year." Laura leaned her head close to the window as she drove slowly down the highway.

Betty snapped another shot of the field of flowers.

"Let's stop and take some pictures of the next great scene."

Laura pulled to the side of the road.

"Stand over there," Laura pointed to a meadow filled with flowers. I'll take a picture of a beauty amongst all the other beauty."

"Here let me get a picture of you this time. I know Christina would enjoy it …and John and Tom." Betty chuckled as she teased.

"You're absolutely infuriating." Laura laughed as she handed Betty the camera and smiled for the picture. They took turns in the midst of the heavenly scene, taking pictures and laughing.

"John called on Monday night and said he missed me. I don't want to get serious, but I felt a little lonely myself that night. He probably just wanted to say something nice."

Laura took the camera back and Betty posed for another picture. They started toward the car.

"If you ask me, the two of you would make a perfect pair."

"You're forgetting, Betty. He hasn't made a commitment to the Lord, and I can't be unequally yoked. Besides, I'm not looking for another husband." Laura seated herself behind the steering wheel, fastened the seat belt and started the engine.

Betty buckled herself in on the passenger side and looked at Laura. "He's an awfully nice guy. We'll wait and see where the Lord takes your relationship. But, I think he's probably the one for you."

"Now, Betty, don't go fixing me up. Besides, how about Tom? At least, we know he's a Christian. Laura stared straight ahead as she drove down the highway. In silence they continued their drive to Johnson City.

"Let's talk about something else and stop trying to second guess the Lord." Laura looked over at her friend, but found her fast asleep. Sleepy herself, Laura needed to keep her eyes open in more ways than one. For now, she must concentrate on the highway.

Betty woke up just before they arrived in Johnson City. They looked through a couple of shops, but the old Johnson house had already closed for the day.

Laura pulled into a parking lot. "Let's eat dinner here at the old Grist Mill. I've heard the food is great." Laura started walking toward the restaurant before Betty could even answer.

The Mill, decorated in fifties fashion, served huge hamburgers and fries. Tonight Laura decided to forget her diet and even eat the fries. The peach cobbler with Bluebell ice cream finished off a great dinner.

"I may never eat again." Betty groaned.

"Me neither. But, I'm sure by morning we'll be starving again." Laura couldn't help but giggle even though it hurt her full tummy.

They drove to the hotel and checked in for the night. They played a hand of Gin Rummy before retiring.

They looked at each other after the game and said almost in unison, "We haven't prayed together today."

They bowed their heads and prayed for healing for Betty and the Lord's will in each of their lives. They mentioned friends, loved ones, even the lady from the doctor's office. They thanked him for the beautiful day, the Bluebonnets, Indian Paint Brushes, all His beauty, and their time together.

The next morning they rose long before the sun painted the eastern sky. The hotel, newly renovated, provided a complimentary continental breakfast. They only nibbled at the luscious treats. They threw their purses and jackets into the car and headed for the Johnson Ranch, which provided to be a testimony to God's beautiful scenery.

The rich and rolling pastureland around the ranch had many acres of fields, grass, and flowers that accented nature's best. They boarded the train that shuttled around the property. The graveyard, groomed immaculately, set beneath tall pine trees. At some points, they walked around and investigated. The old home place, kept as inhabited many years earlier, lent a piece of history for them to savor. Some of the kitchen items brought on nostalgia of their own, remembering things from their younger years at their grandparents homes. They continued to shoot pictures of the magnificent countryside and the other attractions. The low water bridge reminded them of days gone by in towns they had already visited. Concerned that their own pictures might not be adequate, they purchased postcards in the gift shop.

Upon completion of their tour, they drove toward Wimberley.

“Look at all the Bluebonnets.” Betty caught her breath as if in awe. They marveled at all the beauty around them.

“Would you like to stop and take some more pictures?" Laura offered.

“Let’s do. I’m not in any hurry, are you?” Betty laughed as she dug the stowed camera out from underneath the seat.

Laura found a huge field of Bluebonnets and pulled over to the side of the highway.

“Get out there Betty, and I’ll take your picture.”

“Isn’t it your turn?” Betty held up the camera. “I have the camera, so you run on out there in its view.”

“Okay. But you’re next.” Laura smiled as she walked out into the field. Then she took the camera and raised it to get a shot of Betty. A puff of wind blew and Betty's wig flew off her head. It rolled among the Bluebonnets.

Betty grew frantic. "Oh, no, I can't lose my expensive wig. Help, Laura, help me catch it."

The two of them ran into the field of flowers chasing the ball of hair.

A car pulled up. The driver got out.

"Can I help you? Have you lost your dog? Did he get away? Let me catch him for you."

Laura and Betty doubled over in laughter. Finally, Laura stopped laughing. She turned toward the man.

"No, it's not our dog. My friend here lost her hair."

The man looked astonished and then laughed along with them when he saw their predicament. By this time, Betty held her sides. She laughed long and hard.

The man ran after the wig as it blew through the field of flowers. Being faster on foot than Laura or Betty, he chased it down and grabbed it.

"Thank you so much." Laura took the wig from his outstretched hand and passed it to Betty.

"Yes. Thank you. This would have been a long chase without your help. I pray the Lord will bless you for your trouble." Betty spoke sincerely, stopping her laughter.

"You girls be careful. I'll see you in heaven if not before." He walked back to his car and drove away.

When they returned to their own vehicle, Laura turned to Betty. "Do you suppose God sent us an angel to help us catch your wig?"

"He sure acted like one. Let's not forget to pray for him tonight. Thank God, I didn't lose this costly thing. Besides, I lost more hair when I washed it this morning." Betty straightened the wig and plopped it back on her head. This time she fastened it securely with several bobby pins.

By late afternoon they arrived in Wimberley. Hunger pains reminded them they hadn't eaten since breakfast. They stopped at one of the restaurants on the square and ate a nice meal.

"How did you like your linner or dupper?"

"What are you talking about, Betty?" Laura thought she spoke another language.

"When Jim and I combined lunch and dinner, we called it linner. Some people call it dupper - a combination of dinner and supper. Depends on your locality and what you call your meals."

"Betty, you keep me guessing." Laura shook her head and laughed at her friend's joke.

Dusk set in by the time they left the restaurant, so they headed for their rented cabin. A gurgling stream ran through the middle of town, and they got a clear view of the running water from their porch.

Unloading the car, Betty turned to Laura. "Thank you so much for this trip. I've had so much fun, even with the wig adventure. We made a great memory."

"Thank you." Laura looked at her and smiled.

To see Betty this happy after what she had gone through these past weeks delighted Laura more than words could express.

They spent the evening the same way as the night before. When they prayed, the man who helped catch Betty's wig took precedence at the top of their list.

With no breakfast provided the next morning, they visited a cafe in town. This gave them an early start on viewing the shops. They found some special items to purchase. The stained glass store proved to be one of their favorites, and they bought angels for many of their friends. Laura eyed one for a teacher, but resisted getting it for John. However, she did think about him.

They left Wimberley by mid-afternoon so they could see more flowers. Betty again thanked Laura for such a wonderful weekend as they started for home. Betty looked tired. Laura drove home with a feeling of accomplishment. Glad she brought her and for their time together.

They arrived home around nine o'clock. Betty slept from dark until they arrived. She awoke as they pulled into her driveway and apologized to Laura for sleeping. "I'm so sorry. I conked out on you all the way home."

"It's okay. I almost fell asleep myself a few times." She teased Betty.

"I'm sure glad you didn't." Betty carried her things into the house with Laura's assistance.

Then, Laura got into her car and pulled into her own driveway, happy to be home safely. She hoped they could make it for choir the next morning. And she wondered about Betty.

CHAPTER TWENTY-THREE

Things Change

Laura walked into the house to the shrill ring of the phone. She dropped her load in the middle of the floor and rushed to pick up. “Hello?”

“Mother, where have you been?” Christina’s voice rang from the other end of the line.

“Oh, hi, Christina. Roaming around the Hill Country with Betty.”

“I’ve tried to call you all weekend. I was worried about you.” The alarm in Christina’s voice came through loud and clear.

“I’m sorry, honey. I called you earlier in the week, and then, I remembered your library time. After that, I got busy with our plans, and forgot.” Tired, she plopped down into the recliner, phone still next to her ear.

“Mother, how could you forget your own daughter?” Christina’s voice sounded incensed.

“My, how things change. Aren’t those my lines?” Laura wanted to laugh, but stifled the urge.

"Well, Mother, you should let me know when you're going out of town. I worry about you when I can't get hold of you for days."

"Okay, sweetheart. I'll let you know from now on." Laura regretted making Christina worry. "By the way, I bought a cell phone. Take the number. Then, you can reach me anytime or anywhere." She flipped open the phone to make sure of the number before repeating it to Christina.

"Mother, you bought a new cell phone and didn't even let me know?"

"Well, I only got it recently, and now I'm letting you know. Here's my number: 281-555-5093."

Laura eased back into a reclining position. "So, what have you been up to?" The unpacking could wait. She needed to give her daughter her undivided attention.

The angst in Christina's voice spoke volumes.

"Not much. Just studying. I'll be glad when I finish this law degree. I may never go back to school again."

"Now, sweetheart, you'll finish soon. But, you do need to take time to have fun." Laura hoped she would take her advice. *All work and no play doesn't make for a balanced life.*

Christina's tone calmed. Laura hadn't meant to worry her. She promised to let her know where she went in the future. After they hung up, Laura trudged to the car and pulled out her suitcase. *Unpacking can wait until tomorrow.* She got ready for bed and fell asleep as soon as her head hit the pillow.

The next morning, she pulled herself out of bed and made her way into the bathroom. When she finished, she stumbled into the kitchen to fix coffee. The grandfather clock struck nine. Choir would begin in thirty minutes. *I wonder if Betty will make it.* Laura dialed her number. The phone rang several times without an answer. Her heart began to pound.

Finally, Betty answered. "Hello, Laura. No, I'm not going to choir practice."

"Is something wrong? Are you all right?" Laura moved the phone to her other ear and took a cup down from the cabinet.

"I'm tired. My bed feels too good today. I believe I'll visit the church of Mattress Springs today." She laughed lightly, but Laura could tell the chuckle took some effort on her part.

"You're so funny. I'll check on you after church. Is there anything I can do for you beforehand?" Laura poured herself a cup of coffee.

"No, I'll be just fine. Go on to church and out to eat with the others. Or, better still, if John's there, go out with him."

Even when she's tired or not feeling well, she still gives me advice. "We'll see." She didn't want to argue.

When they hung up, Laura carried her cup into the bedroom. No time for breakfast. She flung on her clothes and applied makeup. Then, she hurried off to practice.

Usually, Laura enjoyed choir and church service, but today Betty stayed on her mind. She left as soon as the service ended. She called Betty on the way to ask if she could bring her lunch. No answer. She stepped on the gas and drove well past the speed limit to Betty's house.

The tires squealed when Laura pulled into the driveway. Frantic, she jumped out and ran to the front door. No answer came after several minutes of knocking. Using the key from her ring, Laura opened the door.

"Betty, it's me. Are you awake?" Laura called as she walked toward the bedroom.

No answer. She peered around the door and gasped. Betty lay on the floor unconscious, barely breathing. Laura ran to her side and shook her as she cried, “Betty wake up.” But, no response came. She flew to the phone and dialed 911. Tears clouded Laura’s eyes as she paced back and forth waited for the emergency vehicle to arrive. Laura clenched and unclenched her fist, trying to decide her next action. Then, ran to the bathroom to dampen a cloth. She felt Betty’s forehead. No fever. She ran the cool cloth over her friend’s brow. At least, she could do something. *Lord, she’s got to be all right. Please let her be okay.* Laura prayed as never before.

The ambulance arrived and the paramedics checked Betty’s vital signs and applied an oxygen mask. At the hospital, she kept asking for Jim and seemed to be in a state of confusion. Laura stayed by her side, but Betty didn’t seem to notice.

Dr. Thomas arrived and immediately ordered tests. He patted Laura’s shoulder. “I’m sorry. “We’ll do everything we can to keep her comfortable. You should go on home. Betty will sleep for some time.”

“No, I can’t leave her alone. She has no one else close by but me.”

Laura dozed off and on throughout the night as she sat in the chair beside her friend’s bed. She phoned

Betty's sister, Lorraine, to let her know about the situation, and promised to keep her informed.

"I can come if you think I should." Lorraine didn't sound like she wanted to make the trip.

"Let's wait until tomorrow and see how she is by then."

By morning, a bed in a regular room became available. Glad to leave the emergency unit, Laura gathered Betty's personal things and brought them along.

While in the elevator, Betty stirred and gazed at her surroundings. "Where am I?"

"You're in the hospital." Laura filled her in on the details.

Betty seemed to remember some of what happened, but her short-term recollection was impaired. They arrived at her assigned room. The nurses checked her vital signs and a lab tech drew blood. One of the aides pulled a tray off a rolling cart and gave Betty her breakfast. Usually hospital food smelled awful, but this morning, Laura's stomach rumbled. Her last meal was yesterday morning's breakfast, if coffee counted.

"I'm not hungry." Betty looked at the food and then over at Laura.

"You need to eat something to build up your strength." Laura urged her to eat a few bites of the scrambled eggs and drink some milk.

Betty obliged her, but took only a couple of forkfuls and then turned her face away.

"What about you? Laura, you need to eat something. Why don't you go to the cafeteria, or eat the remainder of mine." As sick as Betty was, she tried to take care of Laura.

The nurse piped up when she entered the room. "Yes, go ahead and finish up the breakfast, I'll record what Betty ate."

Laura ate the watery oatmeal and drank the strong coffee. She dumped some of the cream in both of them along with some butter and brown sugar on the oatmeal to help with the flavor. She didn't want to leave Betty's side to go to the cafeteria.

Dr. Thomas entered the room, and the look on his face showed his concern.

He sat down on the edge of her bed. "How are you feeling?"

"Not good. To tell you the truth, I feel like a Mac truck hit me." Betty tried joking around even though everyone knew she felt miserable. She tried to sit up in bed, but fell backwards on the pillow.

"I seem to have no balance."

"I'm not surprised." The doctor frowned and his eyes looked sad. "Betty, I'm sorry, but the cancer has spread to your brain in the form of a tumor. From the x-ray, it looks inoperable. We want to run a few more tests to be certain."

Laura caught her breath. "What are you saying, Dr. Thomas?"

"It doesn't look good. However, if the tumor is removable, then we'll try. However, if not, we have few options except try more chemo and radiation to shrink it." He looked down at Betty and then over to Laura. He hung his head.

Betty closed her eyes and tears slid from under her lids down her face. She fell silent.

Laura stood to her feet and clasped Betty's hand. "When will you know about the tumor and whether or not you can operate?"

"We'll run further tests today and do another MRI as soon as we can. I'll talk with you more when I get the results and the other tests back." He rose to leave. "Hang in there, Betty. I'm praying for you."

Betty remained silent but nodded her head.

Laura ran home during lunch. A sandwich hadn't tasted this good in ages. The shower revived her, and the clean clothes made her feel better. She didn't take long. She wanted to get back to the hospital. A few phone calls needed to be made. First, she called Christina and let her know the situation.

"Mom, I'm so sorry. I'll pray for both of you. Gotta go now." Christina hung up to run for class.

Laura dialed the prayer chain. Knowing the power of prayer, she wanted everyone to pray for her friend.

Her last call was to John.

"John, this is Laura. Betty's in the hospital. The doctors found more cancer, this time in her brain. They're running more tests." Laura broke into sobs.

"Where are you now?" John didn't hesitate to ask.

"Home, cleaning up, but I'm on my way back to the hospital." Laura checked her watch to see how long she had been gone. More time than she wanted.

"Can I pick you up and take you, or meet you there?" He sounded concerned.

"Why don't you come by the hospital a little later? Betty would like to see you, and you can keep me company for a while, if you like."

"I'll be there whenever you say."

"I'll call you after I get there and survey the situation. Bye." She hated to cut him short, but hoped he understood.

"Okay. Let me know. Bye."

Laura grabbed her purse and jumped in the car. Anxious to return to her friend's side she exceeded the speed limit. Only a few miles away, yet, the drive seemed long. When she arrived, Betty lay fast asleep. *She probably didn't even miss me, but I missed her. Lord, please heal her.*

Medication kept Betty groggy, and she slept most of the time, waking up only briefly when the staff took her for a CT scan.

Laura felt forlorn as she waited for Betty to wake up. Finally, she lifted the telephone receiver in the room and dialed John's number. Betty didn't stir. He answered on the second ring.

"Laura, how's she doing?" John said without even a hello.

She quickly realized he must have caller ID.

"She's sleeping. I need the company more than she does if you still want to come by."

"I'll be there in a jiffy." He hesitated and then said, "Bye." The phone clicked.

***

The next few days, Laura sat by Betty's side. The staff ran more tests. John attended to as many of the two women's needs as possible. He brought magazines, food for Laura, flowers, and stayed either with them or on call. Reports came in slowly. The final diagnosis struck quite a blow. The new tumor had metastasized to other parts of her body. It wouldn't be long.

"Dr. Thomas, I believe Betty would rest more comfortably at home, so can she be released? I'll take good care of her.

"I think you're right. She'll have good days and bad days. Her appetite will probably not return. We'll try and keep her pain at a minimum. A hospice nurse will be assigned and available. I know the next few weeks will be tough."

"I'm not ready to lose my best friend, but I'm sure God knows best." Tears rolled down Laura's face and her chin trembled. She and the doctor stood outside Betty's room.

"I've told her there's nothing more we can do. She's accepted it and indicated her affairs are in order and tells me her sweetheart and her Lord wait for her. She told me about the Bluebonnet trip you took. She treasures the memory." The doctor looked grim, but smiled slightly when he mentioned the trip.

The tears came faster at the mention of the trip. "I'm so glad I took her. She gave me some great memories." Laura pulled out another Kleenex and wiped her face. The doctor squeezed her hand as he left, and she went back into Betty's room.

"I'm ready to go home. I don't want to die in this ugly hospital gown." Betty held out the garment with a look of disdain on her face.

"The nurse will be here to check you out in a few minutes." Laura helped her dress in the clothes Betty had asked her to bring.

When they arrived at Betty's, John waited at the door. He helped situate Betty and carried things from the car. Other friends dropped by. They brought small gifts, food, flowers, magazines, and books.

In the next two weeks, visitors streamed into Betty's home. Everyone loved her and couldn't stay away. Laura suspected they all hated to see the cancer's toll on their friend's body, just as she did, but they came. Since the lab report and the other tests indicated nothing could be done, no follow up visits, surgeries, chemo, or radiation took place. Everything came to a standstill, except the cancer. Hospice arranged for doctor visits. And he ordered medication for pain management.

Only a miracle could save Betty's life. Otherwise, she would be going home to her sweetheart and her Savior.

"Help me finalize my home going. It shouldn't be too hard since I have Forethought. I'm so glad Jim and I bought our funeral plan a few years back." Betty could hardly speak above a whisper.

"Sure, I'll be glad to help in whatever way I can, but I'm still praying for a miracle." Laura didn't want to release her.

Her voice shaky and trembling, Betty managed to get out what she wanted to say. "I've written out some instructions, but help me if I forgot anything." She handed Laura the paper.

Laura took the paper from Betty's unsteady hand and viewed the directions. The first thing on her list was: *I want a praise service with a salvation message.*

Laura found the process difficult as she read through the rest of the list. But she managed to keep things together long enough to help her friend. She took a pen and wrote down other things she thought Betty wanted. A nod of the head showed her agreement at each one. By now, Laura pretty well knew her friend's last requests. Everything would be in order, just the way she liked.

CHAPTER TWENTY-FOUR

Life Must Go On

Laura stayed by Betty's side. She talked to her, read the Word of God to her, prayed with her, and tended to her every need until hospice took over. Friends dropped by daily to visit and sometimes sat with Betty. This gave Laura a moment or two to herself. Betty knew a lot of people, and they all loved her. The pastor never failed to come and pray with the two of them.

"How is she?" Lorraine, Betty's sister and her only living relative, hugged Laura firmly when she walked into the room.

"About the same as when I talked with you earlier." Laura returned the hug as she related the sad news.

"I'm so glad Betty has you. It's difficult living two states away. I've taken ten days off, but then I'll have to be back on the job." Lorraine walked over to Betty.

A weak smile brightened Betty's face when she saw her sister. Laura marveled. *Sick as she is, she still has kept Her sweet disposition, sense of humor, and faith in God during the two-month ordeal.* Her speech barely audible, but her smile never failed.

Each day she grew weaker. For a time she could scratch a few words on note paper, but even that gave way to the cancer's caustic toll on her body. The tumor grew larger, and she drifted into a coma after her sister left. Hospice administered pain medication as often as needed in order to keep her comfortable. Laura felt as if she'd already lost her friend. She sat by Betty's bed and cried for days. Even though Laura didn't want to release her, she knew her friend would be happier in her eternal home. So, Laura turned her loose to God's sovereignty. Then, one day, Betty just slipped away.

Laura lifted her head off the pillow, but could not bear to get off the couch. She flung her arm over her eyes. *I can't believe she's gone.* Shock invaded her as she starred into the darkness. Finally, she rose from her sofa. She knew she had to help with the arrangements, and get Christina there for the funeral. So much to do. She stumbled to the telephone.

Laura could feel the Lord's presence surrounding and comforting her. He encased her in a bubble and made things easier than she expected. After she called her daughter, Christina called her father. And Frank made plane reservations for his daughter. John offered to help in any way he could. He brought tons of food to Laura's house, and she encouraged friends and guests to eat whenever they appeared.

"Wow, Mom, who brought all this food?"

"A friend." Laura didn't want to divulge too much information just yet. *What would Christina think?* How could she explain a relationship she didn't even fully understand herself?

"Everything looks delicious. Wish I felt like eating." Christina walked past the food and went to her room. Laura knew Christina missed Betty almost as much as she did. Almost. No one could miss her more than Laura.

She treasured having her daughter around, even though she would need to fly back to school right after the funeral. The pace of summer school didn't afford her missing more than a day.

The funeral went according to Betty's plans. The pastor gave a salvation message, and praise songs rose to the rafters. The casket remained closed. Betty's beauty riveted from the pictures displayed around the church. However, Laura expected that everyone knew her greatest beauty came from the inside. *Everyone who knew her will miss her, especially me.*

Tears flowed down Laura's face, and she couldn't speak due to the huge lump in her throat. *I don't know if I can make it through this service. This is one of the saddest days of my life. What will I do without Betty?* These questions formed in her mind, yet, she knew the Lord would carry her through. *But, Lord, it is so hard to lose your best friend on earth...* But, Laura knew her best friend, Jesus, would be there for her. *He will remain faithful. His grace is sufficient.*

She will no longer have to suffer. But, at the same time, Laura questioned why God didn't answer their prayers for Betty's healing. Ultimately, she understood God knew best, and with her tears and the Holy Spirit's comfort came the acceptance of His sovereign will. *God looks at death differently than we do. When a loved one dies, we think of missing them, and we look at the temporal more than the eternal. It's hard for us to grasp things beyond this world. We look at death as finality, while God looks at it as a beginning.*

Laura sat with Lorraine and Christina. She saw John enter the church and his presence comforted her. She looked across the aisle and spotted Frank with his girlfriend. *How could he?* But, what could she expect. It had been a year and a half now. The old hurt no longer plagued her. Betty helped her move on with her life.

The words of the minister brought truth and healing to her heart. Betty traded an old body for a new one that walked on streets of gold. She would have no need for shoes, old or new! Even though her own days ahead would be difficult, Laura could release her friend to the arms of God and rejoice to think of her with her sweetheart and her Savior! One day she would see her again – and they would be together forever!

More than once in the days following the funeral, Laura picked up the phone to call her friend. When realization hit her, she knew Betty would say, "You must go on with your life."

It's much easier to say than do. I miss you so much.

When the next canasta group met, Laura made herself go. After she arrived and met Carol, a newcomer in town, she felt grateful. Immediately, Laura liked her. A divorcee in her fifties and a couple of years younger than Laura, she came from Oklahoma. The grapevine had it that her parents lived in the Humble area. Her husband left her a year earlier for a younger woman. After a year of struggling on her own, she finally decided to move closer to family. She had no children.

"Welcome to Humble. We're glad to have you in our group." Laura smiled at Carol as she lay down her discard.

"I think I'll like it here. So far, everyone's been so friendly." Carol answered with a wide grin.

"Can I get you another drink?" Carol offered.

"Thanks. I'm having unsweetened tea." She handed Carol her empty glass.

She's so much like Betty. She's friendly, outgoing, fun, and likes to see others enjoy life - so many qualities like Betty, even down to being a servant. I know no one can ever replace Betty, but I have to realize she's gone.

Between games, Laura and Carol talked and became better acquainted. *I have been praying for a friend and someone to fill the void Betty left.* Carol seemed to be in need of a friend, also.

"I'll call you for lunch soon." Laura wrote down her phone number and passed her own to Carol.

"I'll look forward to hearing from you." Her new friend waved and walked toward her car.

Tom called Laura for a date during the time of Betty's illness, but she couldn't accept. He said he understood. However, now, Betty would want her to continue dating. She even said before she died that she hoped Laura would marry again. She might accept a friendly date with Tom or John if they asked later.

On Tuesday, Laura drove into the Dairy Queen for lunch. John sat there in one of the back booths, but not alone. A woman with beautiful black curly hair, a slim body, a dazzling smile looked across the table at him. *I guess he likes younger women. Besides, he has the right to date others. But, he doesn't need to rob the cradle. Why am I angry? I have no claim on him.*

She glanced their way. They appeared intent on their conversation. As Laura started toward the door, hoping they wouldn't notice her, John called out.

"Hello, Laura. It's so good to see you out and about. How are you?"

"I'm fine. And you?" She turned to look in his direction.

"Great!" John stood from his seat and walked her way.

Laura turned back and placed her order.

"Come over and let me introduce you." John led her to their table.

This is Jane Smith," John stated without any further explanation.

"How do you do?" Laura nodded.

"Good to meet you, Laura. I've heard some good things about you." Jane flashed her smile.

Before Laura could answer, John spoke up. "Laura lost a very special friend, Betty Ivey, recently. It's good to see her getting out."

"I'm so sorry. I knew Betty. A lovely lady," Jane's smile faded.

The cashier called for Laura to pick up her order, and she excused herself.

"Come join us." John sat back down at the table.

"I ordered my food to go. I have a million things to do. Thank you, anyway."

Laura didn't feel comfortable interrupting their time or conversation.

John stood and walked back toward the counter with her. "I'll give you a call soon, if that's okay."

"Fine, I'll talk to you later." Laura picked up her order and headed for the safety of her car and home. She wondered about his companion. *Is he playing the field too? Is he still interested in me as well? How do you figure men, anyway?*

During Betty's illness, he came through for her on several occasions. He visited more than once, called periodically, and even invited her out, although she couldn't bring herself to go.

When Betty died, he not only sent flowers to the funeral, but also a sympathy card and roses for Laura as well. He even attended the service. And brought over gobs of food. She noticed he'd not mentioned the Lord in his card, but it was beautiful. By now, she figured him for a nice man, but without a close relationship with the Lord, or a church home. Something she hoped to find out for sure the next time they dated — *if we date again.*

On the drive home, she pondered her relationship with both Tom and John. She went to lunch only the one time with Tom, but he called regularly during Betty's illness and death, even though his work schedule seemed hectic. He sent flowers for the funeral, as much for Laura, she suspected, as for Betty.

She sensed something special about Tom. Could be because she knew him in the past. But, she suspected the real reason was because he knew the Lord and kept a close relationship with Him. They'd not discussed it openly, but he made references to God and going to church a few times. The sympathy card he sent led her to believe he knew Him. She recognized going to church didn't necessarily make someone a Christian – just like sitting in a garage didn't make you a car.

Maybe dating two men might prove too much of a burden. However, she liked them both and enjoyed their company. *Anyway, it's just friendship. Why couldn't I have several guy friends the same way I have girl friends?* Sounded like a good idea to her. She knew the value of friendship, now that she'd lost her best friend on earth. It made her want more — both guys and gals. However, the fear of losing them plagued her. The deaths of Jim and Betty loomed over her like a cloud. Thirty-two years of marriage down the drain made her life seem empty. At one time, Frank had been a friend. The emotional pain of all the losses together made her want to give up on relationships, but she must keep on keeping on. She decided the risk would be worth taking. Even though the pain was severe, she considered friendship worth the pain.

She thought of the Hill Country trip and reminisced. The pictures they took in the Bluebonnet fields remained one of her biggest treasures. On several occasions, she viewed them and remembered, laughed, and cried. The memories they made together delighted her. Betty must have known Laura would need something to re-live their time together at her departure.

Engrossed in her thoughts, Laura almost missed her driveway.

The rest of the afternoon she worked around the house, neglected for the past few months. She straightened her closet; put in order the things left in a heap, watered drooping plants, and cleaned the coffee pot with vinegar.

The phone interrupted her work, and Tom spoke from the other end of the line. "I'm taking off early Friday, coming to Humble, and taking you to dinner and a movie, if you'll honor me with your presence."

Laura, taken by surprise, hesitated and then found her voice. "I'd like that."

"I'll pick you up at six, so we can start early, and then see the eight o'clock movie. There's a movie I'd like to see with Tom Hanks called *The Terminal.* Have you seen it yet?"

She could truthfully answer. "No." *I almost did.* She stopped herself. *No need going into that.*

"Do you like seafood?"

"Oh, yes."

"Then seafood it is. How does Red Lobster sound? I hear it's pretty good."

"Sounds great to me." She thought about the delicious coconut shrimp the restaurant served.

"I'll see you then. Have a good night's sleep." How nice of him to remember her mentioning trouble sleeping since Betty passed away.

"You do the same." She hung up the phone and dressed for bed.

It will be nice to see Tom again. In more ways than one, I'd forgotten how handsome he is. I'd like to find out more about him as well. I wonder how he's been since his divorce and how it all happened. This is all still pretty new to me.

Laura drifted off to sleep thinking about her upcoming date and wondered what she should wear on Friday night. She wished Betty could advise her. Perhaps Carol would be a good one to ask. She would call her for lunch this week. Then, maybe, she would buy something new along with a pair of shoes. Somehow she had become fixated with footwear lately.

CHAPTER TWENTY-FIVE

Movie at Last

Laura picked up the receiver. She looked at the paper with Carol's phone number. Laying the handset back down, she couldn't make the call. How could she replace Betty? She walked over and sat on the couch. Tears flooded her eyes. *Betty would tell me to move on with my life.* But how can I?

After a good cry, some self-talk, and thinking about what Betty would say, she lifted up the receiver again and dialed Carol's number.

Carol answered on the third ring.

"Let's go to lunch. And do some shopping afterwards." Laura said.

"Sounds good to me. I'm always ready for shopping. And eating too." Carol chuckled.

Laura giggled along with her. "Me too. I just got off the scale and I can tell."

After a pause in the laughter Laura continued, "Foley's is having a big sale. I want to pick up a new pant suit if I can find one."

"Great. I've wanted to shop there ever since I came to town. I've cut out all my coupons for today." Carol sounded excited.

As they spoke, Laura mused about how much she liked Carol. Her new friend provided great companionship and a listening ear. As a matter of fact, she listened better than Betty ever did. *But I must stop comparing Carol to Betty. They each hold a special place in my life, and God sent both for a reason.*

"I'll pick you up, in say—" Laura checked her watch. "An hour?"

"Wonderful. I'll see you at nine then." Carol sounded enthused.

When she hung up the phone, Laura dressed to leave and reflected on shopping days with Betty. All the laughter and crazy stunts they pulled. They modeled their clothes for each other. The good choices elicited a nod of approval, and the bad invoked a hearty laugh. The emotion of their memories almost overpowered her. She sat on the side of the bed. Drawing in a deep breath, she determined to take control of her emotions and move on with her life. Today, she would start anew and make new memories with Carol. *Betty would approve. She'd also be glad I'm dating again.*

The grandfather clock chimed the quarter hour before nine. Laura gathered her things. Wiping the tears from her eyes, she fixed her makeup and headed out the door. She then drove the few short blocks to Carol's.

Carol slide into the passenger's seat.

"Carol. I'm so glad you joined me. We'll have so much fun"

"Me, too." Smiling, Carol peered over at Laura.

The car sputtered away from the curb. "Betty and I used to go shopping all the time. We usually had different taste in clothes, but we had so much fun together. She liked the loud flashy things, but I'm more conservative."

"I'm more conservative than you. Maybe Betty influenced you more than you know. I've noticed you coordinate everything you wear from the jewelry down to the shoes and purse." Carol's observation pleased Laura. The coordination seemed ingrained in her – another gift from the Lord.

"On a spectrum, Betty ranked flashy and bold, middle of the road for me, and you conservative." They laughed at Laura's analogy.

"Do you have coupons?" Laura checked with Carol when they arrived at the mall entrance.

Carol held up her purse. "Oh, yes, I cut out all the ones I could find. How about you?"

Laura searched through her handbag. "I'm sure I put mine in here. Oh, no, I must have left them lying on the kitchen counter. I can't believe I forgot my coupons." She rummaged through her purse, and grew more frantic by the moment.

"Don't worry, Laura. I have enough for both of us." Carol displayed several coupons in her hand and handed them to Laura.

"Thanks, you're a life saver." Laura stuck them in the side pocket of her purse. "Are you sure you won't run short?"

"Actually, I think you only need one today. They hand them back to you, but if not, yes, I have plenty." Carol laughed as they made their charge toward the front door of the store.

They hurried into Foley's like two tourists on a safari hunt.

Laura stopped just inside the door. "Wow, what a

great looking pant suit." She took the stylish light blue Capri pants and their short jacket with cording of white on the edge of both, off the rack and held up the cotton prize for Carol to see.

"Oh, yes, the color brings out your eyes and goes so well with your blond hair and complexion. You must be a summer."

Laura thought out loud as she planned her wardrobe for her date with Tom. "The shoes and purse I bought for my first date with John should be the same color blue. At least, I hope so. My silver jewelry should set everything off just right."

"See what I mean? You always coordinate everything." Carol stood with her hands on her hips. Her green eyes sparkled as she looked at Laura and the pantsuit.

"Guess it's engrained in me. I hope I don't blow my budget for the week, but if the suit fits I'm going to buy it, regardless." Laura walked toward the dressing room to try on the treasure.

When Carol viewed her, she said, "You definitely need to buy the outfit. I think it was made for you."

Laura turned over the price tag. "On sale. Great. I have to watch my spending. I want Christina to fly home for Labor Day, and I plan to buy some things for her. Frank pays most of her bills, but there are things I like to get her."

"I'm sure she'll like that." Carol continued to search through the sale racks.

"Also, I must watch my spending for another reason. I'll tell you about it sometime, a story I don't share with everyone." Laura felt she could confide in Carol.

"Lucky we came today. They have some really good bargains, especially, with the extra coupon. I would love to hear your story. And thanks for wanting to confide in me." Carol's face broke out into a wide grin.

"I've gotten into the habit of going to the beauty and nail shop and that adds up." Laura continued her budgeting resume as she searched through the racks, holding the treasured blue pantsuit in her hand.

"I've been meaning to ask you. Who does your nails? They always look so nice. I'd like to get mine done." Carol walked over to Laura and took her by the hand for a closer inspection.

Laura held her hand steady for Carol to get a good look. "I go to Beautiful Nails. Why don't you come with me this Friday at noon? I'm getting my hair done at nine and nails at noon. We can see if we can get you an appointment."

"Since I'm new in town, I don't have a hair dresser either. Would you mind if I tag along for both the appointments?" Carol raised her eyebrows in question.

"Of course, you can. In fact, let's call now. I have my cell phone with me." Laura took her phone out of the side pocket of her purse. She stood poised and ready to dial at Carol's command.

"Great! That would be wonderful" The relieved and happy look on Carol's face let Laura know she'd done the right thing by including a new friend into her life.

Laura hit the automatic dial for the beauty salon and then the nail shop. She arranged the appointments. "Now, we're all set for shopping and getting beautified."

"You're really getting into this dating game." A bit shocked at Carol's statement, Laura protested.

"You sound like Betty. She'd be proud of me. That's what she wanted – me to move on with my life." Laura grinned.

Thankful for Carol's companionship and support, Laura found herself smiling more than she had in months. *I'm so glad to have a friend again.*

"Why don't we run next door to the cafeteria and grab a bite?" Laura examined her watch. One-fifteen.

"Where has the time gone?" Three hours had passed during their shopping excursion. Her growling stomach told her the watch read correctly.

"That sounds great to me." Carol picked up her bundles and marched in the direction of the cafeteria. Laura trailed right behind.

The noon crowd had already departed, so no long line deterred their progress. Laura and Carol zipped through the variety of choices and sat down in no time. They placed their food on the table from their trays and bowed to pray.

After their prayer, Laura opened up to Carol. "The reason I must watch my spending is two-fold. I'm a shop-a-holic. Sometimes, I don't know when to stop. I sunk my family into debt when Frank and I were married, due to my shopping sprees."

"I can understand how that could happen. I like to shop myself." Carol took a bite of her salad.

"I'm not talking about the kind of shopping we did today. I'm talking major purchases. After Frank started making money as a lawyer, I went wild. I spent money everywhere on anything I wanted. I landed us in debt over our ears. Paying off those bills took us several years, and I went through counseling in order for me, and our bank account, to get back in balance."

"Wow, That must have been hard on you and Frank." Carol eyed Laura tenderly.

"I'm better now, but I still must control my spending, just like a reformed alcoholic. Unlike the alcoholic, I'm glad I can at least spend in moderation. My love for Christina keeps me straight. I want to help her." Laura watched her friend's face for any shocked reaction due to her confession.

"Laura, when we go shopping, I'll keep you under control and help you with the problem. Today, you've done great. You only bought the pantsuit, but look at my stash. Carol looked at all her Foley's bags and then at Laura. I'm the one who needs to watch it. We might need to keep each other in check." She took another bite of her salad. The look of sincerity in her eyes told Laura she understood.

Laura gazed back. Her heart acknowledged Carol as a friend, one she could trust and rely on. "Okay, we will watch each other." Happiness spread through Laura as she and her new friend smiled at each other.

Friday evening came and so did a case of nerves. Her first real date with Tom. She didn't know what to expect. He appeared kind and polite, but some of her single-again friends told horror stories about their dating experiences.

As Laura focused on the times the two of them spoke on the phone, her heart raced and she caught her breath. In fact, whenever he called her heart skipped a beat. Just thinking of him affected her. *He's so handsome, but I never thought a man would get me excited again. Was she acting like a teenager?*

Well, she would find out more about him tonight. Marrying a non-Christian would be a big mistake. *What am I thinking? I'm not marrying him. We're only going to a movie.* However, how many times had she advised younger people, her daughter in particular, not to date an unbeliever? "You might fall in love, and then what?" She knew from experience. *Anyway, I think Tom is a Christian.*

"Lord, help me relax and enjoy this evening. I know you're in control. Help me enjoy my time with Tom. Use it for my good and your glory." Glad no one could hear her, she continued with some self-talk. *I can do this. Tom is an old friend and we can continue as friends. I will find out where he stands with the Lord – with the Lord's help of course! It's just a date. We're not getting married. Anyway, I don't want to get married right now.* She found herself laughing at herself.

She dressed and studied her reflection in the full-length mirror. *Good, the pantsuit looks nice*. She gave herself a confident nod, defraying some of her nervousness. By the time Tom rang the doorbell, she felt cool and calm. However, her heart skipped another beat.

When she opened the door, Tom looked fabulous in his green polo shirt and black sport slacks. He'd never looked better, even in high school. His hair held a touch of gray at the temples, and he had added a few pounds, but he matured into an even more handsome man. He took her hand. She couldn't tell whether or not the shaking rested there or in her insides. Fortunately, if her hand shook, he didn't notice or comment.

"Come in while I grab my purse."

He stepped inside and looked around. "What a lovely place. Just like I expected, neat, orderly, and attractive. Just like you."

"Thank you," she uttered as color flooded her checks. She again hoped he didn't notice.

"Are you ready to go?" His eyes met hers as he and waited for an answer.

"Ready." She switched off the light and flipped the lock on the door.

"Have you been sleeping better?" Tom asked on the way to the restaurant.

"Some nights are better." She didn't tell him the cause lately—him and their date.

He pulled against the curb at the restaurant and jumped out. *I'm glad we're here so he didn't see me blush again.* He appeared on her side of the car and opened the door. *He's a gentleman, too. John opened the door for me, but Tom does it with such ease and grace, like second nature.*

"Wow, what a crowd. Glad I phoned ahead and made reservations." He seemed pleased with himself as he smiled down at her.

Long distance from the Woodlands. Maybe he used his cell phone— the best way to make a long distance call anymore. Cheaper than using the home phone. Why am I going there?

The hostess seated them in a corner away from the crowd, so the noise level decreased. Laura preferred quieter restaurants, but not many existed anymore. Red Lobster served the best coconut shrimp around. The pineapple sauce added the perfect flavor. She decided earlier in the week what she would order, even though the entree didn't follow her diet plan. She would compensate tomorrow.

Tom ordered broiled flounder. *I should have ordered the same and stayed on my diet.* When their food arrived, Tom asked in a normal voice, "Do you mind if I say grace?"

"I would love for you to." *He is a Christian. I don't have to wonder any longer.* She sighed and the evening took on a new meaning for her.

During the course of dinner, they discussed their weeks, the weather, and general things at first. In this quiet corner, they didn't have to shout as they continued their conversation.

"How's your daughter doing in college?" Tom pursued a subject after her heart.

"Doing quite well. Thank you for asking." Laura placed her napkin back in her lap, and smiled up at him.

"And how are your children and grandchildren doing?" She remembered his grown son, a lawyer, and two married daughters with a child each.

"I happen to have pictures of them in my billfold." Tom reached in his back pocket, produced the billfold, and opened to the first picture. He showed her one of each of his children and grandchildren. He beamed with pride over all of them. “Jason wants to establish himself in a law career before he marries and has a family. I think that’s a good idea.”

By the time they finished eating their dinner and talking, they had to rush for the movie. A parking place at the theater took time to find. Did everyone in Humble decide to attend the eight o’clock movie on Friday night? Except for this discussion, the talking ceased.

“Would you like some refreshments?” Tom offered after purchasing the tickets and walking inside.

“No thanks, we just ate.” She laughed at herself. Of course, they’d just eaten. “I seldom pass up popcorn, but I couldn’t eat another thing.” She chuckled again. *This might be the first movie I’ve ever attended without popcorn.*

They laughed together at the funny lines throughout the movie. A love story of sorts captured the big screen, but Tom Hanks didn’t get the girl this time.

When they left the theater, they ran into Janice. Laura knew her vaguely as the quiet one from the canasta group. She spoke to them, acted a bit peculiar, and then hurried away. Tom spoke as if he knew her, but hung his head and said nothing else. Some type of exchange happened between the two of them.

Tom took her straight home and stopped the car in front of her house. "I would invite you out for coffee, but I have an early day tomorrow. I'm driving to Dallas to visit my youngest daughter and grandchild for the weekend."

"That's fine. I'm a little bushed myself. It's been a busy week." Laura held her hand over her face to stifle a yawn.

"I enjoyed the evening. Let's do it again soon. Next time, I'd like someplace we can talk without all the noise. I want to get to know you better." Tom turned toward her.

Laura blushed again. This time the dark hid her embarrassment, so she didn't worry about his seeing her. "I- I would like that too."

Tom slid out and opened the car door for her. He walked her to her doorstep and waited until she got inside. He didn't even try to kiss her goodnight. Instead, he turned and walked down the sidewalk, got in his car, and drove away.

Mixed feelings invaded her. On the one hand, she felt relief and knew she wasn't ready for a goodnight kiss from any man. On the other, she wondered what a kiss from him would be like.

How will I ever sleep tonight!

CHAPTER TWENTY-SIX

Mid-Week Date

Laura tossed and turned most of the night. The shrimp from dinner weighed heavy in her stomach. Tom and John weighed heavy on her mind. A special choir practice would start at nine in the morning, and she hated the thought of getting up early. She dozed off and on until the alarm sounded at six-thirty.

Around seven, she eased herself out of bed and dressed. Instead of fixing breakfast at home, she stopped by the local donut shop to treat herself to a bear claw, something she rarely indulged in.

She walked into the shop and heard her name. "Good morning, Laura."

She turned around, and John stood there with a wide grin on his face, dressed in lake attire. *Even in fishing gear, he looks pretty striking*. He managed to keep a nice slim physique for a man of 60. His gray hair peeked out around the edges of his cap, which made him look distinguished. One could drown in his sea blue eyes. They reminded her of a refreshing swim in the Pacific Ocean.

In some ways, she felt more at ease with John than Tom. He didn't make her heart race the same way Tom did. Maybe because she saw him more often. John appeared always the same while Tom posed a mystery to her.

"G…G…Good morning." She managed to stammer. You're out early today. Looks as though you're on your way fishing."

"Yes, I'm going to try and nab some of those Crappie they say are biting. Maybe next time I cook for you, we can have a fish fry. By the way, why don't we do that this Thursday night? I'm having another couple over for Canasta. We could make it a foursome, and I'll cook my catch." He grinned from ear to ear and appeared quite pleased with his ideas.

Laura attempted to puncture his smugness. "What happens if you don't catch any fish?" She tried to hold back her smile and act serious.

But John took the teasing in stride. "Guess we'll just have to punt and eat hamburgers again, or I'll buy some fish. But, I do plan to catch Crappie, if they're cooperating!"

She couldn't let him cook twice in a row without contributing something.

"This time why don't you let me make the dessert?"

"Great. Then you're accepting my invitation?" He drew his head back and peered at her.

"Well, yes, I guess I am. Sounds like a great evening. Do I know the other couple?" She walked to the counter to place her order.

"You probably do. They live right here in town, or at least she does. Her name is Janice Johnson and his is Tom Lockhart. He lives over in the Woodlands, actually."

Laura's face felt hot. Blood rushed to her checks, and then she felt weak. Finally, she found her voice again. "Oh, yes, I know Janice. She's in my women's Canasta group, and I went to high school with Tom."

"Are you okay? You look a little pale." He obviously didn't have a clue as to why she turned colors.

"Yes, I'm fine. Haven't had breakfast yet, maybe I'm a little hungry." She didn't think of her explanation as a fib. She was hungry.

"Well, get on up here and get your order before you faint." He quickly moved aside to give her plenty of access to the counter.

She picked up her two bear claws and a decaf coffee. And then turned back to him and their conversation.

"I'd stay and join you, but my fishing partners await. Better not miss the Crappie if you want them for dinner on Thursday. See you then. I'll pick you up at six."

"It isn't necessary for you to pick me up since you're cooking. I'll drive over and bring my dessert." She thought about what she would fix.

"Are you sure?"

"Yes, I'm sure. It'll be fine."

"Okay, see you then." He waved goodbye and headed for the door.

"Okay." She waved back. The clerk handed her the pastries.

Now, what am I going to do? This could be embarrassing for everyone. Why did I have to accept his invitation? Maybe I'll call and say I'm sick.

Laura pondered her situation. As a Christian, she knew she couldn't tell a lie. *No wonder Janice and Tom acted so funny the other night. Had they been dating for a long time? This dating game is getting complicated. I told Betty I wouldn't be good at this. It's hard to date different people after being married for so long. Well, I'll just have to make the best of things. Sure hope everyone else can do the same.*

Even though she resolved to make the best of things, during the week her thoughts strayed to the encounter with Tom and Janice. She envisioned how each person might respond. Janice might mention seeing her and Tom together at the theater? Would John find out she and Tom dated? Or would Tom act as if nothing had happened between them? She hoped it wouldn't be an awkward evening.

She meditated on the upcoming event throughout the week. *It's best to get the dinner over with and see what happens, instead of torturing myself.* She quoted Scripture when her thoughts ran away with her. *Casting down imaginations, and every high thing that exalteth itself against the knowledge of God, and bringing into captivity every thought to the obedience of Christ.* (2 Corinthians 10:5 KJV)

Laura's week, filled with activities, sped along. On Wednesday evening, she made her dessert, an Italian Crème Cake – her favorite. Usually, men liked it as well. *She had two men to impress*. She couldn't believe her thoughts. *Where did that come from? The devil must really be working on me overtime. I must be walking in a miracle.*

Thursday arrived. Around four-thirty Laura started getting ready. She wanted to look as good as Janice, an attractive woman with striking red hair, a slender figure, petite statue, and clear skin, with the exception of a few freckles. Not that she wanted to compete, but she did like to look as good as possible. At least, she dressed without asking anyone else's opinion for a change. She smiled at her progress in building her confidence. *After all, it's just a fish fry and Canasta game.* She decided on designer blue jeans and a colorful cotton blouse. She slipped into her slides to match the shirt, and wore simple gold jewelry. She hoped the outing would be as simple as her outfit.

The clock bonged five thirty, and she surveyed her appearance one last time in the mirror. Not wanting to be the first one there, she sat down to wait a few minutes before leaving. At five- fifty-five she left her house. On the way, she gave herself a pep talk and prayed. Running away crossed her mind, but she knew the problem couldn't be avoided forever.

At the time she arrived, her pulse had slowed to normal, and she felt calm. Either that, or she figured she must be in a stupor. At any rate, she checked her hands, and they didn't shake.

Laura rang the doorbell. When the door opened, Janice stood there in apparent shock. By the startled look on her face, Laura knew she didn't know John had invited her as his date for the evening.

"Hi Laura." Janice seemed to regain her composure. "John and Tom are in the backyard frying the fish, so I answered the door."

"Thank you, Janice. I'd better set this cake down before I drop it." Laura stood on the outside of the door holding the heavy cake platter.

Janice stepped aside for her to enter. The silence between them hung in the air like a balloon filled with helium.

Laura walked into the kitchen where she could see John and Tom through the patio window frying fish and talking. Tom caught a glimpse of Laura and smiled, but the Coke can in his hand took a tumble. He scurried to retrieve his drink from off the patio floor. Apparently, he hadn't expected her either. He turned to John. She couldn't hear what he said. He must have announced her arrival because John peered at her through the sliding glass door. A wide smile spread over his face, and in one movement he bounded inside to welcome her, probably the only one really glad to see her. The awkward moment passed, and all recovered, or so it seemed.

"How can I help?" Laura said, and Janice chimed in. "Yes, how can we help?"

"Everything's all ready to go." John opened the refrigerator to reveal the salad. John's colorful everyday dishes adorned the table, and the baked potatoes lay on the counter along with a tray of condiments. John's culinary skills and organization exceeded any Laura ever witnessed.

Frank couldn't find the saltshaker most of the time. Laura and Janice set the salad on the table and filled the glasses with ice while John scooped the fish onto a lovely platter and carried his prize catch into the house. He placed a grand mound of crappie before them.

Laura complimented John as everyone gathered round the table. "I see you had a good day fishing on Saturday." She glanced over at the platter of fish, and all eyes drifted in that direction.

"You must have brought me good luck. The fish were really biting, and My friends and I caught over fifty. They sent them all home with me. I think they just didn't want to clean their share. There's more in the freezer.

Let's sit down and eat before they get cold. Crappie tastes the best piping hot." John held Laura's chair, and Tom helped seat Janice.

When they were all seated, Tom offered to say grace. Laura suspected John wasn't accustomed to this, but as a polite host, he accepted Tom's offer and handled everything graciously. Janice's eyes darted from one person to the other, but she bowed her head. She looked uncomfortable, and Laura wondered about her.

This helped Laura realize some things about each of them. Apparently, Tom was a believer, but John wasn't, or had drifted away from serving the Lord. She must find out which. There are no accidents with God, so He must have put each of them in her life for a reason. She suspected the same in regard to Janice. Laura hoped she could fulfill His purpose.

She decided then and there she would have a good evening and enjoy each participant. Laura trusted the Lord, even though, she wondered about His plan this evening.

John outdid himself again. The dinner was delicious. The Canasta game that followed made her laugh, and she and John came through as victors. Tom and Janice, caught off guard in more ways than one, possibly had lost their concentration.

Janice remained cool to her, but Tom acted attentive and friendly after he recovered from the shock. He even asked about Christina, which Laura appreciated. *Janice may just be shy or else insecure.* She usually didn't say much at their regular Canasta games. Tonight she was even quieter.

Anyway, what would I do with two men? With Janice in the picture, maybe I won't have to make a choice.

CHAPTER TWENTY-SEVEN

No Explanation Needed

The phone rang and pulled Laura from a deep sleep. She had planned to sleep in since she had nothing pressing for the day. She grabbed the phone and looked over at the clock. Eight-thirty. At least she had slept beyond her usual seven. Sleep hadn't come easy last night for she tossed and turned, analyzing the evening. She tried to figure out each of last night's participants place in her life. *The Lord has a plan, for He always does. Each person occupies our lives for a reason, a season, or a lifetime.*

Tom's voice came across the wire. After their initial greetings, Tom poured out his explanation. "I suppose you're wondering why I didn't tell you about my dating Janice. We have dated for a while, but I don't believe she's God's choice for me. I wanted only friendship, but she intends for something more. I've tried to break it off, but it isn't easy. I don't want to hurt her."

Laura shifted the phone to her other ear as she struggled to get out of bed. "I see. I understand. I wouldn't want to hurt anyone either."

"We planned the evening at John's a few weeks ago. I wanted to back out." Tom hesitated and then continued. "Once I make a commitment I like to keep it. I hope you weren't too uncomfortable."

"Thank you for thinking of my feelings, Tom, but I'm just fine. I enjoyed the evening. I don't need any explanation." She sat up in bed. *After all we're just friends. I may not be the right one either.*

"Well, I know you must have wondered when we ran into Janice at the movie the other night, and then at John's. That's the story." He ended with a nervous laugh.

"I think it's okay for each of us to see other people, we're all just friends." She thought aloud. However, she wasn't exactly sure how she felt. Did she want to be more than friends with Tom, or John? She started surveying her own heart and mind.

"I wish we could keep things that way, but Janice wants something more. I'm not ready to commit to anything right now. My divorce hurt too badly. Perhaps, I'll feel differently in a little time, and if I find the right person." His voice took on a tone of sadness – something new for the Tom she knew. In high school he kept everything jovial. *He must have suffered a great deal.*

"Excuse me, but I've got to get to work." Tom

interrupted her thoughts with another explanation. "Before I go…" He still sounded a bit nervous, "I would like to know if you would have dinner with me tomorrow night? I want to talk further over a leisure dinner."

"That'd be very nice." She stood to her feet from the bed and headed toward the bathroom. Grateful for a cordless phone.

"Great. I'll pick you up at seven and make our reservations for seven thirty. See you then."

"Okay. Have a great day, Tom!"

"You, too, Laura. Bye for now."

"Bye." She hung up the phone. She wondered what he wanted to talk further about. He probably needed someone to listen, and listening seemed to be one of her ministries. People came to her and unloaded. She never thought of herself as a good listener, but perhaps the Lord changed that. She knew she could definitely relate to a broken heart and the sadness of divorce.

The rejection, which came with her divorce, proved to be the most awful feeling she ever experienced. A fate worse, she believed, than the death of a spouse. In that case, at least the loved one, in most instances, left in love. She pictured Betty and knew her sadness at the loss of her precious husband, but she never felt rejected or unloved. Laura, on the other hand, felt like an old discarded shoe that no one wanted anymore. She continued to recuperate from the trauma.

Finally, she came to grips with people knowing she and John dated. Maybe everyone would quit talking about them shortly. No one knew about her dates with Tom, not even John. Well, as she told Tom, they could date other people with no explanation needed. She wanted to play the field for now and enjoy both of their friendship. Maybe God had one of them in mind for her and maybe He didn't. She definitely didn't want to be out of His will ever again. She yearned to know John's story about his relationship with God, or if he had one. Maybe in a little time she would find out his whole story.

Laura wanted to look her best now that she dated. She kept her standing beauty shop and nail appointment every Friday or Saturday, depending on her social calendar. Not only did she want to look good for her date, she found her hectic schedule didn't allow for time to do her hair and nails herself. Retirement kept her busier than when she worked fulltime. The ministry work gave her a sense of fulfillment and joy.

Her days packed with activities didn't afford her time to worry, a good thing. Water aerobics class at seven on Monday got her up and out early. Then she dressed for Bible study, spent from nine until twelve there, and ate lunch with the other ladies in the group. She stopped by the grocery store on her way home and bought groceries. She tried to get in some housework, ironing, and yard work the remainder of the day. Most times the day expired before she got to the latter.

Tuesday morning she walked on the treadmill before breakfast. Exercising faithfully kept her fit. She packed her lunch, but still hoped Carol would call so they could eat together at the nearby tearoom. When she arrived at the area ministry donation store at nine, the place buzzed with activity. Not finding time to even call Carol, she thankfully ate the sandwich she packed. Pricing, sorting, and reselling the items brought to the store kept her busy until the store closed at five. Arriving home, she plopped into her recliner and vegged for an hour until dinner. The rest of the evening she spent watching a movie on Television.

Wednesday morning, water aerobics again. Carol and Anna from the canasta group would come for coffee at ten, so, Laura hurried to bake the cake for the dinner party at John's, along with some cookies for the women. After her guests left, she visited the nursing home. The residents clapped when she showed up. When she sat down at the piano to play and sing, everyone gathered around to listen. Mrs. Rosie was missing. When she finished, Laura walked back to Mrs. Rosie's room. When she discovered Mrs. Rosie left the evening before for her eternal home, tears pooled in Laura's eyes and sadness filled her for a few moments. Then, she remembered how Mrs. Rosie longed to go and be with her Lord. *Well, Rosie, you're walking those golden streets with your Savior.* Then, a smile twitched across her lips.

On her way home, Laura thought again of Mrs. Rosie when she put her check for deposit into the carrier at the bank. She had planned to buy new house shoes for Rosie when she received her retirement stipend, but now there would be no need for shoes of any kind. She could walk those golden streets without shoes.

With such a full day, Laura almost stayed home from Choir practice, but couldn't neglect her commitment to the group and the church. After she got there, the time singing praise songs to the Lord and then pastors sermon brought refreshment to her weary bones.

The phone rang off the hook on Thursday when Laura filled in for the receptionist at the Christian radio station. Hurting people phoned for prayer. From nine to five, calls poured in with prayer request. A few asked her for song requests or to speak with one of the D Jays. Laura loved helping however she could, but she recognized that only God could meet each need.

Friday, Laura planned to run errands, do her banking, read a good book or scrapbook, and bake and send goodies to Christina. Hopefully, she could even get in some shopping at the mall. But her plans were interrupted.

Getting off the phone with Tom, her doorbell rang. Laura rushed from the phone to answer. Janice appeared on her front door step. Laura's mouth fell open in surprise. *Maybe she's coming to apologize for her coolness last evening.*

Laura quickly recovered from her shock. "Come in and have some coffee and a bite of breakfast with me." Pleased she picked up pastries at the store on her way home from the nursing home on Wednesday, she offered some to Janice. Eating them alone would only add unwanted pounds to her already overweight figure. She liked to keep a handle on her weight. She really did believe God wanted her to maintain a healthy body.

"Thank you, Laura. I will have a cup of coffee, but I'll skip the pastry." Janice stood in the doorway of the kitchen where Laura led her.

"Have a seat here at the table." Laura motioned Janice to the table, where she sat down. Laura couldn't help but notice Janice's small, petite frame, and now knew one reason why. She could pass up the pastry. Something Laura found difficult, but not impossible. But after all, she had not had breakfast. *I'm making excuses.*

Laura took a seat beside Janice with two steaming cups of hot coffee. One she sat before Janice.

"Are you interested in Tom?" Janice blurted out just as Laura took a bite of her sweet roll. Laura almost choked. However, she took a breath and swallowed her food before answering.

"Tom and I are friends. We've known each other since high school. We lost track of each other for years. We reacquainted recently. Why do you ask?"

"Well, I saw the two of you at the movie the other night together. Tom and I have been dating for some time. I really like him. I thought he might make a commitment to me eventually, and then you came along. I should've listened to him when he said he only wanted friendship. Now, I'm miserable because I've let myself fall in love with him." Her lips curled downward, and she looked as though she might cry at any second.

"I'm sorry, Janice. Maybe you need to give Tom some space. You definitely do not want him, if he isn't the one for you. I'm sorry." Laura apologized but made her statements with authority.

"What do you mean? Not the one for me? Do you think everyone has a special someone just for him or her? How do you make that decision?" Janice looked at her with sincere interest, a quizzical look in her eyes, and a questioning sound in her voice.

"I think through prayer and the Lord's leading you can find the special someone God ordains for you." Laura took another drink of her coffee to give Janice a moment to soak in her answer.

"I suppose I don't think God really cares about matching up people. He's too busy with all the other problems in the world." Janice stared at her coffee cup and then looked straight at Laura, waiting for her response.

"You know, Janice, I used to feel the same way, but I've found out that God cares about our every need. He's a personal God. He developed a perfect plan for each of our lives." Laura looked into Janice's green eyes to get a reflection of how she felt about her answer.

"I sure wish I knew His plan for my life right

now." Janice looked back at Laura as if she expected her to have her life's plan.

"You can know through His guidance, studying His word, and getting to know Him in a personal way." Laura laid her hand on Janice's as if to reassure her it could be done.

"I go to church every Sunday." Janice moved her hand away but did not yank it away. This gave Laura a good indication that she wasn't too offended, maybe just a little shy or embarrassed.

"I'm not talking about going to church. I'm talking about knowing the Heavenly Father, and acknowledging what He did in giving His son to die on the cross for you, on a personal level. Inviting Him into your heart and fellowshipping with Him. Talking to Him everyday as you would an earthly father." Laura whispered softly as she saw Janice relax her body and take in what she said. Then, she tensed again.

"You mean get saved? I was born a Christian." Janice repeated something Laura had heard before, and she was prepared with the answer.

"Janice, no one is born a Christian. Jesus said, 'You must be born again.'"

"How can I be born again? I'm 45 years old.

How can I be born again?"

"What you say is similar to what Nicodemus said when Jesus told him 'you must be born again.' Let's go to the Scripture and see what Jesus answered." Laura walked to her recliner and reached for her Bible lying on the floor beside the chair. She carried it back toward the kitchen table, opened it, and found the Scripture.

"Okay." Janice agreed and seemed to have her curiosity peaked. For she turned her head toward the Bible and watched Laura turn to the Scripture.

Laura read John 3:3-7 from the King James Version: *Jesus answered and said unto him, Verily, verily, I say unto thee, Except a man be born again, he cannot see the kingdom of God. Nicodemus saith unto him, how can a man be born when he is old? Can he enter the second time into his mother's womb, and be born? Jesus answered, Verily, verily, I say unto thee, Except a man be born of water and [of] the Spirit, he cannot enter into the kingdom of God. That which is born of the flesh is flesh; and that which is born of the Spirit is spirit. Marvel not that I said unto thee, Ye must be born again."* When she finished reading, she looked into Janice's eyes.

"I see the peace and faith in your life, Laura, and

I've often wondered about it. Is this what being born again can do for you?" Janice looked back at Laura as if she wanted to see that peace for herself again.

"Yes, it is, Janice." Laura stared back at her and smiled.

"Then, I want to be 'born again,'" Janice emphatically stated.

Laura reached for Janice's hands and took them in hers. This time Janice did not pull away or even flinch. "Then, pray this prayer after me."

Janice shook her head up and down in an acknowledgement of Laura's request. "Okay." Then, she bowed her head in anticipation.

"Father, I thank You for sending Your Son to die in my place. Thank You, that my sins are forgiven as I ask You to forgive me. You were crucified, died and was buried that I might have eternal life. Come into my heart and take over my life, so that I might be born again. In Jesus Name." Laura led and Janice repeated the words. From the look on Janice's face, Laura knew she meant every syllable. Then tears of joy flowed as they laughed and cried. Brand new relationships began. More than one for Janice!

CHAPTER TWENTY-EIGHT

Visiting and Sharing

Laura instructed Janice about the days ahead. "Janice you need to read the Scriptures, pray, look for God's guidance, and fellowship with other believers. God through His Holy Spirit will lead and guide you into all truth." Laura took Janice's hand and again she didn't pull away.

"I'm so glad to have you as a friend, Laura, and to think, I almost hated you for your interest in Tom. I will wait for God's plan. If what you say is true, and I think it is, I know the Lord will guide us both, and Tom as well." Janice sounded like a new person already.

Laura wondered if living out what she voiced would be that easy.

"Wow, you learn fast, Janice! You're right. God will show each of us His best for our lives. I don't want to cut off any friendship with Tom. You don't want him if God hasn't ordained him for you. Let's watch what God does. I'm sure it will be good."

"Gee, I must get home. I'm sure you have things to do, also. I need to do some ironing, washing, and make cookies for a bake sale at church tomorrow. Wait until I tell the minister what happened to me." Janice drew a deep, excited breath.

"You reminded me. I need to bake cookies to send Christina. I haven't sent any in a while. I don't want to disappoint her again this week. I must get them in the mail. I wish she hadn't decided to go out of state to school. The time between visits keep getting longer. We do talk often. Never thought I'd be so happy for a cell phone."

"They come in handy." Janice rose from the table and started for the door.

"I'm so glad you decided to come today, Janice. God has done a wonderful thing. I can see the difference in your eyes. They're lit up like light bulbs. Anytime you have questions or need prayer, feel free to call." Laura walked with Janice to the door. She patted her on the shoulder. "May I give you a hug?"

"I would love it." Janice turned and embraced Laura like a long-time friend.

"Laura, I can't thank you enough for taking the time to listen and for pray with me. I feel like a different person." They finally released each other.

"You will find you are a different person. Read 2 Corinthians 5:17 later, and you'll see what I mean." Laura scribbled the reference down on a piece of paper and handed the note to Janice.

"Okay. I will." Janice tucked the paper into her pocket and walked toward the door.

When they reached the door, Laura hugged Janice once more. Janice returned the hug with tears in her eyes, not the first ones today. What a morning. The hours passed quickly, and noontime approached.

Laura gathered the ingredients from the cupboards for the cookies. Then, the phone jingled. This time John's voice came across the line. He jumped right into the reason he called. "Laura, are you busy this evening?"

"If I don't get these cookies finished and some errands run, I will be. However, I should be done by evening. What do you have in mind?"

"I would like to come over, talk, and get further acquainted with you, or have you come here. We've always had others around, cards to play, or movies to watch. I would like to just visit." John sounded sincere, yet casual.

W*ow! Everyone wants to visit today.* Then, she checked her thoughts. God ordered her steps, so this must be His plan. Hadn't she realized by now He sent people to her so she could listen and tell them about Him?

"Sure, John, come on over about seven-thirty. I'll save cookies for us and fix a pot of decaf coffee. I hope you like hazelnut."

"That sounds great." She heard excitement in his voice. "I'll see you then."

Laura pondered after she hung up the phone. *What does John have on his mind*? Did he need someone to tell him about the Lord and His goodness, being 'born again' or had he found out about her dating Tom? Could be an interesting evening.

Laura finished her chores and dinner. She didn't have time to change again, but freshened up a bit. Ready or not, the doorbell rang promptly at seven-thirty. She hurried to put on lipstick, her finishing touch. She opened the door. John held a beautiful bouquet of flowers – her favorite – yellow roses.

"T—thank you. They're beautiful! Let me put them in some water. Come in and make yourself at home."

John followed her into the kitchen. "You have a lovely place here. Your kitchen looks so homey. And the smell of those cookies and coffee! Makes a person hungry, even when they're not."

"Would you like some now?" Laura reached into the cupboard, took out two cups, and placed them on the counter.

"I do think I'll have coffee, but no cookies, not yet anyway. I just finished dinner." He poured himself a cup.

She reached for a vase from the lower cabinet, then stood and arranged the flowers as she drew in a deep breath to take in the sweet aroma.

John watched closely, making her uneasy as she pondered what he wanted. Grateful she hadn't pricked herself with a thorn, she carried the roses to the kitchen table. Her hands shook as she placed the arrangement in the center, not spilling a drop of water. He stood quietly and she wondered about his thoughts.

***

As John watched Laura, he felt all warm inside and jiggle, like Jell-O gelatin. She made his heart pound. No other woman affected him this way in his entire life. Something about her made him want to know her better. Although she pleased the eye, his attraction went deeper than looks alone. *I don't want to frighten her*. His feelings must be kept in tow. She made her intentions plain. She only wanted a friend. Maybe someday soon, he could change her mind.

Then, his thoughts turned. I would like to attend church with her, but I know some of those people too well. Where were they when my mother needed them? No one ever came by to see her. The pastor prayed for her healing, and I prayed my heart out, but God didn't listen. Why should I trust in a God who doesn't hear? My father called himself a Christian, but he left my mother for someone else. He deserted us. I know many men at the church who have stepped out on their wives. So, how can I trust them?

***

"Would you like to sit here at the kitchen table or would you like to move to the living room?" She fixed her eyes on the beautiful roses, then, turned back to face John as she waited for his answer.

"What? Oh, either's fine with me." He sat his cup on the counter. "May I pour for you?"

"That would be great. Why don't we move into the den and get more comfortable. I have two recliners. You can't fall asleep on me though." She laughed at her own joke.

"I don't think there's any danger of that. I came to talk and find out about you." He pointed his finger at her as he marched toward the recliner.

"I'd like to get to know you too, John." She placed her coffee on the table beside her recliner and sat down.

John did the same. Then, he looked over at her. "Ladies first. Tell me about yourself."

She raised her cup, took a sip, and then began. "Okay, where do I start?"

"Just jump right in." He nodded toward her and then picked up his cup and brought it to his lips for a swig.

"I grew up here. I have always been a caregiver. Mother said as a youngster I took care of all the hurt animals. However, I didn't want to be a veterinarian. After graduation I attended college at Baylor University and received my nursing degree. I met Frank in high school. He attended law school. Then, we married and moved back here, where he started to practice law. And I worked at Northeast Medical Center Hospital as a nurse. We had Christina, but then complications kept us from having any other children."

"I'm eager to meet Christina." John turned up his cup once more.

"She is the light of my life. Frank found it hard to stay true to one woman. However, I stayed with him for thirty-two years. But I never could prove his unfaithfulness, or perhaps, I didn't want to know for sure, until toward the end of our marriage. My family never believed in divorce. I stayed for Christina. And I hoped he would come to his senses. He finally decided he wanted his freedom." She squirmed in her chair finding the truth a bit uncomfortable to discuss.

"He must be crazy to leave you for someone else." A gentle glow in John's eyes showed his sincerity as he sipped from his coffee cup.

"At first, I felt so rejected, discarded like an old shoe, but I'm doing better now. Betty helped me a great deal. She always urged me to get on with my life. My faith helped me through the divorce. Wow, I have been going on and on. Tell me about you!" She waited for him to begin.

"I grew up right here in Humble. Never wanted to go anywhere else. You know how native Texans are." He laughed.

Laura caught his humor and laughed. "I know. We Texans do show our pride. There's no place like the Lone Star state." She tipped her cup toward him and then brought it to her lips.

He returned her gesture as he lifted his cup to her toast. "You got that right." Then he continued to give her information about himself. "I went to school at the University of Houston and got my teaching degree in Social Studies. I taught here in Humble for thirty years and then retired. I still substitute teach occasionally. I miss the young people. Many of them still come to me for advice."

"I have noticed you talking with some of the young people—like the young lady at the doughnut shop. I think that's great." A warm surge of admiration flowed through her.

"Sometimes, I don't know what to say to them, but I listen. Most of the time, people only need someone to pay attention to them, and hear what they say." He took another sip of his coffee. Laura nodded in agreement as she sipped her own.

"I've traveled both in the states and abroad, but I always come back home to Humble. My mother lived with me after she got sick." He sipped his coffee and a far away look came across his face. “My father left us when I was very young and Mother never remarried. She had Alzheimer’s close to the end, which was hard, but I didn’t want to put her in a home. So, I kept a nurse with her during the day while I taught.” The sad far away look in his eyes grew more intense. Could he still miss her?

“How difficult that must have been.” She reached over and touched his hand briefly.

“Yes, one of the hardest things I’ve ever faced.” He looked into her eyes and their eyes held for a moment, but then he continued. “I almost married once, but things didn’t work out. Since then, I’ve not found the right one for me, until now. I think maybe I have now.”

Laura didn’t know what to say. She picked up her coffee cup and started to drink again. What could she say? She wasn’t sure of her own feelings toward him. So, she didn’t respond to his statement. The awkward moment finally passed.

“I guess I place my faith in myself. I tried the church and God, but that didn’t work for me. My mother died. During mother’s sickness and death, I asked—How can a loving God let anyone suffer that way? I prayed for her to be healed.” She saw a trace of a tear in his eyes. But he recovered quickly.

"Where I went to church, there were too many hypocrites." He took a breath and downed some more coffee.

"John, I can't tell you why your mother wasn't healed. But I can tell you God is sovereign. He knows what's best for all of us. One thing I've learned: God looks at death differently than we do. To Him, it's the beginning of eternity; for us it seems final until we understand His Word and His ways. I don't know all the answers, but He does." She held her hands out for emphasis.

John looked at her and seemed to listen intently.

"As far as hypocrites, I can tell you a couple of things: One, they need to be in church worse than anyone. And two. If you let a hypocrite stand between you and God, he's closer to God than you are. Sorry." She hunched her shoulders and put her hands over her mouth.

John sat quietly for a few minutes. *Have I offended him?* Maybe, he's just mulling over my words. He finally spoke. "I'll have to think this all over. I do know I've gotten along the last few years just fine on my own. Oh, there have been times, when I felt rather empty inside, but doesn't everyone feel that way at times?" He looked at her and shrugged his shoulders.

"I can truly say, since I made Jesus Lord of my life, I never feel empty. Oh, there are times I feel lonely, but I never feel alone. I know God watches over me. I enjoy the fellowship of other Christians as well. I miss Betty so much, but I know I will see her again. I also know God will take care of me. I used to think Frank would take care of all my needs, but no one takes care of me like Jesus." She smiled as she spoke and thought about His wonderful name.

"I remember when I felt close to Him. And the peace I had. I will think this over and get back to reading my Bible. Maybe, I will even try church again. Laura, you're the kind of Christian we need in this world. Someone, who not only 'talks the talk' but 'walks the walk.'" John nodded his head as if he agreed with himself.

She could sense he didn't want to discuss spiritual matters any further. "Say, how about those cookies with a fresh cup of coffee."

He gave her a look of appreciation. "That sounds great! Just the smell makes my mouth water. What are they, chocolate chip?"

"Yes, with lots of walnuts." She remembered he loved walnuts and plenty of them. Another trait they had in common.

"Wow, my favorite. I like almost anything with nuts." John followed her to the kitchen.

They discussed the weather, Christina, John's great fish catch and how they beat Tom and Janice at cards the evening before. Laura wanted to tell him about Janice, but knew it was Janice's story to tell. She didn't want to overload John this time. She hoped that like Janice, someday soon, John would trade an old life, not serving Jesus, for a new one, like she had traded some of her old shoes for new.

CHAPTER TWENTY-NINE

Stood Up

John stayed and talked late into the night. On Saturday morning, Laura shook herself, finding waking up difficult. She bolted out of bed at seven-thirty when she remembered her beauty shop appointment at nine. She threw on her robe, spent a few minutes in the bathroom, and trudged to the kitchen where she ate a bite of breakfast, then, dressed to go. She scheduled her nail appointment for ten-thirty and hoped her beauty treatments would end by noon. She wanted to compose herself before her evening date with Tom.

I must find time to practice my solo for Sunday morning. Why did I invite John, this of all weeks? When she returned from her beauty trip, she fixed a ham and cheese on oat-nut bread topped with loads of tomato, lettuce, and mayonnaise. She devoured the sandwich along with some of her favorite chips, Kettle Honey Dijon. Then, she allowed herself some extra time to practice her singing. She popped the sound track into the CD player and began. *Something Beautiful,* one of her favorites, came easy for her. Still, butterflies always gathered in her stomach when she sang alone. She hoped to do her best and not appear too nervous, but, most of all, not forget the words. John didn't ordinarily make her nervous, but she wanted to make a good impression on him, probably because she wanted to see him back in church and serving the Lord. Did she have ulterior motives?

Practice in front of the mirror helped. Pleased with the way her beautician did her hair, she walked closer to inspect the job. Looking closer, she spotted facial hair growing on her chin and upper lip. She never noticed until now. Was the discovery because she had grown more conscientious about her appearance in the past few months? *This dating game is a lot of trouble!* Horrified, she searched for her tweezers and plucked with vengeance. *This is a lot of pulling and pain.* Carol asked her earlier if the nail shop did face waxing. She found out today they did. *Next week, I'll get waxed.*

Oh, Carol. I said I would call her back the other night when we talked. And I still haven't. Where is my mind going? She reached for the phone and dialed. After the fourth ring, the answering machine came on with a blessing for the caller. *I'd like to put something like that on mine.*

Laura decided Carol probably went shopping and felt a quick wave of temptation to join her. *No, I've bought enough new shoes and clothes lately.* She needed to fight the old urge of overspending. Perhaps she had gone a little overboard the last few months, but not like she once did. Smiling, she thought about her acquisition of so many pairs of new shoes.

Laura wandered into the bedroom, examined her closet, and observed how the space overflowed. *Surely, in all that I can find something decent to wear tonight.* She decided upon a pink Capri outfit. One of her most flattering colors made a comeback this year. *I have some shoes that might match.* She dug out her pair of pink sandals and examined them. *Close. Not perfect*. But *Close enough.*

At least, she didn't have to buy new ones. No one would ever notice the difference. They were old shoes, but still good. *Like people. Even though, we get old, we can still be good for many things.* This one pair she didn't have to trade in. Sometimes, it's okay to hold on to old things. However, she tried not to hang on to her old feelings of rejection. Besides, the fact that two men pursued her built her self-confidence and feeling of acceptance, even if they were *only friends.*

Later in the day, worried that her solo wasn't quite ready, she started back to her practicing when the phone rang.

Carol must be returning my call. She answered just before the answering machine started. To her surprise, a male voice spoke instead of Carol.

"Laura, I'm glad I caught you. I'm so sorry, but I'm going to have to cancel our date for this evening. Something came up unexpectedly."

"That's okay." She felt a little dejected, but hoped her voice didn't give away the emotion.

"I'll explain later. Please forgive me. I'll get back to you tomorrow or next week." Tom pleaded.

"I hope everything's all right. I hope no one's hurt or anything." Laura pressed to make sure everything, or everyone, was okay.

"Oh, no. It's nothing like that. I'll tell you all the details later. I've got to run right now. Talk to you in a few…" The phone clicked in her ear.

Her curiosity aroused, she wondered what urgent circumstance prompted Tom to cancel their date. Some old feelings of rejection wanted to surface, but she refused to fall into Satan's trap. *I will not buy into the rejection game again. I'm accepted in the beloved and that's all that counts.* Laura remembered a verse in Ephesians chapter one verse six she learned from Betty after Frank walked out: *To the praise of the glory of his grace, wherein he hath made us accepted in the beloved.* She needed the encouragement then, and now.

If she kept her Savior first, everything else would fall into place. An inward peace flooded her as the power of the Word of God filtered through. She refused to worry about being stood up, or, anything else for that matter.

Well, I can practice more on my solo for Sunday. I'll try Carol again later and we can talk. I wonder what she found today. I could still go myself. If I promise myself, I won't overspend. She jumped into her most comfortable shoes, cut out her coupons, hurried to her 1999 tan Buick LaSabre and headed for her favorite store. Just the therapy she needed to tame her negative emotions, especially, since she had lost those few extra pounds. Returning to her desired size twelve gave her ego a boost and an excuse to look for something new. *I won't buy much, and only if it's on sale.*

Why don't I call Carol on her cell? She Flipped open her phone and spoke her desire as she drove to the mall. "Call Carol, mobile 1."

The voice answered back. “Did you say call Carol, mobile 1?”

“Yes.”

“Calling.” The line rang, but Carol’s voice mail message came on after four rings.

Laura flipped the phone shut. *Probably busy buying bargains and didn’t hear the ring. I’ll just surprise her at the store if she’s there.*

When she arrived, Laura walked straight to the sports clothes department. Carol plied through the sales section. “I tried to call, but I guess you didn’t hear the ring. I thought I might run you down. I tried to call you at home earlier, too. I figured you were out shopping.” Laura reached to give Carol a big hug.

“No. I never heard the phone. How are you, Laura?” Carol hugged her back. “You’ve been so busy. I haven’t been able to catch you by phone. What have you been up too?”

“Well, I have been busy with church things as usual and a few other things, I suppose.” Not knowing just what to say about her social calendar.

“I’ve heard the gossipers talk. You’ve been dating. Rumor says you have two guys on the string.” Carol smiled.

"Wow, things sure get around in a small town, don't they? Who told you?" Laura took her by the arm urging her to tell her right away.

"I ran into Janice here earlier. She couldn't stop talking about you. All good. She told me about what happened at your house on Friday morning, and I've never seen her so excited. She looked like a different person. She glowed." Carol stepped back and looked at some clothes that interested her.

Laura joined Carol in looking at the rack of clothes. "Well, I'm so happy for her. I'm not sure I have two guys on the string. One stood me up tonight."

"Stood you up?" Carol sounded indignant. She placed her hands on her hips as she shifted from one foot to the other. "I can't believe someone stood you up. When we finish here, let's go next door for a glass of tea or cup of coffee. You can tell me all about it." Carol turned back to investigate the items on the sale rack.

"There's not much to tell." Laura looked at the next rack. "He called and said something came up and he would give me the details later."

Carol picked out a blouse, held it up for Laura to see. "How do you like this?"

Laura shook her head. "Not your color."

Carol put the blouse back and motioned Laura to follow her.

"I'm getting a little tired and need something to drink, but first let me show you the bargains in purses and shoes today."

Laura shoved the blouse back in the rack and followed Carol. "Let's go." What a blessing to have a friend like Carol. Laura regretted not finding enough time for her lately. She missed their girl talk, and their shopping sprees.

Laura wagged the package with her pair of shoes and purse, and watched her friend do the same as they drifted over to the cafeteria for something to drink.

"My, it's dinner time already." Laura felt her stomach growl. She looked at her watch. No wonder. "Why should either of us eat alone? Let's have dinner here and then we can finish bargain hunting."

"Sounds good to me." Carol walked to the serving line, and Laura followed. They filled their trays and found a place to sit.

"Okay, Laura, who stood you up?" Carol unfolded her napkin and placed it on her lap.

"A guy named Tom. He's an old friend from high school. I don't know what happened, but he said something unexpected came up." Laura poured Splenda into her iced tea.

"Maybe unexpected for him. But Janice told me his ex-wife, Ellen, came back into town. She probably called him up, and he's still vulnerable where she's concerned. Janice says he always jumps when Ellen hollers frog. Matter of fact, he probably wanted to know, how high?" Carol picked up her fork and dove into her dessert.

"What do you mean?" Laura looked at her, then turned and forked the baked whitefish from her own plate.

"Well, I hear Ellen broke off with the guy she left Tom for. It didn't work out. He refused to leave his wife, so Ellen got left in the cold. She's probably trying to get Tom back." Carol paused and took a sip of her coffee. "Janice thinks he's a pretty good catch. She told me he's a pharmaceutical salesman making a good income, a God-fearing man, and one of the best looking guys around." Carol looked over at a gentleman walking by and commented. "Now, there's a handsome one."

Laura smiled and clucked her tongue. "Carol, I can't believe you said that!" Then she lowered her voice to a whisper. "Someone might hear you."

Carol laughed, shrugged her shoulders, ducked her head, and continued working on the pie on her plate.

Laura loved Carol, despite her gossiping. Carol couldn't resist listening to and repeating a story, even if all the facts weren't completely verified.

"Now, Carol," Laura shook her head and lifted her hand in protest. "You don't know if this is all true, do you?"

"Well, no, but from what Janice says, the scenario makes sense to me." She took another sip of her coffee to wash down the pie.

"Let's just wait and see what Tom says before we go jumping to any conclusions. He told me he would call either tomorrow, or next week. I'm sure he has a good reason for standing me up." Laura refocused on her food. *At least, I hope he does.*

As they finished their dinner, they talked about the things they bought, the weather, their last card game, and what the Lord was doing in each of their lives. Laura couldn't help but wonder if at least part of Carol's story might be true. She hoped the same thing wouldn't happen to Tom that happened to her. Ellen might tear his life apart again, and then cast him aside like an old shoe. From what he said, Laura knew Tom had suffered enough. But, God could put a marriage back together, even after a divorce. However, she had heard rumors about Ellen. *Now don't judge her. A person can change.*

CHAPTER THIRTY

Cake and Eat It Too

Laura's hands shook and her knees threatened to give way when she got up to sing. John sat in the middle section of the church directly in front of her. His reassuring smile helped calm her nerves. He somehow conveyed everything would work out okay. *Guess that's the teacher in him, or maybe something more.* At any rate, she sang with ease and the message of the song seemed to minister to the whole congregation, for many shed tears and responded with 'Amen.' A few even raised their hands in praise. Even though John never lost his smile, she thought she spotted a tear in his eye, but couldn't be sure.

After the service, a group of 'single again' adults gathered at the door to pass the word regarding lunch. Laura usually went with them, but today John found her first and asked if she would have lunch with him. She thought he might want to talk about the service, so she accepted his invitation. After all, she had invited him. At least, she told herself that.

John opened her car door and then slid into the driver's seat. "Would you like to go to Red Lobster for some coconut shrimp?"

Laura didn't hesitate. "That sounds great! I can always eat coconut shrimp." With that settled, John said, "What a great voice you have. I sure enjoyed your solo." He went on and on about her voice and the song she sang, but mentioned nothing about the rest of the service. Disappointed, she didn't press the issue because she hoped he would continue to attend. She didn't want to scare him away or turn him off.

As they ate, they discussed the hot weather along with its high electric bills, Christina and her upcoming Labor Day visit, and John's fishing escapades during the week.

"Did you catch a lot of fish?" Laura remembered the huge catch of crappie.

"Nah. Not a one. They weren't cooperating this time. I didn't run into you for good luck. As a matter of fact, I had bad luck."

"How so?" Laura searched his face, thinking she might find the answer to her question.

John hesitated, but finally told the story. "I got my line tangled in a tree over the lake. So, naturally, I climbed the tree to get it loose. The limb broke and dumped me into the lake— watch, billfold, and all."

Laura snickered and then laughed with gusto. "I can see the picture in my mind. Wish I'd been there with a camera." She held up her hands as if snapping the scene he described. "I could have sent the pictures to the humor section of a fishing magazine."

"At the time, it wasn't funny, but now I can look back and laugh. I did make quite a spectacle." He gave a hearty chuckle.

Laura liked John's humor. She hadn't laughed much in the past year, first the divorce, and then Betty's sickness and death. She wanted to enjoy herself again. Betty's advice continued to ring true. She did need move on with her life.

The dessert tray came, and she knew she couldn't resist the Italian crème cake, especially if John wanted dessert.

"Let's just have our cake and eat it too, today." John snickered. He ordered the Italian crème, and she joined him, gladly participating in eating the cake. Another thing they had in common.

After they polished off the dessert, they talked a while longer. Then, John piped up. "I'd better get you home for your afternoon nap. I hear most church goers take a Sunday afternoon nap before going back for Sunday night service." John seemed to know the routine, even if he didn't participate.

"I usually do. I hate to admit it, but there does seem to be something about Sunday afternoon and naps. I never take one during the week, only Sunday." She scooted out of the booth.

"I never sleep in the afternoon, not even on Sunday. I sometimes read a good book, but otherwise, I stay busy around the house or watch sports on television." He took her hand and helped steady her to her feet.

She couldn't resist the urge to ask. "Will you be going back to church this evening?"

"No, not this time. I promised one of my former students I would help her with a college entrance application and reference. She's coming over at six thirty."

"I see." *At least he said not this time. Maybe there will be a next time.* She certainly hoped so. She liked John, but didn't want to become entangled with someone not serving the Lord.

John drove her back to the church parking lot to pick up her car. He waited to ensure the engine started before he took off for home. When the motor purred, he waved goodbye and sped away.

The phone rang as she unlocked the door to her house. She dropped her purse and Bible on the sofa, wishing for Caller ID. She didn't want to talk to a salesman. Her bed called her for the nap she and John discussed.

"Hello?"

"Hello." She recognized Tom's voice. "I called to apologize for standing you up and to explain."

"Explanations aren't necessary." She held the phone to her ear, took off her earring and changed sides. "Only if you wish to talk about it."

"I want you to know what a mixed up situation you're getting involved with." He laughed nervously, sounding alarmed.

"What do you mean?" She laid her earring on the table beside her chair.

"I think I'd better explain. Where do I start?" He cleared his throat. "Guess I will just jump right in. When I called you yesterday, I had just received a call from Ellen, my ex-wife. She said she wanted to see me right away, and it was important. Thinking it must have something to do with the children, I agreed."

"I can understand that." Laura pulled the other earring off and switched the phone to that ear. She thought the conversation might take awhile.

"Well, when I arrived, she'd been crying. She said she had made a huge mistake leaving me and wanted to know if we could start over. She seemed so sincere and repentant, but I could not welcome her with open arms. I told her I would give it some thought and prayer."

"That sounds like a good idea." She nodded in agreement, even though no one could see her.

"To make a long story short, we agreed to date occasionally, but I did not agree to date only her. I let her know I dated others, and I wanted the Lord's guidance. I wanted you to know, since I would like to continue our relationship." He paused.

"I see. So you want to have your cake and eat it too?" Laura laughed, but didn't think her statement really funny.

"Look at whose talking. You're dating John. Don't you want your cake and eat it too?" Tom gave a nervous laugh.

"We're all just friends. This is your ex-wife we're talking about. If you decide you want to make up with her, I certainly don't want to stand in your way."

"At this point, I'm not sure what I want," he admitted.

"I will pray and seek the Lord on His direction for both our lives. I want to remain friends, but I don't see any other future for us. As I told a young lady recently, it's all up to the Lord!" She failed to mention the young lady was Janice. *No need to complicate things any further.*

"I, too, want the Lord's will in this." He hesitated briefly and then continued. "I truly only want His will for my life."

"By the way, what about Janice?" She couldn't resist mentioning her. "Have you told her your plans? All this should make a good three-ring circus and something for the town to talk about for awhile." She tried to make a joke, but sensed a touch of sarcasm in her voice.

"Haven't you heard about Janice? She started dating Mark, a guy from her church. She's really changed since our fish fry at John's." He sounded amazed.

Laura smiled to herself. She knew the reason for the change in Janice's life. *So the Lord is already giving her direction in her life and possibly the person He has for her.* "That's great!" She could hardly contain herself. She wanted to tell Tom the story, but thought this might not be the right time, or her story to tell.

"When will you let me know, if you want to continue seeing me, Laura?" He sounded anxious.

"I'll pray and give my answer later this week. You seek the Lord as well, Tom."

"I definitely will. I've tried things my own way before, and nothing works out too well. Like not at all!"

Laura felt better that he too depended upon the Lord for an answer. *Maybe he doesn't just want his cake and eat it too, after all! We have love for the Lord in common.*

CHAPTER THIRTY-ONE

Hard to Say No

Several times during the week, thoughts of Tom and the decision she must make crossed Laura's mind. If he and Ellen had a chance to reunite, she couldn't continue to see him. She knew God hated divorce and intended one woman, one man, and one set of children—His perfect design for marriage.

Even though they were divorced, their marriage may have a chance. She didn't want to hinder any reconciliation in any way. On the other hand, she hated to see Tom hurt again by his ex-wife. Neither did she want to hurt Tom, which made the decision difficult. According to their phone conversations and their talk at lunch, he had been quite devastated by the divorce. However, she would leave it entirely up to Tom, Ellen, and the Lord. She knew what she must do. She must bow out of the picture, at least for now.

"No"— a hard word for her, but she learned to use it more often in the last few months. She discovered "no" to be a perfectly good word. Each time she practiced, she found it a little easier, especially in regard to some of

Frank's request over their property settlement. On several occasions, she reminded herself of two Scripture passages. One she found in James, chapter five and verse twelve. *But most of all, my brothers and sisters, never take an oath, by heaven or earth or anything else. Just say a simple yes or no, so that you will not sin and be condemned for it.* Matthew chapter five verse thirty-seven contained the other. *Just say a simple, `Yes, I will,' or `No, I won't.' Your word is enough. To strengthen your promise with a vow shows that something is wrong.*

Just the same, she hesitated calling Tom. Finally, on Thursday, she forced herself to dial his number.

"Hello?" Tom's masculine voice came across the line. Apparently, he didn't have Caller ID, or else he didn't want to sound too familiar.

"Hi, Tom. This is Laura. How are you?"

"Okay, I guess. How are you doing?" He responded slowly and with much hesitation. She could tell by his voice he wasn't in the best of moods. Maybe he expected a "no" answer.

"I'm just fine. I called to give you my answer about seeing you in the future."

"And what have you decided? I hope you're going to continue to see me." Tom's voice carried a hint of pleading.

"I'm sorry, Tom, but I don't think that would be for anyone's good. If you and Ellen can work out your differences, I don't want to stand in the way. I know God wants marriages to continue, if at all possible. We both want His will for our lives. I'll be praying for you and Ellen. Give me a call sometime and let me know how things are going for you. In the meantime, we still can be friends, you know."

"You're probably right about what you've said and your decision." He hesitated again. "I'd like for us to continue to be friends, and I thank you for that."

"Be blessed, Tom. I'll talk with you later." She didn't want to prolong the conversation.

"You too, Laura. Bye for now."

She didn't understand why she felt like crying. Maybe she felt the sting of a lost relationship that had only just begun. She could tell Tom experienced reservations about everything. She wanted to comfort him, but knew she'd better keep the conversation short. For now, they each needed to go their separate ways. She understood how Tom felt. He cared for Ellen, and for her.

She could relate. She felt the same about him and John. How complicated life could become in this dating game. She whispered under her breath, "Betty, why'd you get me into this mess? I was doing just fine in my own little world, and you made me come out and face the real one again."

At least this time she hadn't been rejected, at least not yet anyway. In a circle such as this, someone ends up left behind sooner or later. She prayed no one would get hurt. They all had faced this type of pain in their lives, even Ellen. When her boyfriend rejected her, she came crawling back to Tom. Her actions may not have pleased the Lord when she left Tom for another man, but still, she had faced rejection too. *I hope she has come to her senses, and she and Tom can make a go of things.*

I can't dwell on these rejection issues. She moved on to something more positive. She remembered Philippians chapter four verse eight, which told her to dwell on things good and lovely and of good report. One of her favorite Bible verses.

She looked for John at the mid-week service last night, but he didn't show up. His apparent anger with the Lord for not healing his mother might hold him back, as well as his disappointment in other Christians.

I wish John knew he could see his mom again, just as I'll see Betty again, next time forever. Neither of them would have the old bodies that suffered so long. However, it's hard to think in those terms for us mortals.

Here she went again, thinking these internal and eternal thoughts. Were they insights or vain imaginations? She needed to get busy doing something. Her mother always told her as a youngster that idle hands were the devils workshop and idle lips his mouthpiece. She had better locate that Scripture sometime. She knew such an important truth must be in God's Word.

Well, no time like the present. She got down her Bible from the shelf and searched diligently through her concordance. She was not able to find the particular Scripture. *I need to get on the Internet. They tell me you can find references a lot faster. However, I first must learn more about the computer. I sure am behind in my technology. Maybe I'll take a course soon.*

Several verses she did find brought comfort and solace. Yet, she couldn't locate the verse she set out to find. Perhaps, her mother's saying wasn't in the Scripture after all. Just another of her wise comments like where there's a will there's a way. The ringing of the phone cut short her search time. Again she wished for Caller ID.

She picked up the hand piece. *I will call as soon as I get off and have the phone company hook me up.* However, this call wasn't an unwelcome one. At least, she thought not.

"Hi, Mom."

"Oh, Hi, Christina. How are you? It's so good to hear from you. I planned on calling you tonight." Laura sat in her recliner and leaned back.

"Yeah, I haven't heard from you in a while, Mom. Instead of worrying about you I thought I would call."

"I'm sorry, darling. Guess I lost track of time. I've been pretty busy with church, choir, my volunteer jobs, and other things." Laura eased back in her chair and changed the phone to her left ear. Now she could hear better.

"What other things, Mom?"

Laura hesitated and then confided in Christina. "Well, I've been seeing a couple of nice gentleman here. One from Humble and one lives in The Woodlands."

"You've been dating?" Christina's voice rose. Laura didn't have any trouble hearing now!

"Well, yes. I meant to tell you, but guess I forgot." Laura pulled the lever on her chair and pushed back into an upright position. Sounded like she needed to be alert and on her toes. Christina didn't seem to take this news lying down so maybe she'd better not either.

"You can't be serious. You're dating?" Laura could hear the shock in Christina's voice.

"Why are you so shocked? I get the feeling you don't approve." Laura walked to the kitchen to pour herself a cup of coffee.

"No, I don't approve. Have you already forgotten about Dad? I thought you two would make up and get back together." Laura could hear the familiar edginess in her daughter's voice.

"Christina, you know your Dad chose to leave and he had someone else, even before we separated. Our divorce has been final for several months. We have no intention of reconciling. As a matter of fact, he and Jane are living together." Laura blew on her coffee before she sipped, as if the action might cool it, Christina, and herself.

"I know, but they're not getting along, and I hoped you would get back with him." Christina paused and then continued. "Maybe he's tired of her and wants to come home."

"What makes you think he'd want to, or that I'd want him to? Besides, you know we haven't gotten along for a very long time. I think we have grown too far apart over the years. Anyway, I don't love him anymore and wouldn't be able to trust him again." Laura tried to sound convincing and hoped Christina would understand.

"I just can't think of seeing you with someone else, Mom." Sadness replaced the anger in her daughter's voice.

"Maybe you'll change your mind when you meet John on your trip here for Labor Day." Laura offered.

"What's his last name?"

"Talbot." Laura sipped again from her cup.

"I remember him from high school. One of the history teachers, as I recollect. I never really knew him, but the kids in his class seemed to like him."

"I think you will too." Laura emptied her cup and sat it back on the counter. She walked to her recliner again and leaned back.

"We'll see. You said you were dating two men. What about the other one?"

"Well, I was dating him, but we're not seeing each other right now. He's going to see if he and his ex-wife can work things out, so I told him that I wouldn't date him as long as there is a possibility of them reuniting."

"See, Mom, that's what you and Dad should do." Christina's remark sounded smug.

"No, Christina, we won't be getting back together unless the Lord speaks to me in an audible voice and says otherwise." She raised her own voice with conviction and determination, but not in anger. "Let's talk about your homecoming. That would be more interesting. I can hardly wait to see you. It's only two weeks away. I'm sure the time will go fast, but in some ways I know it'll drag. It's been too long since you left."

"Yes, the spring does seem like a long time ago. Even though we talk on the phone, I'll be glad to see you too." Christina confirmed. "I better go now, Mom. I'll call you again before I come home, if I can catch you between dates."

Laura couldn't tell if she were kidding or being sarcastic. Judging by the conversation it could be either. Christina, always her father's daughter, liked to control everything. However, Laura felt relieved she could tell Christina "no" in her own way, and let her daughter know she couldn't rule her mother's life. She had no plans to get back with Frank. *I can say "no" on both counts and move on with my life.*

CHAPTER THIRTY-TWO

The Visit

Laura's busy schedule kept her on the go. Only two weeks and her daughter would be home. She yearned for the homecoming, so, in that respect, time seemed to drag along. The two dates with John both pleased and worried her. She found him becoming more and more serious. By now, she knew his commitment to the Lord wasn't what she wanted. Maybe, the Lord would use her to lead him into salvation the way she had Janice.

He kissed her on their last date. However, she hadn't minded. Showing affection for someone she liked came natural, yet, she felt a little uncomfortable. Her feelings vacillated between joy and fear. How far should she let things develop? Did the kiss indicate their relationship had developed into a romance instead of just friendship? John seemed to think so. Could *she* call them just friends anymore? Still, she didn't want to make any kind of commitment. She didn't know if a long-term relationship with John would please the Lord. After all, he didn't go to church or serve the Lord, at least, not in her way of thinking. Even though, he was a nice enough man and a good person, still… *Goodness without Godliness is worth nothing.*

She liked John a lot. He showed kindness, patience, and certainly proved to be a gentleman. But she knew in order for her to marry again the person would need to be devoted to the Lord for the union to work. She believed with all her heart that a good marriage took three—the two partners with the Lord at the center. John did visit church again last Sunday, but made very little comment about the service, other than to compliment her special song. He did ask a few questions in regard to her faith, which she thought a good sign.

"How do you know it isn't just chance instead of God at work in your life?" He asked her one evening as they sat in her kitchen sipping coffee.

"I just know that I know, and chance, or luck, is just another name for God at work." She poured them another cup. "I can look around me and see all God's creation and know He's real." She spread out her arms to emphasis her feelings. "I know within me, in my heart of hearts, there is a God." She pointed to her heart. In the book of Romans Paul says we are without excuse because these two things are true—we see God's creation all around us, and our heart tells us He is real."

"I will have to read the book of Romans." He stated in a matter of fact manner without further comment.

Laura hoped and prayed he would. Showing an interest in reading God's Word seemed like a good sign to her, for she knew God's Word would not return void.

Not a word from Tom, but through the grapevine she heard Ellen had returned to her old boyfriend. *Wonder why he hasn't called? Guess he's lost interest, gone on to someone else, or feels too embarrassed. Maybe I'll call and see how he's doing.* On second thought, she felt it wouldn't be a good idea. She wanted to leave her future in God's hands. Whatever He had in store would be the best for her. Besides, her upbringing taught her women do not call men, even though in this day and time most accepted the behavior.

Laura took the time to think, reflect, and plan for Christina's visit as she drove to the airport. *I'm just going to forget about this dating thing and concentrate on enjoying my daughter*. As usual, the self-talk helped her focus on the situation at hand.

She arrived at the gate and saw Christina exit the plane. Laura felt a lump in her throat when she came down the gangway. *She looks different than in the spring.*

My baby has become an adult. Laura thought her dark auburn hair cut short into such a sophisticated style made her look like a lawyer, even though she wasn't dressed in the usual attire an attorney wore.

Blue jeans and a tee shirt, her favorite casual dress, made her look like Laura's child. Laura recognized again how much Christina resembled her father in looks, mannerisms, and personality. Still some of Laura's own traits came through, especially kindness. Laura wished she would make a commitment to the Lord. She, too, was a good person, but what about godliness?

"Hi, Mom." Christina reached to give her a hug.

Laura squeezed her tight and planted a kiss on her cheek. "You look great, sweetheart."

"So do you. Wow, you've really fixed yourself up." Christina stood back and looked her over. "Maybe this dating isn't so bad after all. You've started keeping your hair and nails up again. You've lost some weight, and that new outfit and shoes really becomes you."

"Well, I decided to trade in some of my old things for new. I wouldn't want to embarrass you. You're the one who looks great." Laura put her hand on her hip and surveyed Christina. "I like your new hairstyle. You look like a lawyer!"

"I'm not one yet." She shrugged her shoulders. "But hope to be soon." Christina smiled.

"It won't be long. Just the rest of the year and then you'll be able to practice law." Laura's voice resounded with pride in her daughter's achievements. "Have you thought about where you'll work? I hope in this area. Maybe in Houston, or better still, Humble."

"I'm not sure. Maybe I'll stay on the East Coast." They walked toward the luggage area. "Massachusetts is a beautiful place and so are several of the New England states."

"Christina! That's too far away. I thought our separation would be over when you finished school." Laura stopped and turned to face her, placing both hands on her hips this time.

"I'm just not sure, Mom." Christina shrugged for the second time. "I do like the area and all."

"Have you found someone special, you haven't told me about?"

"Well, I think so. I just met him, so I'm not sure yet. I'll have to wait and see what develops during the rest of the year." They reached the conveyor belt and Christina stood looking for her bags.

"Tell me all about this on our way home. I can hardly wait to hear." Laura looked for Christina's familiar bags.

"I don't have much since I will only be here for a few days." Christina pulled her medium sized suitcase off the turnstile.

"Yes, I wish you could stay longer, but I know you have to get back to school. I wish you had chosen a school closer than Massachusetts." Laura reached for the makeup bag, which she recognized as Christina's.

"I know, Mom, we've been through this before. I think I remember this same conversation from several other occasions." Christina's slight laugh let Laura know there wasn't any need in belaboring the point.

"I know. I know. I won't keep harping on it. Let's just enjoy the time we have together. What would you like to do while you're here?"

"Just hang out. Maybe see some of my old friends. Relax and eat some of your home cooking." They walked toward the car.

"I've cooked up some of your favorites—brownies, chocolate mousse. We can have the chicken dish you love one night, and I've made a big pan of your special lasagna." Laura knew Christina would be pleased but would probably protest the calories.

"Wow, Mom, you're certainly going to fatten me up while I'm here. We could probably eat on the lasagna the whole time." They reached the car and prepared to drive home.

"If it's okay with you, I would like to have John over for dinner to meet you tomorrow night." Laura met Christina's eyes.

"I guess it'd be okay with me but don't expect too much. I still have hopes of you and Dad getting back together." Christina smiled smugly and folded her arms over her chest.

Laura didn't want to waste time with the same conversation of two weeks earlier via telephone, so she chose to drop the subject. At least Christina agreed to meet John. Chances were she'd like him, and Laura wanted her daughter's approval. *What a switch*. Only a short time ago, she'd been the one to give the approval, or disapproval, for Christina's boyfriends. She never dreamed the tables would be turned. Then she never expected to end up divorced and dating. She hoped the chance would come again for her opinion, even though

Christina grew more independent each day, and headstrong, another of her father's traits.

Laura drove away from the terminal toward home, and the conversation turned to Christina's new friend. The questions came fast. "Tell me about him. What's his name? Where's he from? Is he handsome, a law student, or what? Give me all the details."

"Mom, you sound like your friend Betty. She always wanted to know everything. I sure miss her. I know you must." Christina looked at her mother with tender softness in her eyes.

"Yes, I do, but let's talk about you and your new fellow." Laura didn't want to be sad just now.

"Okay. He's from Massachusetts, a law student, very handsome, and smart, tall, slim, brown hair and brown eyes. He'll make an excellent lawyer. He asks all the right questions. We hit it off right away." Christina squirmed and twisted in her seat. She smiled, and her eyes lit up with excitement. "We met at a birthday party of a mutual friend. He brought someone else but talked to me a great deal of the evening. He asked for my phone number and called me the following week."

"Wow, he's a fast worker." Laura interjected.

"We went to a movie together." Christina told Laura the name of the movie. "That was last week. I think we made a connection. He said he'd call me when I return after the holiday." Christina stopped for a breath.

"I saw the same movie myself recently." Laura blurted out instinctively as she made the turn onto Highway 59.

"Oh, did John take you?" Christina looked around, and Laura knew she observed the familiar, but now almost strange, landscape. "Wow, everything looks so different. They keep doing construction."

"No, I went with Tom on our first date." Laura volunteered and then added, "Yes, our area continues to progress. Soon everything will be concrete. Instead of the livable forest, Kingwood will be the livable concrete. Humble practically is already."

"Talk about fast work, Mom. You are the socialite here." Christina looked at her mother with a shocked look on her face.

"Aw, Christina, we're all just friends. I'm not looking for a wedding in the near future, unless it's yours." Laura laughed and headed the car down the street toward her home.

"I don't think you have to worry about that for a while. I intend to get my law degree and set up a practice before I think about marriage. I plan to put my career ahead of everything for now. I think Nathan feels the same."

"You've always been goal oriented. Guess that's one thing you get from both your father and me. We always put our goals first. However, my main project for many years was a family. I do hope you won't wait too long to have children. I sure would like some grandchildren."

"I don't think I'll have time for children for a while, if ever…" Christina mumbled the 'if ever' spoken more softly under her breath.

Laura heard but ignored her statement. Christina knew she wanted grandchildren. She didn't want an argument with her daughter. Laura wanted to enjoy their time together, in spite of the short time frame.

She pulled into the driveway. They barely entered the house, when Christina went upstairs to unpack. Laura put the coffeepot on. She glanced out the window as a familiar car sailed onto the concrete slab. Laura's eyes widened as Tom walked up the sidewalk. Handsome as ever, but the spring in his step seemed lost. He rang the bell and Laura shouted to Christina, “I’ll get it.”

CHAPTER THIRTY-THREE

Indecision and Decision

"Hi, Laura." Tom stood looking forlorn as she opened the door. "I'm sorry to drop in on you like this, but I wanted to see you so badly. I've been too depressed and embarrassed to call."

"Come on in, Tom, and I'll fix us coffee and some brownies. My daughter, Christina just arrived for a visit. You can meet her while you're here." Laura directed him towards the kitchen.

"I'd love to meet her, but I guess I picked a bad time to come by for a talk. I can call you later." Tom halted his steps and turned around to face her. "I'll have that coffee and brownie, meet her, and then be on my way. Is it okay if I call you next week?"

"Sure, you're welcome to call anytime, Tom. We're still friends, remember." Laura turned to look at him. "Give me a call and I'll be glad to talk with you."

"Thanks, Laura. I sure need to talk with you and would greatly appreciate the opportunity." He lowered his eyes to the floor as if embarrassed to look at her.

Her heart went out to him. She'd never seen him so downcast. She knew, however, this would not be a good day to talk. She hoped he'd be all right until next week. "Sit down here at the table, and I'll pour you a cup of coffee. I'm brewing a fresh pot. It should be finished by the time I find the cups."

He sat at the table and waited, but the coffee took longer than she anticipated. So, they spent a few awkward moments. "A watched pot never boils, I've often heard." She wanted to break the silence and turned her back on the coffee maker to make her point.

He laughed. But not as heartily as the old Tom would have. However, he relaxed some. "I've heard that all my life and it seems to be true."

When she placed a brownie on a plate for him, the coffee finished perking and she poured him a cup. "I'll call Christina now."

She hurried to Christina's room, opened the door, and peered in at her daughter.

Busy unpacking, she looked up when Laura spoke. "Christina, Tom's here and would like to meet you." Laura kept her tone low.

"I thought you told me his name was John." Christina's voice projected louder than usual.

Laura hoped Tom didn't hear. She lowered her own voice even more, hoping Christina would do the same. "The one coming to dinner tomorrow night is John, but this is Tom. I told you about him, the one who tried to patch things up with his wife. Looks like things didn't work out. He seems distressed. Be kind to him, okay?"

Christina lowered her voice to a whisper. "Mother, you know I'm always kind to others. I may not like him, but I'll be courteous."

Laura's voice stayed low. "Yes, you're right. You're courteous, but please don't show your dislike too much. He's having a hard time, I suspect."

"Okay, Mother. I'll meet your friend and try to be nice." She rolled her eyes as if to say, oh, brother, or, oh, mother.

"Thanks." Laura breathed easier and continued to whisper. She hoped Tom didn't overhear the conversation.

Christina followed her into the kitchen. Tom rose from his chair. "So this is Christina. I've heard a lot about you."

"Well, I hope Mom hasn't told all of our family secrets." Christina tried to be funny. She managed to do a good job. She exhibited more kindness than Laura expected. She tried in her own way to cheer Tom up. *Guess she's her mother's daughter as well as her father's, after all.*

Tom chuckled and Christina offered her hand to him. Laura made the introductions. "Christina this is Tom, a friend of mine. We went to high school together."

Tom shook her extended hand. "Speaking of school, how's it going for you, Christina?" Christina probably thought he tried to make small talk, but Laura knew he showed a genuine interest, for he asked several times about Christina and law school.

"It's going well. It looks as though by January we'll have another lawyer in the family." Laura didn't expect Christina to put it that way.

"How is Frank doing? You know we went to school together, also. I'd like to see him sometime." Tom didn't take her bait. He showed an honest interest in her father.

Laura knew Christina's plan to keep her dad in the picture, but it hadn't worked the way she hoped. Laura and Tom discussed earlier the circumstances of her divorce. He knew Laura wouldn't consider any possibility of rekindling their marriage. He probably knew by first hand experience that sometimes too much water flowed under the bridge to salvage a marriage gone wrong. *I'll probably learn more about that next week.* She fixed coffee and brownies for Christina and herself, offered Tom a refill, which he politely refused, and they joined him at the table.

They talked for a short time about school, the weather, and general things. Tom finished his coffee and stood to leave. "I'll let you girls get back to unpacking and visiting with each other. Thanks for the coffee and brownie. I'll talk with you next week, Laura. Christina, I enjoyed meeting you."

Christina nodded. "The same here."

"Glad you came by." Laura walked him to the door.

Tom seemed to have more of a spring in his step. *Perhaps the visit has done him some good.* Laura hoped so. But how would she handle things next week?

Tom took her hand when they reached the doorway. "Thanks, Laura, for the coffee, delicious brownie, the conversation, and lifting my spirits."

She shook his hand and patted it with her other one. "I'm glad you're feeling better."

"I'll call you on Tuesday." Then, he walked out the door and headed down the sidewalk. He stepped into his car and waved goodbye as he drove away. When Laura re-entered the house, she expected to find Christina in the kitchen. She planned to ask her how she liked Tom, but her daughter had already gone back to her room to finish unpacking.

Laura suspected Christina didn't want to discuss Tom further. Christina avoided issues, especially, if she found them uncomfortable or not to her liking. Like a lawyer, she sometimes spawned evasiveness. If she didn't want to acknowledge something or someone, she ignored the subject. Perhaps, she didn't want to validate another man's interest in her mother.

Laura's traits proved quite the contrary in recent months. She wanted to face things head on and come to a resolution. Something she learned after Frank walked out on her. Laura admitted she used to be more like Christina. She tried to ignore trouble and didn't want to acknowledge unpleasant things. If Christina couldn't control the situation, she ignored it, like her dad. Christina would hopefully learn with time to face things the way they were.

Laura didn't want to press the issue, so she left Christina to work things out on her own. She let her finish unpacking while she made preparations for dinner.

She thought about what she would say to Tom if he asked to start seeing her again. Would it be fair to John? Did she want to complicate her life more than it was? What if Tom wasn't the one for her? What if John wasn't either? Well, why couldn't she be a friend to both of them?

The conflict raged on and on the more she dwelt on the situation. She finally decided she wouldn't think about her guy friends anymore until Christina left. They'd spend time together, enjoy each other, and set other things aside. However, she'd invited John to dinner tomorrow night. *Well, at least then Christina will get to meet them both. Maybe she could help me make a decision. If it comes to that.* She caught herself and wondered when she had become the child and Christina the mother. No, she wouldn't play that game. She'd have to make her own choices, using the Lord's guidance, of course.

Christina still didn't make any comment regarding Tom during the dinner of Honey Dijon Chicken, steamed rice, asparagus and Romaine-Broccoli salad with homemade dressing, one of her favorite meals. Salad with walnuts always delighted Laura.

"Mom, you must give me these recipes. I think Nathan would enjoy this meal."

"Sure, I believe they're on the computer, so I'll run off copies for you. I'm finally getting used to using that thing a little more. Guess I'll take some classes at the college. They hold senior classes for just a small fee. I might be computer literate the next time you visit."

"Great, Mom, we could even email each other and talk on IM." Christina took a sip of the peach flavored tea to rinse down the salad.

"Hold on, now don't get too fast on me. I don't even know what IM is. I'll need several classes before I'm able to do all that." Laura held her hands up to Christina motioning for her to halt, or at least slow down.

"Oh, Mom, you're smart. You'll learn in no time." Christina laughed, even though her mouth brimmed with the delicious chicken. When she swallowed, she continued. "IM stands for Instant Messenger. We could write back and forth on it."

"I think I would rather talk with you on the phone." Laura hesitated as she chewed up her own bite of food. "By the way, when will you be coming home again? Will you be able to come Thanksgiving and Christmas?"

"I'll just have to wait and see how things go, Mom." Christina continued eating, but gave no explanation.

"Do you mean with school or with Nathan?" Laura guessed her thoughts.

Christina shrugged, indicating it could be either or both. "It may also depend on what you have up your sleeve. You're the busy one. Dating two men at once. Who knows, you may bring in some others on me. Dad may even join in the circle." Christina sounded wishful.

Laura felt her temperature rise, but tried to remain calm. "Oh, Christina, you exaggerate.

I'm just friends with Tom and John. Besides, I've no intention of bringing in anyone else, especially not your dad." Laura lowered her voice as if sympathetic with Christina. "I know you'd like to think that, but it's the furthest thing from my mind or desire. I'm sorry, Christina, I don't want to upset you, or burst your bubble, but your dad's not in my plans anymore." Laura held her ground even though she hoped her statements wouldn't upset her daughter too much. She tried to soften her voice, but held firm.

"Well! Just do what you want. I can see you will anyway. It doesn't really matter what I think or how I feel!" Christina threw her folded cloth napkin beside her plate, got up from the table to leave. "I have some more work to do. I'll talk to you later."

She hurried to her room without even looking back. "Aren't you going to have some dessert? I have chocolate mousse." Laura called after her.

Christina slammed the door, not with a bang but louder than usual, letting Laura know she didn't want to deal with her any further at the moment.

She still has the same way of dealing with me; as her father did – just get angry, shut me out and off. Laura cleared the table with tears in her eyes and pain in her heart. However, she knew she couldn't let Christina, or anyone else, make her a doormat any longer. She'd follow only the Lord's direction. She'd been under someone else's rule far too long. She always gave in to Frank. Christina learned well from him how to get her way. However, Laura didn't intend to allow their antics to work on her any longer.

CHAPTER THIRTY-FOUR

Making Up

Laura didn't pressure Christina to come out of her room. She sunk into her cushioned recliner after she cleaned up the dishes. Then turned on the television and started watching a movie. She considered eating some of the chocolate mousse, but needed to watch her calories. She'd already indulged in the brownie earlier in the day when Tom visited.

When she thought of Tom, she pondered a response to the question he would most likely ask. How could she avoid hurting him or John? Why couldn't they all be friends? She wasn't planning on marrying either of them, not in the near future, anyway. John acted more serious lately, and she felt concern. She didn't want to be a heartbreaker. Neither did she want her own heart broken. *Betty, I told you I didn't want to play the dating game. Things get so complicated. Now, my daughter's even upset with me.*

The tiff with her daughter went beyond the dating game. Christina wanted to control her actions, but Laura refused to allow her to manipulate or run her life. *Why must I fight for any independence I get?* The realization that all independence came with a price hit her. Even countries fought for their liberty and freedom.

After a short time of laying in her recliner with the television blaring, fretting over her dilemma, she decided to turn the idiot box off and pray. W*hy worry when I can pray.* She remembered the song with those words. She set her mind on the Lord and His answers. She leaned back, closed her eyes, and uttered her prayer. "Lord, forgive me for worrying instead of praying. Help me to turn each of these situations over to You. Help me to rely on You and Your answers for each one of these relationships – with Christina, John, Tom and anyone else you choose to bring into my life." She hesitated, wiped away a few tears, and then continued. "I want only to do Your will. Please help me do what You'd have me do, say what You'd have me say, pray what You'd have me pray, go where You'd have me go, and be what You'd have me be. I want to be totally and completely Yours and in Your perfect will for my life. I pray in Jesus Name. Amen!"

Just as she said amen, Christina walked into the room. Laura detected a changed mood. Christina came over, sat on the floor beside Laura's chair, took her hand in her own and whispered, "I'm sorry, Mom."

Laura turned, took her in her arms, and held her close. "So am I, Christina. You're so important to me. I love you with all my heart. I'm concerned about what you think, and I want you to be happy, but there are some things I have to do for myself."

"I know, Mom." Christina slowly pulled out of her mother's embrace and faced her. "What time is your friend, John, coming tomorrow night?"

"I thought we'd have dinner around seven. So I asked him to be here at six-thirty. Is that okay with you?" Laura waited for her answer as they faced each other. She searched Christina's face to make sure she agreed.

"Yes, that'll be fine. I plan to see Dad in the morning, but I should be back by around two in the afternoon. Then we can spend some time together, either shopping or just hanging out, if you like."

"Let's go shopping. I'd like to buy you something new for your next date with Nathan." Laura chuckled.

"That'd be great, Mom. I could sure use a new pair of shoes."

At that Laura laughed. Christina looked at her with a puzzled look on her face. "What's funny about a new pair of shoes?"

"It's just something I'm going through lately. Right now, you probably wouldn't understand, but I'll tell you later when I figure it out myself." Laura leaned back in her chair again.

"Oh, come on, Mom. Tell me what's so funny about a new pair of shoes."

"Okay, I'll tell you what I know. However, I suspect the Lord's not finished with the story yet." Laura hesitated.

"Oh, Mom! You always think the Lord's doing something." Christina sounded more than a little defensive.

"Yes, Christina, He always is, but maybe we better just hold the story for later. How about some chocolate mousse?"

Christina ran her tongue over her lips. "Umm, that sounds good."

They walked back into the kitchen, Christina leading the way. Laura took the dessert from the refrigerator and Christina took down the special bowls from the cupboard her mother always used to serve it.

"Would you like some coffee or tea with your mousse?" Laura waited for Christina to answer before preparing one or the other.

"I believe I'll have water. I haven't had my quota today."

"Sounds good to me, too." Laura thought about the several glasses or bottles of water she drank each day, and knew she hadn't today. "Shall we go into the den and watch the movie or just talk?"

"Let's just talk for awhile, and then I need to get back to some of my studies." Christina picked up her dessert in one hand and her water in the other and carried them toward the den sofa.

Laura followed her back to the den and they sat down on the sofa next to each other. "Tell me about your classes at school and what else you've been up to lately."

Christina talked as they both ate their chocolate mousse. "Mom, I believe this is the best mousse you've ever made."

"That's just because you haven't had any for awhile." Laura smiled. Glad to please her daughter.

After a time of visiting, Laura listening to Christina's adventures, laughing, and eating their chocolate dessert, Christina went back to her room to study. Laura realized the hour grew late and bedtime approached. She needed her beauty sleep. After all, tomorrow would present another day to work on relationships and enjoy her daughter. She cleaned the kitchen, turned off the lights, and made her way to the bedroom.

When she undressed and took off her shoes, she thought about the shoes she would buy Christina tomorrow. She remembered Christina's reaction to her reference to the Lord and the shoe story. Christina's relationship with the Lord, or lack of, concerned her. Were the school and the world's philosophies clouding her judgment toward Him? Maybe her father's attitude influenced her. *Lord, how can we make her see what's important in life?*

Then she remembered she gave Christina to the Lord, asked Him to help her, and she knew He would. For the shoe story, she would be excited to see where the Lord took it. She knew He wasn't finished yet. God works in all His children's life, including hers. The work never completed until they met Him face to face.

CHAPTER THIRTY-FIVE

What's Cooking?

Laura heard Christina rise early the next morning. Eager to visit with her father, or else, she wanted to get back early to go shopping for her shoes. She refused Laura's offer to cook a big breakfast. "Can we just have some cereal, please?"

This suited Laura. Cereal, her breakfast of choice, helped keep her weight in check and added needed fiber to her diet. She chose Raisin Bran along with blueberries and half a banana. They provided potassium and the blueberries had an anti-aging ingredient, something important to her. *At fifty-five, I can use all the help I can get.* "How about some blueberries?" She offered the bag to Christina.

"No, but I'll have half your banana." She watched her weight too. Not that she needed to, she wore a size seven.

Laura poured one percent milk over her cereal. "When you return from your father's we'll go shopping, perhaps we can find a dress to go with the shoes."

"Make it a suit and I'll go for it." Christina added the low fat milk to her own mixture. "I need a new suit for interviews and when I start my internship. I have a birthday next month. You can make the shoes and suit my present."

"Sounds good to me! I wondered what to get you. That makes my decision easier. What color suit will you be looking for?" They each carried their bowl carefully to the table, in order not to slosh the milk, and sat down.

Christina brought her spoon to her mouth but before she tasted she answered Laura's question. "I think navy, black, or gray. I want to stick with the basic colors. I can use different colored accessories and blouses to enhance the look."

Laura smiled. She taught her a few things about coordinating her clothing. Christina chomped down before Laura could offer thanks. Laura wondered if she taught her the most important things in life.

She bowed her head and Christina hesitated but followed by lowering her own. Laura offered the day to the Lord and asked for His blessing upon them and their activities.

When finished, Christina placed her empty dish in the sink, trotted back to her room, gathered her purse and keys, and then left for her father's. Since he lived in Kingwood, only about ten miles away, she didn't have far to go. Laura again cleaned up the kitchen. *This is getting to be a habit, Christina running out and me cleaning up. Well, at least she put her bowl in the sink this time.* For a short visit Laura didn't mind, but hoped Christina wouldn't make a habit of running out on her. Christina usually helped. Laura noticed her lack of consideration this visit. Maybe she had other things on her mind.

Before Laura left the kitchen, she prepared for the evening meal. She wanted to spend as much time shopping with Christina as possible. Perhaps they would run by the antique shop. They both enjoyed looking there. She didn't want to hurry home and rush getting ready for dinner or, worse yet, be late. John's punctuality she could count on. Something she admired. He exhibited several good traits, only one thing amiss – his lack of commitment to the Lord. *I think I will invite him to church again tomorrow.*

She prepared the salad, except for the dressing and tomatoes. Put the lasagna together, and set the completed dish in the refrigerator ready for the oven. Buttered the French bread. Her dessert sat ready in the refrigerator - chocolate mousse. Satisfied she finished everything she could; Laura drew water for a relaxing bath and planned for Christina's return. When the tub filled to her usual waterline, the phone jingled. *I am definitely going to get Caller ID next week.* Not knowing what she'd find on the other end this time, she shut the water off before she answered.

"Hello?"

"Hi, Laura, it's Janice."

"How in the world are you Janice? I haven't heard from you in a few weeks. I've missed your calls. Hope everything's okay." Janice ordinarily called at least once a week. She had adopted Laura as her spiritual mother since she led her to the Lord. Whenever Janice faced a problem, Laura would pray for her over the phone.

"I'm doing great. I could use your prayers though. James asked me to marry him.

"That's wonderful!" Laura sat down on the bed.

"I'm pretty certain he's God's choice for me. You said God would send the right one, and I believe He has. I'm so happy. He's a strong Christian. We go to the same church. He's exactly what I need and want in my life." Janice's voice simply bubbled with excitement.

"Wow! Congratulations! When's the wedding?" Laura caught the excitement. She bounced with excitement on the bed.

"We haven't set an exact date yet, but we hope before Christmas. I wondered if you'd be my Matron of Honor?" Janice's voice took on a hopeful sound.

"I'd be thrilled Janice. Just let me know, so I can mark my calendar and not schedule anything else then." Laura knew her water grew cold, but Janice's happy moment trumped her preferred bathwater temperature.

"I've got to run now. James is waiting for me to go shopping for wedding rings. He wants me to pick out my own. So, I'll talk with you later."

"Okay. Thanks for calling and sharing the good news. I'm really happy for you.

"Bye. I love you."

"Bye. And I love you too." Laura hung up the phone and made a dash for the bathtub, grateful to feel the lukewarm water surround her. She wanted to linger in the tub, but knew time wouldn't permit.

She laid her head back on the end of the tub for just a few minutes and almost dozed off. She sat up with a start and finished bathing. After getting out of the tub, she dressed, in case Christina came early. She dabbed on the finishing touches of her make-up and heard the front door open.

Christina's voice drifted into the room, "I'm home."

Laura glanced at the clock overhead. Only 12:45. They could shop most of the afternoon. Laura would grab a pretzel at the mall. She didn't need much to tide her over since she planned a big dinner this evening.

Christina, eager to go, started for the front door. She liked getting something new. She walked to the driver's seat. Laura didn't object. She knew this let Christina feel in charge. Laura didn't mind in this instance. Laura didn't enjoy driving much anyway. She discovered years ago, with Christina you picked your battles. She certainly wouldn't fight over this. They locked the front door, climbed in the car, and headed out to the mall.

Christina headed straight to Dillard's, her favorite store. When they walked in, she strode to the suit department first, picked up a lovely basic black suit, and showed it to Laura. "I like this one."

Laura spied the special sale tag. Something she liked.

Christina took the suit into the dressing room and tried it on. She came back out and modeled the outfit for Laura to see.

"It's lovely, honey, but don't you want to look around a little more? You might find something you like better." Laura couldn't imagine buying the first thing she looked at. She generally surveyed several before she decided. Then, she remembered the pantsuit she bought at first sight with Carol. *I guess sometimes you just know.*

"No, mother, this is exactly what I wanted. I don't have to look and compare like you. I can save time this way." Christina tucked the suit under her arm.

"Okay, if that's what you want. It's fine with me. I like the price, and the suit is nice. It looks great on you." Laura looked at her daughter. *And a lovely thing she is*.

"Let's pay and go to the shoe department, then." Christina sprinted toward the shoes. Laura could hardly keep up. When she stopped to look at other things on sale, Christina proceeded on her journey. If it took too long, Christina stopped and tapped her foot impatiently while her mother looked.

Finally arriving at the bottom floor and the shoe department, Laura eyed, picked up, and even tried on several styles and types of shoes. Her new passion for shoes evident. She commented several times, "Aren't these cute?"

Christina just said, "umm," and went straight to a pair of black pumps in the Easy Spirit section. Laura knew her daughter. They were basic, attractive, comfortable, and durable. No frills, but what Christina wanted. She found a pair, tried them on, and stood ready to go again.

"Well, Mom, I've accomplished my mission. What do you want to do now?"

"I'd like to get a pretzel. And then I'd enjoy going to the antique shop, and just browse."

Christina shook her head in agreement. "Sounds good to me. Dad was too busy for lunch, so I haven't eaten anything."

"Why didn't you tell me? I didn't eat either. Let's go buy our pretzels, or would you like to have lunch?"

"No, a pretzel will be fine. Aren't we having a big supper? Isn't your friend, John, coming for dinner?"

Christina's reasoning sounded like her own. "Yes, that's what I thought. So a pretzel it is, my treat!"

They walked toward the outside of the mall and their car, eating their scant lunch. They would head toward the antique shop. Laura didn't know why she enjoyed looking. She didn't need to purchase anything. Once she bought only a small table as an accent. But something about looking at them brought her joy.

On the ride over, they talked about the good price on the suit and how much Christina liked it.

"The shoes are exactly what I need. They're durable, comfortable, attractive, and basic."

Laura wanted to laugh but refrained. She had guessed right about the shoes – almost in the exact order.

When they walked into the antique store, a gentleman almost ran Laura down. He kept looking back at a particular antique serving table he liked. When he bumped into her, he apologized several times. "I'm so sorry. Are you hurt?"

"No, I'm fine. That's a lovely server. I've been admiring it for sometime myself." She pointed toward the piece of furniture.

"I came into town yesterday. I saw this antique shop, and knew I must get back here. My late wife and I loved antique shopping. I don't own many, but I love looking." He blurted out his thoughts and history.

"That's so funny. I'm the same way. I know of several antique places in the area and once in a while I make the rounds."

"As I said, I just got into town yesterday. By the way, I'm Anthony Blake. I'm the new pastor for the First Church here in Humble." He stuck out his hand to shake hers, and she clutched his warm hand.

"It's great to meet you. I'm a member there. I'm Laura Olson. I didn't recognize you. I saw you once when you came to preach a few weeks ago. Glad to meet you."

"Guess I look a little different in the pulpit. I like to dress comfortable when I look for antiques. How about showing me around to some of those other shops you spoke about, at your convenience, of course? Some Saturday maybe?"

"Sounds like fun. Oh, this is my daughter, Christina. She's home for Labor Day from law school in Massachusetts."

"Hi, Christina, glad to make your acquaintance." He extended his hand to her, as well.

"Hi. Nice to meet you, too." Christina took his outstretched hand.

"You girls have a good time. I won't detain you any longer. See you in church tomorrow morning."

"We'll be there." Laura called after him as he departed the shop and walked to his car.

"Well. Mom, looks like you have another guy on the string." Christina looked at her. Laura couldn't tell if she were being facetious or serious.

Laura looked back at Christina. "What do you mean? He's our pastor and I'm just taking him antiquing."

"Mom, he's a man, widowed, about your age, and I saw how he looked at you." Christina chuckled lightly and rolled her eyes.

"Oh, Christina, you're imagining things. He lost his wife a few months ago and he's probably lonely. Why shouldn't someone in the congregation show him around to things of interest to him?"

"I think you're the thing of interest, Mom. I always knew I had a pretty mom, but didn't know she would attract all these men."

"Christina, you're embarrassing me. Lower your voice. Someone may hear you." Laura felt her face turn hot. She imagined the color of catsup.

They stayed a while at the shop and then rushed home to cook dinner. The lasagna barely placed in the oven, Laura hoped for a smell, so John could guess what was cooking. *I wonder what else the Lord has cooking for me.*

CHAPTER THIRTY-SIX

Pleasant Times

At six-thirty sharp, John rang the doorbell. Laura opened the door. "Come in John. Dinner will be a little late, but it's in the oven. Come in and meet Christina."

Walking into the den where Christina stood, John extended his hand. "It's so good to finally meet you. I've heard so much about you. All good, of course."

"Mothers are a little prejudice. Aren't they?" She took his extended hand and laughed.

"From what I've observed she has a right to be proud of you. She tells me you have maintained a 4.0 average in your law school. I'd say that's quite an accomplishment." Laura smiled to herself, happy to have him compliment her daughter.

"Thanks. I do study a lot." Christina held a note of modesty in her voice. "You know, my father's a lawyer. Guess I take after him in that area."

In other areas as well, she continues to bring up her father. I wish she would let it go. Laura laughed but felt uncomfortable. "Why don't you continue your conversation as I prepare the rest of the meal? I'm not quite as organized as you when it comes to cooking, John."

Christina looked surprised as she glanced from one to the other. "You've been cooking for mother? Bet that was a treat for her."

"We enjoyed a fish fry with some friends, and I made her some burgers one night. She hasn't tasted my gourmet dinners yet. Wait until she tastes my spinach soufflé…" Laura watched John beam as he described his cooking fetes. She walked to the kitchen, checked on the progress of the Lasagna, and let them talk.

The drone of their voices made a pleasant sound, and Laura smiled, hoping they enjoyed getting to know one another. Only about fifteen more minutes until the pasta finished. Time enough to set the table, finish the salad, and warm the bread. The French bread sat buttered and ready to stick into the oven. She wanted things to finish at the same time, so it would be piping hot. No way could she compete with John's cooking, but she could prepare a decent meal.

Laura laid aside the apron she wore and entered the den. "Dinner's ready."

John held out his hands. "I should wash up."

"I'll show you to the bathroom." Christina popped up as Laura opened her mouth to give directions.

After a few minutes, John returned and sniffed. "Aw, lasagna." His face lit with pleasure. "I haven't had homemade lasagna in a long time. Not since my mother made some before her illness. I usually pick up some from the frozen department at the grocery store or go to one of the Italian restaurants."

"Don't know if this can compete with the restaurants or not." Laura laughed as she cut the dish into serving size pieces.

Just then Christina reentered the kitchen. "It's much better. Mom makes the best lasagna around. She makes it for me every time I come home."

Her daughter's compliments seemed like music to her ears. Not a regular thing. *Especially since she found out about my dating. Maybe she'll like John and that will change.*

Laura loved the way dinner turned out, and the light and comfortable conversation warmed her inside. John remarked several times about how he enjoyed everything, especially the lasagna. "You made it as good as my Mother's. God rest her soul."

At least he mentions God.

When dinner ended, John and Christina pitched in to help Laura clean up the dishes and voted unanimously to eat dessert later. "I'm stuffed. I couldn't eat another bite right now." John rubbed his stomach and moaned.

"Have you met my father, John?" They walked into the den.

Here we go again. I thought she would be over this by now. Guess she's checking John out like she did Tom, or else she wants me to know she's not letting go.

"No, I haven't had the privilege, Christina. I understand you visited him this morning. I know he was glad to see you."

"Oh, yes. He's quite a family man. He enjoys his family." Her voice rose emphatically.

He didn't even have time to take her to lunch. What's she trying to prove, anyway? I think we're going to have to have another talk about this.

Laura liked the way John handled Christina's comment about her father with grace and understanding. He accepted the intrusion and seemed to pass the test Christina put before him.

"Would the two of you excuse me? I need to hit the books. But don't forget to call me for the chocolate mousse." Christina rose from her chair and started toward her bedroom.

"Sure." John stood to his feet. "Wow! Chocolate Mousse another of my favorites. Tonight I feel as though I had died and gone to Heaven. What more could any guy ask for – two lovely ladies, homemade lasagna, delicious I might add, and one of my favorite desserts."

I wish he'd think more seriously about Heaven. I sure hope he's made his reservation. I'm becoming quite fond of him, but I can't be unequally yoked.

After Christina left the room, John patted the sofa beside him, inviting Laura to join him. When she did, he placed his arm around her shoulder and gave her a squeeze. "What a lovely, pleasant evening. I feel so comfortable in your home. There's such peace here. I'm becoming quite fond of you, you know."

Laura did not know how to respond. She drew back on any type of commitment. She didn't know how she felt about John, not a practicing believer. Her feelings mixed. She snuggled closer into his arms and purred peacefully.

The dessert, one of Laura's best efforts, brought Christina back to the den. She seemed to enjoy the conversation, and the mousse. They spoke of ordinary things – like fishing, their shopping spree, antiques, the new pastor coming to town. Laura held her breath. The weather, baseball, who would win the World Series, and Christina's education …

"Guess I better let you girls rest. Tomorrow's another day and I know you'll be getting up early for church. By the way, if it's okay with both of you, I would like to join you tomorrow and check out this new pastor. If I'd not intrude, I'd like to take you to lunch afterward." John announced nonchalantly.

"Sounds great to me." Laura turned toward her daughter. "What do you think, Christina?"

Christina's lips turned up in a smile, and Laura knew it pleased her that they included her in the decision. "That'd be fine. How about having some Mexican food?"

"Mexican food it is! I know Laura leaves early for choir practice. I can pick you up, Christina, and we can meet her there. If it's okay with you two."

Laura liked John's plan and his decisiveness. Yet, he asked Christina and her for their opinion. She liked someone who carried the ball, but shared it with others. She liked the feeling of teamwork and equality. Even more, she grew excited he'd be going to church again.

"Sounds great!" Christina and Laura looked at each other and they all laughed as they spoke in unison.

CHAPTER THIRTY-SEVEN

The New Pastor

Laura bounded out of bed at the sound of the alarm clock. Time to dress for choir practice. Excitement fluttered through her, and she felt the day would be special. She hurried to bathe, find her best outfit, choose the right shoes, and fix Christina some breakfast. She suspected Christina, like herself, was still full from last evening. A glimpse in the mirror told her, her hair looked okay. A little fluffing and some hair spray should do the trick. After all, she had just gone to the beauty shop on Friday.

She woke Christina to join her at the table for breakfast. They ate a repeat of the day before, only in a smaller portion. Neither wanted much.

"You're up mighty early." Christina rubbed the sleep from her eyes and peered over at her mom.

"Yes, choir practice before Sunday school, remember? I'm so excited John's coming to church again. Thanks for agreeing to go with him. I know you'd rather spend your time alone with me." Laura reached across the table and held Christina's hand.

"It doesn't matter to me. John's an all right guy. I rather enjoyed his company last evening. He's easy to talk to and doesn't try to intimidate anyone." Christina released her hand and shoved a bite of cereal in her mouth.

Laura wondered if she realized her father did intimidate and control. "You noticed that about him too. I think that's one of the things I like about him. He makes me feel like an equal." Laura smiled with relief that Christina liked him.

Christina changed the subject. She would never say such a thing about her father or even admit such a thing to anyone else. Laura never wanted to say anything critical or derogatory about him to Christina, so they moved on to other topics.

"Does John usually not go to church?" Christina sounded a little surprised.

"No. He used to go some with his father as a youngster. I think his mother's illness and death made him angry with God. I pray that will change. Please pray with me about that."

"Okay. You better get going. I know you want to look your best. I sure have a nice looking mom, and I'm glad you're taking care of yourself again."

Another compliment from Christina, not a regular occurrence, this certainly has started out as a most unusual day. I suspect there are more good things to come.

Laura finished getting dressed, fluffed and sprayed her hair again for good measure, and carefully applied her make-up, hoping to look her best for this special day. *Just getting my daughter and John in church will make it a special day.* She knew Christina hadn't gone to church regularly in Massachusetts, and John hadn't been in years. *God at work!*

She bid Christina goodbye with, "I'm off now. See you later in church." Laura didn't try to push her or John to make Sunday school, at least not for now. Elated they would attend church; she floated out the door to her car. When she turned the ignition, the car engine roared. She backed out of the driveway and headed for church. She sang all the way, rehearsing some of what the choir would sing today, but mostly just praising the Lord for His wondrous works. And what she felt He was going to do. She continued to sense in her spirit God planned something special.

With traffic backed up because of road construction, Laura took longer than usual. She hated the idea of being late. When she arrived, she sprinted into the building, and almost ran head long into Pastor Blake.

"Whew, we've got to stop meeting like this." He held out his hands to steady her and laughed. "We're making this a habit."

"I'm so sorry." She fought to get her breath. "I got caught in traffic and now I'm late for choir practice. Good to see you Pastor." His blue green eyes reminded her of an ocean off the coast of Hawaii as she looked into them, so clear and calming. She felt blood rush to her face. Embarrassed that he caught her staring, she quickly turned her head as a sudden heat lit her cheeks.

"I still want us to go antiquing one day whenever you can. Check your calendar. I'll call you this week." He released her and stepped back close to the wall.

"Yes, give me a call. Welcome to your new church home, Pastor. I'd better run. See you later." She dashed down the hall to the choir room.

Life was getting too complicated. She only wanted to be friends with the pastor. But, she'd heard this before, from herself, no less! She wanted to stay friends with the guys she cared for, and she surely didn't want to have to choose. But she knew the day would come when she would have to. She sure missed Betty. Probably time to call Carol again. Maybe next week for lunch. She needed some advice. *Lord, I'm depending on you to help me make the right choices.*

A new revelation came – Laura really liked men. To her they were fun creatures. However, she knew she couldn't have them all. Maybe she did want her cake and eat it too. She stuck with one man all these years, and now she found many interesting ones out there. Was she supposed to play the field, be friends with several, or did God have a special one for her?

Laura's mind wandered as she tried to sing the songs. She couldn't help think about Christina, John, Pastor Anthony, and even Tom. Finally, she made a decision to put each of them at the Lord's feet and not take them back. She knew the not taking them back would be harder said than done. However, she planned to try.

She breathed a prayer to that effect. Her singing took on a new tone and her heart a new melody as she surrendered her friends and loved ones to the Lord. She saw Christina and John sitting in the audience about mid-way back and flashed them a smile. They both responded with a tiny wave and a return smile.

After the choir finished singing, Laura made her way back to sit with them. She sat in the middle. John, sitting on the end of the pew, stood up and let her in beside Christina as she scooted down to make room for Laura. It all seemed so natural, almost like a family. She wondered what others might think seeing them together, especially the pastor, as she saw him glance their way. *Stop that.* She remembered she gave them all to the Lord.

Pastor Blake delivered a good message about the lost sheep coming home. To Laura's surprise, amazement, and joy, John walked the isle when the invitation came. Pastor requested for those who strayed to come home. John never cried or became emotional in her presence, but today was different. Tears streamed down his face as he went to meet the pastor at the altar.

She witnessed the Lord perform a good thing in his heart, and she shed tears of her own. Even Christina seemed touched. Laura saw her wipe her eyes. John stayed a long time with the pastor, talking with him, and rededicating his life to the Lord. *I knew today was a special day, and there could never be anything more special than for a lost sheep to come home to our Father God.*

Other people came to the altar, and the prayer team prayed with them. However, John and the pastor continued their conversation until everyone else went back to their seats. Finally, John headed back down the isle to where Laura and Christina sat waiting. The tears dried by now, Laura beamed as John re-entered the pew beside her. He took her hand in his and gave it a squeeze. She squeezed back, and they looked into each other's eyes. Holding back tears, even his eyes seemed to smile.

The pastor dismissed the congregation, and all filed out of the church. He met them at the door for a handshake.

Members and guest alike complimented him with words such as: "What a great service." Many seemed sincere, but other's words came across as just rhetoric.

When John and Laura came to Pastor Blake, John shook his hand first and the pastor said, "You have made a great decision today." He reached to give John a hug and John hugged back.

The pastor then turned to Laura. "Call me and we'll make that trip to the antique shops."

Laura blushed but responded. "I'll get back with you." *I hope John will understand that I'm just being nice to the new pastor.* She then wondered why she cared so much about what John thought.

John organized lunch plans as they walked to their cars. "Christina, why don't you ride with me back to the house to pick up your mother? We can decide where to go for lunch."

Laura loved the fact John included Christina in their plans. It appeared they had become friends. She could tell Christina liked the inclusion and went merrily along. During the short drive home, Laura reflected on the morning's service and happenings. John actually made a decision to follow the Lord! Joy unspeakable filled her soul.

She wondered what Pastor Blake had in mind. Was it a friendly antiquing time, or a date? What should she say if John asked? *How do I get myself into such dilemmas?*

CHAPTER THIRTY-EIGHT

Old Things – New Creation

"We had Italian last night so today we'll have Mexican. Does that make us international?" John joked as he opened the car door for the ladies to exit in front of the restaurant of their choice, Pappasitos, one of the best around. The noise level exceeded what Laura liked, but Christina didn't mind. They'd talk about more serious things later. Right now, Laura anticipated an enjoyable evening with atmosphere, good food, and each other's company.

Christina and Laura decided upon Taco Salad and John went for Fajita's. After getting their salad, Laura wished for the Fajita's and borrowed one from John's plate. When she remarked how good they looked, he offered her one, and she took it. Christina looked at them quizzically when they shared from the same plate. She didn't know their history for sharing. Laura hoped she didn't embarrass her daughter.

"They sure do look good." Christina held a gleam in her eye.

John pushed his plate toward her. "Try one."

"I believe I will." She reached for a tortilla to make it. "You may not have any food left by the time we get finished." She giggled as she forked a piece of fajita meat.

"That's okay; I can just help myself to your salads." He scooped out a forkful from Laura's plate and then Christina's. They all chucked as they ate from each other's plate.

"I've been told since childhood a person should share, so here we are." John laughed again.

No lunch tasted any better or brought Laura any more pleasure in her estimation. She sensed John and Christina felt the same way. They didn't discuss it, but this was a very special occasion. John decided to make his life brand new spiritually. Laura more than delighted, knew Betty would be so proud. Laura anticipated what the days ahead would bring.

The church had a new pastor, who wanted her to go antiquing to look at old things. Tom wanted her to call next week and talk about their old and new relationship. John became a new creation. She anticipated the days ahead would be full of decisions for her. *God please guide me and show me how I fit into each of these lives and how they fit into mine. Just how do the old and the new come together?*

When all the food disappeared, even the Flan for dessert, John spoke up. “I’d better get you ladies home for your nap or some visiting. I know Christina must leave tomorrow evening, and we want to get back to church tonight at six.”

Laura could hardly sit still. John mentioned going to church. She wanted to jump and shout. Would this be a regular thing from this time forward? *God does come in and change hearts and lives. He does make old things new.*

“John, you made the best decision today you could ever make. I’m so happy for you. I think you will find much happiness from it.” Laura looked over at him.

“I feel so good and so free. I never knew what I missed all this time. It’s hard to describe, but I feel so light and wonderful.” John looked over at her with a big grin on his face. “I feel as though my life has just begun.”

“In a way, it has.” She smiled back.

“Congratulations.” Christina didn’t say anything more.

Laura watched her and could tell she mediated on the whole situation. She looked out across the room and seemed in deep thought.

"I'm so stuffed. I could use a nap. However, I do want to visit with Christina as much as I can. Maybe I'll forego the nap this Sunday. I can sleep other times, but I can't always be with my daughter." She reached over and gave Christina's hand a squeeze. "I so hope she'll be home for Thanksgiving or Christmas." Laura looked at Christina. She pleaded with her eyes. She hoped Christina would listen.

"Maybe I'll bring Nathan here for one of the holidays, if that's okay with you. I'd like him to meet both of you." Christina looked from one to the other.

Another breakthrough! Laura could not think of a thing to say. Finally, she got her wits about her again. "Oh, Christina, that'd be super."

Laura could tell by the look on John's face Christina's statement pleased him also. "I'd be honored to meet your young man. I tell you what. You let me know which time you'll come, and I'll do the cooking at my house. Laura can take care of the two of you, and I'll furnish the special meal."

"Sounds great to me." Laura chimed in.

"Me, too! Now if we can just get Nathan to agree. He's pretty close to his family. But we'll see. I'll start working on him as soon as I get back and let you know."

John insisted on paying the bill for all three of them. Christina headed toward the door.

What a special day. God always works, but I can surely see it today. Pleased Christina wanted to come and bring her boyfriend. And especially blessed she liked John and the two of them hit it off so well. Laura grinned to herself and thanked God in her heart.

They left the restaurant, got in John's Toyota Avalon and headed home. On the way, Laura, feeling contented and happy, fell asleep. Christina and John chided her about falling asleep on them. She shook herself awake and laughed with them. She didn't tell them, but she felt peace about what God planned for all their lives, and it gave her a sense of contentment.

John helped them out and walked them over to Laura's car. "Happy sleeping or talking. I'll see you both at quarter 'til six. We can all ride together tonight."

Laura laughed. She felt so thankful because John continued to include them both and seemed eager to get back to church. Overjoyed, she could not resist giving

John a hug. It caught him off guard, but his face beamed as he hugged her back.

Then, Christina reached over and gave him a hug as well. "Thanks for the ride and the lunch. Thanks for the day. See you at a quarter 'til six," she added.

Laura thought she might have trouble persuading Christina to return to church for the night service. God intervened and took care of that concern. *He certainly does perfect those things that concern us as it says in Psalms 138:8: The LORD will perfect [that which] concerneth me: thy mercy, O LORD, endureth forever: forsake not the works of thine own hands. (KJV).*

John waited to make sure Laura's car started. They all waved goodbye and headed home.

No sooner were they inside the door than Christina turned to her mother with a request. "Mom, why don't you go ahead and take your Sunday afternoon nap. I've got some studying to do, and I want to call Dad and Nathan. You and I can visit later this evening and tomorrow?"

"Sounds okay by me." Laura did feel a nap coming on. "If I oversleep, please wake me by five, so I can get dressed."

"Be glad to, Mom. See you in a few." They each went to their respective bedrooms.

Laura had barely taken off her church clothes, and Christina hadn't started her phoning when the phone jingled. *I must get Caller ID as soon as Christina's visit is over.* She had no choice but to pick up if she wanted to know who occupied the other end of the line. She thought about letting the machine answer, but then thought it might be John, Frank, or important. She lifted the phone and said, "hello?"

A voice on the other end responded. "Hello, Laura, this is Anthony Blake. Hope I didn't catch you napping already."

She realized she sounded a bit groggy. "No, just fixin' to. Time for that Sunday afternoon nap, you know."

"I couldn't help thinking about the antique shopping and wanted to go ahead and schedule a date with you before my calendar gets filled. I'm eager to see all the places around here and get to know you better as well."

Laura caught completely off guard hesitated for a moment. "Wha…What day did you have in mind?" She stammered.

"How about Friday afternoon?" He asked and continued. "I would be ready to go tomorrow, but I know you want to spend time with your daughter."

"Yes, she'll leave tomorrow evening. Friday afternoon would be fine with me. We could probably make one between Humble and Kingwood and another between Kingwood and Cleveland. We could try those two at least, if you'd like." She stepped out of her shoes to get more comfortable. Thinking she would be closer to getting ready for her nap. She didn't want to waste anymore time, or else time would run out.

"After we take a look at those, how about having dinner with me? You could also show me a good restaurant in town."

"That would be fine." He certainly liked to plan things out.

"Okay. I'll see you at church tonight then. Have a good nap." He chuckled.

"Thanks, See you later then." She quickly picked up her shoes as she hung up the handset, dashed for the bathroom, and undressed for her much needed nap.

She settled in bed and barely dozed off when the phone rang once again. She let it ring for a short time, hoping Christina would answer, but when she didn't by the fourth ring, Laura again wished for Caller ID and picked up the receiver.

"Hellooo?" Her voice grew groggier by the minute.

"Laura, is that you?" Tom spoke on the other end.

"Yes, it's me. How are you Tom?" She sat up in bed.

"I'm better, but I do need to talk to someone. I have a busy week, but would like to get with you on Friday night, if possible."

"I'm sorry Tom, but I have another engagement on Friday night. Is there some other time we could talk?" She wanted to set a time and get back to her nap.

"Well, what about Saturday night then?" He suggested.

"Saturday would be fine." She couldn't believe her calendar was getting so full.

"I hate to ask this, but would it be okay if we ordered in at your house, so we can talk quietly without interruption? I could order pizza."

"That would be okay as long as we aren't up too late. I have choir practice early on Sunday." She wanted to let him know of her plans.

"I want keep you up past ten-thirty. I promise. How about I come over around seven?"

"Okay, Tom. I'll see you then."

The minute Laura hung up the phone she knew there could be a potential problem. What if John wanted to take her out Friday or Saturday? How would she fit him into my schedule? *Wow, this dating game wears me out.*

Laura tried to get back to sleep. Shortly, she heard Christina talking on the phone before she dozed off. *At least no one can call while she's talking. I don't have Caller ID, but neither do I have call waiting.* She considered ordering both of them, but she might skip the call waiting for now.

These old and new things kept her on the move. What would the rest of the day or week bring? She would find out later when she awoke from her nap.

CHAPTER THIRTY-NINE

Time to Go

The next thing Laura knew, Christina shook her awake. “Mother, it’s time for church. John will be here in fifteen minutes.”

“Oh, my, why didn’t you wake me? I’ll never be ready in time.”

“Sure, you will. Jump up and put on something, fluff your hair, and put on some more perfume and jewelry. You can make it,” Christina urged.

Laura jumped off the bed and rushed around as best she could, but John rang the doorbell before she finished getting ready. Christina graciously answered the door and invited John in. Laura heard them talking.

“Mom, will be here in a few minutes. She overslept. Have a seat.” She invited John into the den. While they waited, Laura could hear their conversation.

“That’s okay. We still have a few minutes before we’re late. What time will you be leaving tomorrow, Christina?” The recliner creaked as he sat down to wait.

Christina filled John in on her plans. “My plane leaves at four so we’ll leave here by two. I hope to see my Dad in the morning, but Mom will drive me to the airport."

"That's right. Your Dad lives in Kingwood."

"Yes, we plan to eat breakfast together at LaMadeline's. I haven't told Mom yet. She's slept this whole time, except while she talked on the phone. I hope she doesn't mind. I'll return to visit with her between ten and two."

"I'm sure she'll understand. She doesn't strike me as being selfish of your time, even though, I know she likes having you. I've certainly enjoyed getting to know you." John hesitated, probably checked his watch.

"The feeling's mutual. I look forward to your home-cooked meal at Thanksgiving or Christmas."

"You'll have to let us know all your favorites. You might even find out what your young man likes in the way of food."

"Wow, this is going to be something special. I can hardly wait." She sounded excited. "However, I do have a lot of school work to do between now and then."

John must have checked his watch again. "We have only about ten minutes to make it on time. Wonder what's keeping your mother?"

Laura stepped out of her room and hurried to the den. "Sorry. Here I am. Is everyone ready to go? Sorry to keep you waiting."

"We enjoyed our visit, but, yes, we'd better get going, if we want to be on time." John walked toward the door with Christina following.

As they hurried, Laura remembered she forgot her Bible and ran back inside to get it. She expected John to be impatient with her, but he seemed to take her forgetfulness and tardiness quite well. *What a wonderful switch from days gone by. I hope this will last.* Did she mean just his patience or their relationship? Right now, she wasn't sure.

The superb message at the service uplifted and encouraged Laura. She liked this new pastor. John seemed to enjoy church as well. She sensed a new fire stirring within him. She prayed it would continue. She knew many times when someone came to the Lord, or back to Him, the enemy attacked with discouragement and overwhelmed the new believer like a flood. She vowed continued prayer for John each day, at least for a while.

Christina seemed to experience a renewal of her own faith also. She didn't go to the altar or make any outward signs, but Laura knew her well enough to know the Lord stirred her heart. The tears she shed when John went forward earlier in the day encouraged Laura. She already prayed for her daughter everyday and would continue, even more fervently.

Laura was relieved when the pastor didn't come by and mention their date on Friday night. She didn't know how John would take it. She contemplated how to break the news to him.

On the way back from church, John asked if they wanted to stop for something to eat.

"Why don't we go to the house and make a sandwich?" Laura offered.

"I'm still pretty full from lunch," Christina said. "Besides, I need to study and pack."

John made his request known as they drove toward Laura's house. "Some coffee and something sweet sounds good to me."

"I think that's a winner. I'll make a pot of hazelnut, and I have brownies and chocolate mousse left." Laura laid out the dessert menu.

"Now, go light on the brownies. I can take some of them back with me." Christina laughed.

"The chocolate mousse sounds perfectly fine by me." John drove a little faster.

When they entered the house, Christina headed for her bedroom.

"Won't you join us Christina," Laura urged. "You can pack in the morning."

"Oh, yeah, Mom, I forgot to tell you. I'm having breakfast with Dad in the morning, but I should be back by ten so we can visit some more. But right now, I could sure do some studying."

"Have it your way, then. I don't want to keep you from your studies. If you change your mind, you can join us."

"Maybe I'll carry some mousse with me to eat while I study, if that's okay." Christina walked to the kitchen with them to get herself the dessert. She piled some in her dish and took leave to her room.

Laura busied herself making the coffee and John served up the mousse. *He's sure handy to have in the kitchen.* "Not too much for me." She instructed him.

They sat at the table while the coffee perked. For a moment complete silence prevailed, except for the noise of the coffee maker. They caught each other's eye and smiled with contentment.

"This has been a good day," Laura finally said. "A very special day, indeed!"

"Yes, an extra special day for me," John looked at Laura with a new sparkle in his eyes. "Laura, you know you are very special to me. I do hope God's plan includes something for us together in the future. We blend so well together. You make me feel as comfortable as an old shoe but as dazzling as the latest style."

"Thank you, John. I care a great deal for you too. However, I don't want either of us to rush into anything." She busied herself with the pouring of the coffee. She didn't really want to pursue this line of conversation too much further. She wanted more time to sort out all her feelings and all her friends. *Where does everyone fit into this picture? What about Tom and Anthony? What exactly is God up to? Why is John comparing me to shoes? Are we made for each other?* Only God knew the answers to her questions.

She did know she was becoming attached to him. She felt he had always been there, even though they had only known each other a short time. He fit into *her* life like a comfortable old shoe too. And he gave her that dazzling feeling as well. Could she be falling in love again at her age?

John must have noticed her discomfort because he didn't pursue the conversation any further. She changed the subject. "Let's take our coffee and dessert into the den and get more comfortable."

When they went over to pick up their dessert bowls, Laura spotted only a small dab in her bowl. "What's this? You stinker. When I said not much, I meant more than a spoonful."

John broke out laughing. "Well, you said not much."

Laura took the ladle and gave herself a good helping. She probably piled on more than she would have otherwise.

Seated in the recliners, they made small talk about Christina's leaving on the morrow and their plans for the week. John planned a fishing trip, and Laura volunteered to work at the radio station and the area ministry for two days of the week.

"One of the men in the church told me about a group of men meeting this next weekend at something called Promise Keepers and invited me to go with him. I think I may accept the invitation. So, I'll be tied up this weekend, but I would like to see you during the week or next weekend." He looked to Laura for an answer.

"That sounds good to me. I've heard those Promise Keeper meetings are great. Many of the men, and their wives, rave about them. The women like the outcome and the changes in their husbands. I think you'll enjoy it." She hesitated and wondered if she should tell him about her weekend or not. She decided it wouldn't serve any purpose at this point. Not that she wanted to keep anything from him, but she needed to pray and sort out her place in each life. She depended on God to give her some direction.

When they finished eating, John spoke up. "We need to make it an early evening. I plan to be up at four for the fishing trip. I know you must want more time with Christina, so, I will say goodnight, now. Perhaps we can continue our earlier conversation about our feelings after the weekend." He gathered up his dishes and took them to the kitchen. He asked if he might say goodnight and goodbye to Christina.

"I'm sure she would like that. I'll get her." Laura walked to Christina's room and knocked on the door to tell her John was leaving.

Christina came to tell him goodbye. Unlike her usual behavior, she walked over and gave him a hug. "It has been such a pleasure to be with you this weekend."

John smiled and hugged her back. “The feeling is positively mutual. Let us know what you want for the holidays. Your Chef will try his best to fix what you like.”

“Okay. I will take you up on that.” She laughed as she headed back to her room and waved goodbye to John. “See you.”

Laura accompanied John to the door. He kissed her on the check and left. She watched him walk down the sidewalk to his car. Her heart felt heavy as if she were deceiving him. *Maybe I should have told him about my dates with Tom and Pastor Anthony.* She didn't want to hurt anyone. She considered Tom a friend and Anthony as just the new pastor in town. Still she felt disloyal, as if she were cheating.

CHAPTER FORTY

Something Missing

Christina left early for breakfast with her father. Hopefully, she had given up on the idea of getting her parents back together. Laura knew they'd never work out and maybe Christina had come to the same conclusion. From what Laura could see Christina liked John. But what if God had other ideas than John? How would Christina be affected? Laura pushed the concern away. *I must follow God and my heart and not let anyone else influence my decision.*

Christina came back before Laura could turn around, since she slept until almost eight, late for her. By nine-thirty, Christina returned obviously mulling something over. Laura watched her from the kitchen. Her demeanor led Laura to believe something had upset her. Christina sat down on the sofa and stared out the window into the back yard. At last, she walked into the kitchen, leaned on the granite countertop, and opened up.

"Mom, I'm sorry I tried to put you back together with Dad." Christina scowled, and her next words indicated her disgust. "He doesn't know what, or who, he wants. I think he's even fooling around on Jane now. I knew they weren't getting along, but he brought another woman to breakfast with us this morning. He introduced her as a fellow lawyer, but I bet something is going on between them."

"Honey, I'm sorry you had to witness that. Your dad does struggle with decisions in his life." In some ways Laura felt sorry for Frank. "I think we need to continue to pray for him. The main problem, in my estimation, he hasn't made a commitment to the Lord."

"Mom, I don't want my life to turn out like that. I want to be committed to the Lord. I thought about turning my life over to Him when John went to the altar, but I hadn't quite made up my mind." She took a deep breath. "You're right. That's what we all need in our lives, and I want to make a final decision today before I leave. Would you pray with me, Mom?" Tears coursed down her checks.

"Oh, Christina, I would be overjoyed to pray with you." Laura reached over and hugged her tightly. Tears rolled down her own face. "This is the answer to my most important prayer. I wanted you to sell out to the Savior, for I know the difference it can make in a life. Honey, just talk to God and tell Him your heart."

Laura held her daughter and led her in the sinner's prayer. "Lord Jesus, I ask you to come into my heart, forgive me of my sins, and take over my life. Thank you for dying on the cross for my sins. Thank you for shedding your blood, so that I might be saved." Laura led and Christina repeated her words.

Then, for a long time, Christina poured out her heart to the Lord. Finally, she lifted her head, her eyes shining with joy. "Mom I feel all clean and light, like a new person."

"That's what Jesus promises, that He will make us a new creation." Suddenly all barriers between them seemed to dissolve as they prayed together, and then talked with new openness until time to get ready to leave for the airport.

After loading the luggage and Christina's carry-on filled with brownies and other goodies, they drove through Chick-Fil-A for a sandwich then made their way to the airport.

Christina tried to talk with her mouth full. "Mom, I really do want to come home again as soon as I can, but Christmas might be more special with you and John."

"I don't know if there will still be a John and me by Christmas. What if the Lord has other plans? You know I have to follow the Lord in whatever decision I make."

"I understand, Mom, but I do hope our future includes John." Christina sounded a bit wistful. "I really like him, and I see he likes you and treats you the way you deserve. He's patient, kind, loving, accepting, and not demanding. If he were a few years younger, I might go for him myself."

They both laughed. "You remind me of Betty trying to sell me on John." Laura took a bite of her sandwich. "I guess you're picking up where she left off. I sure miss my friend. Have I told you about my new friend, Carol?" She turned to look in Christina's direction in time to see her take a huge bite.

Christina continued to chew for a few seconds before answering. "No, Mom, I don't think you've mentioned her."

"She's been a real friend to me since I lost Betty. I need to call her this week. She helps keep me on track, sort of like you and Betty. By the way, I plan to go tomorrow and get Caller ID on my phone." Laura filled their last moment together with a host of information.

Christina laughed. "You're getting so many callers these days. It might help you keep everyone straight. Just be sure and answer when I call, okay?"

They both laughed. Laura knew she didn't need to answer Christina's last question. It felt good to enjoy her daughter's company and not be in conflict. *The spiritual battle between us has ended, and we are now on the same frequency. But, I'll need to keep her ever present in my prayers, now more than ever or the enemy will try to devour her.* She remembered she hadn't prayed for John today and paused to say a silent prayer for him.

"Mom, thank you for this weekend and thanks for being there for me. I knew I lacked something in my life, and it took this weekend for me to find the peace I know I'll have walking daily with Christ. The peace you radiate in your life witnesses to those around you."

Laura treasured the numerous compliments Christina gave her during their visit.

But, this proved by far the best. She thought of the Scriptural promise in Proverbs 31:28 she wished to exhibit in her life. *Her children arise and call her blessed; her husband also, and he praises her.* Christina called her blessed! She wondered if a husband would praise her, or if there would be one.

"Thank you, sweetheart, that's the best compliment ever. And you have given me a lot this weekend. It helps me more than you know." Their eyes, misted with tears and radiating love and contentment, met.

"I meant everything I said. You're the greatest, Mom. You're a very pretty woman, and, I'm not just prejudiced. Just look! You have three men chasing you. I pray God will show you which one is worthy of you. I'm rooting for John."

Lost in her own thoughts about John, Laura didn't answer for a moment. So Christina continued. "You'd make a great pastor's wife, and I suppose Tom would make you a good living, but he'd travel much of the time."

All of a sudden Christina jumped in her seat, making the car lurch. "I know, Mom, you need to sit down and write down the pros and cons of each one!"

"Christina, you're so funny and analytical," Laura laughed. "You know that might not be a bad idea. However, again, it's in God's hands."

"I believe God would want you to have the best. He would want you to have someone who loves and treasures you and treat you like a queen. So don't settle for second best."

"All this advice from my daughter, my how things have turned around in our lives!" Laura said with amazement. "You remember this great advice you're giving me when you decide to choose your own husband, Christina."

"You have a point there, Mom. I'll try and do that. I'm eager to see Nathan. I do hope he's the one God chooses for me. I'll start my list as soon as I see him again."

When they arrived at the airport, Laura found it difficult to let Christina go. She didn't want their time together to end, especially in light of Christina's decision to follow Christ. "I hate to let you go. I wish you lived closer. But I feel happier than ever before, knowing we have a new spiritual relationship."

Christina's look of compassion warmed Laura's heart. "I know, Mom. I feel the same. But, we'll be together for some of the holidays."

Laura hugged Christina close and Christina hugged back with more emotion than Laura remembered her showing in a long time. Holding each other for as long as time allowed. Bittersweet tears formed in both sets of eyes, tears of happiness, as well as sadness. Laura knew their relationship soared to a higher level than just mother and daughter. Spirit proved thicker than blood. Laura's only sorrow lay in the fact they lived miles apart, for at least a few months, possibly longer.

After Laura left the airport, she headed home. *I must call Carol.* She missed her friend and could hardly wait to share her good news of all the exciting things God did. Carol would rejoice with her. The more she thought about the call the more urgent the phone call became. She couldn't wait, so she flipped open her phone and called as she drove.

"Hello?" Carol answered without calling her name, the way Betty used to do. *She must not have Caller ID, or else my cell phone doesn't register.*

"Hello." Laura practically sang with happiness.

"Laura, it's so good to hear from you. What've you been up to?" Carol sounded unusually happy herself.

"I'm coming home from the airport. I took Christina to fly back to school. What a great visit we enjoyed. I have so many things I want to share with you. Can you come over and visit this afternoon?"

"I'd love to, but I'm tied up right now." Carol hesitated. "Can we do it tomorrow afternoon? We're just fixin' to eat some barbeque Tom cooked on the grill."

"Well, I won't keep you, then." Laura hoped the disappointment didn't show in her voice. "How about coming by tomorrow for lunch? I'll make some sandwiches, and we can talk."

"That sounds great. I've got a few things to tell you too. See you then." The phone clicked in Laura's ear.

Laura pushed the end button on her phone. She wondered about Carol's mystery guest. She didn't know of a boyfriend in her life right now. *This must be something new. Can't wait to find out. Well, I will know tomorrow.*

Laura arrived home to an empty house. *Everything's quiet again.* She thought of phoning John, for she missed him being there almost as much as she did Christina, but reconsidered. Her old fashioned upbringing about calling men interfered again. She busied herself around the house, picked up from the weekend, and set things in order for the week.

Sitting down in her recliner to watch television, she couldn't keep her mind focused. She dug out her checkbook and balanced it, then, she took a book from her bookshelf she had been meaning to read. *Maybe John will call.* But he didn't.

She fell asleep and woke when the book fell on her chest. Yawning, she decided to dress for bed. The week ahead a busy one, her calendar full, she knew God held more excitement in store for her. Tomorrow she would relax, but after that, off to the races. But in the morning, she would call the phone company to install Caller ID. Then, she'd fix lunch for Carol and have a nice visit with her. *Who is her mystery guest?*

CHAPTER FORTY-ONE

Match Maker

Bright sun streamed into Laura's bedroom. The glare woke her. She shuffled to the window and declared with a yawn, "What a lovely day?" Thinking of the weekend's happenings warmed her insides. A hint of fall in the air revived her and added to her joy. Thankful for the cool mornings this time of year, still, she expected the heat of the day would most likely elevate to around ninety by the afternoon. She looked forward to the chill, and her daughter, November most likely would bring.

Pulling on a pair of shorts after bathing, something she wore around the house about nine months of the year. If not shorts, then peddle pushers, or Capris, their most recent name. She reflected on her younger days when people called them peddle pushers. If one waited long enough, things cycled in and out of style, only to be revived under a different name.

Laura finished her usual breakfast, then, started preparing lunch for Carol. She decided on fresh tuna salad over a delicious tomato along with her favorite club crackers. Something light would be appropriate for both watched their calories – most of the time. Having deli meat sandwiches almost everyday for lunch, she looked forward to this nice change. Not wanting to give up dessert, she fixed a low calorie blueberry pie. No more of that rich stuff like she ate over the weekend.

Her thoughts tumbled back to the weekend again. Why hadn't John called? She remembered how much he enjoyed the chocolate mousse, and the time spent together over the weekend, but she sensed something troubled him. Maybe they were getting too serious and he decided to back off a bit.

She wasn't quite sure how she felt about that. *Here I go again with these vain imaginations. I cast them down in the name of Jesus. I will just wait and see what God has in store for me.* She breathed a prayer. "Lord, you open or close the doors whatever is best for John and me."

Thinking about phone calls, she remembered her pledge to call the phone company to install Caller ID. Finished making the pie, she picked up the handset and dialed the phone company. The procedure, easy and painless, made her wonder why she hadn't done it sooner, instead of all the fretting. The representative told her it might take a few days to connect. A Caller ID phone already in place to register the calls, so all that remained consisted of the phone company turning the feature on from their computer. She looked forward to knowing who called before she answered.

She straightened up around the house, put on her make-up, and prepared for Carol's visit. While she waited for her friend, she worked on her Bible study lesson for the week. Laura enjoyed the challenge of reading through the entire Bible once every year. God's Word, always fresh, brought new revelation each day. Something new leapt off the pages, like His mercy, every day.

Today she decided to read in Proverbs. When she needed wisdom, she turned there. She read Proverbs 20:24 from the New American Standard Bible. *Man's steps are {ordained} by the LORD, How then can man understand his way?* This further confirmed her thought of letting God be in charge of her life. This brought to mind one of her favorite songs with the refrain, *Rejoice for the steps of a righteous man are ordered of God.*

Knowing God had everything in control gave her peace and made her realize she didn't need to orchestrate things herself. Learning how to let go, so God could work, always posed a challenge. She prayed for Christina and John, determining to do her part to help keep them from the enemy's clutches, especially in view of their new commitment to the Lord. A feeling of love flooded her when she remembered the decisions they both made.

She wanted to keep her vow by praying for them everyday, confident He also directed their lives and ordered their steps. As she went down her prayer list she prayed for the new pastor, Tom, and for her friend, Carol, who would arrive soon.

Just then, the doorbell rang. Carol arrived earlier than expected or else the time slipped away as she became entrenched in her Bible study and prayer time. She checked the clock over the mantle. Quarter to twelve. She liked the fact Carol came a few minutes early, so they could talk longer before sitting down to lunch. She hoped to catch up on Carol's life, especially her mystery guest.

Laura closed her Bible, laid it on the end table beside her, then rushed to the door. Carol stood there beaming. And she looked great. "What have you done with yourself?" Laura gave her a big hug. "Come in. You have lost a lot of weight and you look fantastic. Where are your glasses?"

"Well, I have been going to a weight loss program and have lost twenty-five pounds." Carol's voice held a hint of pride in her accomplishment.

"Come let's sit for a few minutes and talk." Laura ushered her into the den. "Tell me all about your success. I could learn a few tricks."

Laura took Carol's hand and looked her over again as they sat down next to each other on the sofa. "I'm so proud of you. Tell me more."

"Well, I've been doing this program. I lost some weight and decided to work on my appearance. I went to my eye doctor and got contact lenses, had a facial, bought new make up, bought myself some new clothes, plus you introduced me to your nail lady and hairdresser. So, I guess you could say I've had an extreme makeover."

"Wow." Laura could hardly believe her eyes. "You look absolutely radiant."

"I guess my efforts paid off because I met Tom Lockhart. Remember, the guy who stood you up one time." Carol hesitated and then continued. "He's really a great guy, just had some tough times. We seemed to click. We've had quite a weekend. We went to the movie on Friday night. He came over and fixed my leaky sink faucet on Saturday, and I fixed dinner for him. Then on

Sunday we went to church together. Monday he cooked barbeque for us on my grill."

Carol paused, out of breath. Laura felt stunned, but hoped it didn't show on her face. Then Carol continued. "We are supposed to see each other on Friday night. He's a really nice guy, Laura."

"Yes, I think he is, too." Laura didn't know what else to say.

"He told me the two of you have a date for this Saturday night, so if you're seeing him and interested I can back off. But, I'm confused. I thought you were dating John."

Laura sat with her mouth open. She didn't quite know how to answer Carol for a moment. When she finally found her voice she said, "I am seeing John. Tom came by last Friday and wanted to talk, but we couldn't talk right then. Christina had just gotten home. When did the two of you meet?"

"We met at church on Wednesday night in the singles group. Then, he called me Friday afternoon and asked if I wanted to take in a movie."

"Oh, I see." *Boy, that sure was fast.*

"I guess he chose me to talk to when you were tied up." Carol continued.

"He probably wants to talk to me on Saturday night about you then." Laura offered.

"I'm not sure. We do seem to get along great and fit together. I feel so at ease with him. He treats me like a queen. When we're together everything seems natural, as if we're a pair of comfortable old shoes."

"Maybe you're what Tom's been looking for. Maybe God ordained this. You know there are no coincidences with God, only God instances." Laura shook her head to clear her thoughts.

"He lives in the Woodlands. Oh, I guess you know that, but for some reason on Wednesday night he decided to come to the singles group at our church. " Carol continued to fill her in on the details.

"Does he go to a Baptist church in the Woodlands? I never asked him about his denomination. I just knew he was a Christian."

Carol shifted in her seat. "Yes, we're both Baptist. That seems to make things easier, being of the same denomination."

"Well, I'm sure Tom must want to talk to me about you." Laura did believe that must be the case. She didn't know why she felt such relief, but she did. "Carol,

I'm so happy for you. God seems to be giving me some insights too."

"What do you mean?" Carol's face showed a question mark.

"I've been asking Him to open and close doors for me, and I believe He's doing just that. I don't believe Tom is the one for me. Apparently, he's the one for you. How neat. I think we can all be friends."

During their time together, Laura and Carol talked about a variety of things: other friends, fashions, God's leading, John's and Christina's dedicating their lives to the Lord, their mutual friendship, Christina's new beau, Laura's new pastor and their antique date. They tried to catch up on everything happening in each other's lives. The clock gonged one before they finally realized they hadn't eaten. Carol clapped her hands together when she discovered Laura prepared a low calorie meal, allowing her to stay with her eating program.

Laura thought of how God even arranged the food. "Thank You, Lord." They spoke in unison. *Apparently, He remains the greatest matchmaker and planner ever!*

CHAPTER FORTY-TWO

Avoidance or Rejection

After Carol left, Laura cleaned the kitchen and finished the laundry she neglected during Christina's visit.

Suppertime rolled around and the day ended. John still failed to call. *Is he avoiding me?* Pangs of rejection filled her mind and heart. Some of the old sensations returned, especially after she found out Tom started dating Carol. The rejection tape played loud and clear with a vengeance. Satan's song kept repeating itself. *Nobody really cares about you because you aren't worth it.*

In her heart of hearts, she knew God's perfect choice for her wasn't Tom, even though a Christian and very handsome. Their temperaments didn't match. For fear of running ahead of God, she didn't want to say who she thought did. She had strong feelings for John whom she'd grown very fond of and missed terribly. *Maybe I should make the list Christina talked about.*

She sat down at her desk and pulled out a piece of paper and started writing. Without even thinking too much about her actions, she listed three names across the top – Tom, Anthony, John. *Now, I am to put pros and cons for each of them.* She made two columns under each name. One for Cons, and another for Pros. *What am I doing?*

She held the paper in her palms, ready to rip it into shreds, thought for a second, then put the paper back down. *Take a more logical approach Laura.*

Under the cons column for Tom she wrote:

Can't make up his mind just who he wants.

She had to laugh because in that way they were just alike. She entered more cons:

Doesn't seem to fit

Likes Carol

Different denomination

Then she wrote pros:

A Christian

Makes a good living

Handsome

We have history

A nice guy

Another con streaked through her mind:

Away from home a lot.

Laura smiled and spoke aloud. "Well, looks like he comes out about even."

I can't believe I'm doing this!

Now, for Anthony.

So far, I don't know him that well. She proceeded to list cons:

Not as good looking as Tom and John

A pastor's wife lives under pressure

Some church members won't like him marrying a divorced woman

"Now there's a big one," Laura said, her laugh echoing through the empty house.

Then under the pros she wrote:

Beautiful eyes

Likes antiques as much as I do

Spiritually strong

"Well now he's even too."

She hesitated a moment before doing John's profile. *What if he comes out even too? I've just wasted my time. Oh, well, there isn't much else to do right now.* So, she proceeded.

Not able to think of any cons right off, she started on the pros side.

She wrote quickly without stopping.

Pros:

Handsome

Kind

Thoughtful

Punctual

A Christian

She drew in a deep breath. Relieved she could say this now.

Makes my heart sing

I feel comfortable with him

We have many of the same interest

Christina likes him

We like the same food

He makes me feel like a queen

"And he even treats me like one."

Laura was tempted to stop there. But to be fair, she should weigh in on the negatives, too. *But what are they?* She couldn't think of any! *They say love is blind.* The realization hit her unexpectedly, and she had to admit she loved John. *I have fallen in love with John!* She leaned back in the chair, closed her eyes, and pulled in a deep breath.

I haven't even heard from him in two days. I might face another rejection? Maybe she needed to guard her heart. She hoped to see him tomorrow night at church. Perhaps she could tell more then.

Snapping on the television, she settled into the sofa and flipped through the channels, but nothing drew her interest. So, she made her way back to the desk and since she had paper and pen ready she decided to write some letters. She penned a long letter to Christina, even though they parted only yesterday, she wanted to encourage her and stress how much she enjoyed their visit.

Her friend Mary wrote a few days earlier, so Laura answered that letter. Other friends came to mind, and she scribbled notes to them. She told them about her and Frank's divorce. She informed her friends about moving on with her life and assured them things were going well for her. She wrote of Christina's visit, but did not tell them about John. She wanted to know where their relationship stood before spreading that news. She peered toward the phone several times, willing it to ring with John on the other end. Yet, it remained silent.

Finally Laura headed for bed. Her time at the radio station tomorrow would require her to get a good nights rest. She looked forward to the Christian atmosphere and some of her favorite people's company.

The day would be long. When she finished around four, she would need to rush home, grab a bite, and then rush to church for the midweek service. She could hardly wait to see John.

***

Laura arrived at church a few minutes early. Pastor Anthony caught her in the hallway. "I'm so glad I ran into you, at least this time not literally, but I wanted to tell you something came up for Friday. The board wants to go over some things with me, and I don't know how long the meeting will take. I better request a rain check on our antique shopping. Can we do it again some other time?"

"Of course." She smiled. *His eyes don't look quite as clear today.* Could the Lord be closing another door? *I hope he doesn't close them all? Still, no John.*

Laura sat through the service on edge for the first half, her stomach doing flip- flops. She glanced nervously at the door every time it opened and someone walked in. *God is in control.* She reminded herself once more. Then she relaxed and listened to the Lord instead of her pounding heart.

When she arrived home, the answering machine didn't blink any messages. She lifted the handset to make sure the phone worked. The hum of the dial tone convinced her. She punched the button for the Caller ID to see if it registered yet. Sure enough, it did. Knowing the apparatus worked gave her a moment of hope only to have it slashed when she viewed the list of calls. Sears, American Express, Clothing Donations, and some other places of advertisement she didn't recognize registered. But, no calls showed up from the one person from whom she longed to hear.

***

She drove toward the station the next morning, convinced that staying busy would keep her mind off John's lack of response. However, curiosity overcame her and she went by John's house. His car, parked in the driveway, made her even more curious. Maybe he rode with someone else. He mentioned another guy asked him to go to Promise Keepers. She thought of several scenarios and found herself worrying. Then she remembered the Scripture in Philippians chapter four verse six about not worrying. *Be anxious for nothing, but in everything by prayer and supplication with thanksgiving let your requests be made known to God.* So she prayed for John, and herself.

The day at the station went quickly. Before she turned around, the clock read four o'clock. On her way home, she passed John's house. No car occupied the driveway. Perhaps, he left for Promise Keepers early. She couldn't imagine why he didn't call and keep in touch. He usually kept her abreast of his whereabouts.

She relied on staying apprised, and now it drove her crazy not knowing. Tempted to call his cell phone, old-fashioned guilt shot through her. *Girls don't call boys.* So, she resisted. He would return home by Sunday and attend church. She wondered if she could wait until then. When she arrived home, no messages showed on the answering machine. She checked the Caller ID and saw some calls listed. She scrolled through. No call from John, but she did receive one from Christina.

Shaking off her sadness over no call from John, she could hardly wait to phone her daughter. She slipped off her shoes and sat down to rest for a moment, and then reached for the phone.

"Hel loo?"

Laura's heart sank deeper. Concerned now with her daughter's despair. "Christina, are you all right?"

"No, Mom. Nathan and I split up. Apparently, he's not the one for me. I thought he might be, but guess I thought wrong. You know it sometimes hurts when God closes doors."

"Yes, sweetheart, I know." She smiled to herself, knowing all too well.

"When I brought up coming there for Thanksgiving or Christmas, he wouldn't hear of it. He's such a mama's boy." Christina's voice rose with disgust. "I can't believe anyone could be so selfish. I knew right away by his attitude, things would not work out between us. I would turn into a doormat to please him, or else we would argue all the time. I noticed his self-centeredness in other things as well."

"God does have the best for you. Don't settle for second best. Wait for His timing, and He'll bring the right mate for you, honey." Laura shifted in her seat, wondering if she could take her own advice.

"Mom, you sound like a voice of experience, but I wonder how good you did." Before the words could sting, Christina offered her an apology. "I'm sorry, Mom, I didn't mean that. I guess I'm just a bit upset."

"I know, honey." Laura lowered her voice and continued. "I'm putting things in God's hands now, instead of trying to do it myself. I've messed up so far, but now I'm trusting and relying on God. We both should. Frank could have been God's choice for me. But sometimes, we don't all cooperate with His plan. I know one thing, out of our marriage came a very good thing – you!"

"Thank you. You're probably right, Mom," Christina sounded a little more perky than when the conversation began. "I'll get over it in a few days. Anyway, I have my studies to think about. Also, I can come home at both Thanksgiving and Christmas, if we can afford it."

"One way or another, we will afford it!" Laura's voice rose with excitement about the thought of Christina's homecoming.

"By the way, the next time you meet a nice young man you might try the pros and cons you told me about."

"Why, did you try it?"

"Yes, Christina, I admit, I did." Laura smiled with chagrin and felt a flush of heat rush to her face. "I won't tell you the results right now, but soon I'll let you know the outcome. I don't know everything for sure myself yet!"

"Mother, this sounds rather intriguing." Christina's voice increased in volume. "Why don't you tell me now?"

"I need to wait a few days, honey. Then I'll let you know if it really worked or not." Laura switched the phone to her other ear. She realized they both ached from all the calls during the day.

"I think the best thing we can do is continue to trust the Lord." Christina repeated Laura's earlier statement. Her tone now on the eleventh floor, instead of the basement.

Laura puttered round the house after she hung the phone. Food didn't look too appetizing, but she ate anyway. The small salad and half a sandwich filled her empty spot. She bathed. Happy to get into her nightgown and robe, she relaxed. Flipping through the mail, she found only advertisements – or junk mail she called it. She landed at her desk once more to do her Bible study. One of her favorite Scriptures, Proverbs 3:5-6, caught her eye. *Trust in the Lord with all your heart and lean not on your own understanding; in all your ways acknowledge him and he will make your paths straight.*

The pros and cons method helped her realize her true feelings. But ultimately, she knew the Lord directed her path and would make it straight.

Now, with no date on Friday, she decided to go shopping. She hadn't been to her clothing stores since she and Carol met several weeks ago. She might experience withdrawal from one of her favorite past times. She located her kitchen sheers, clipped the coupons from the paper, and got ready for tomorrow's entertainment. A form of enjoyment rather than an obsession, yet, she knew she must watch herself.

Laura shifted in her recliner and tried to focus on the movie on television, but soon her eyes grew heavy and she dozed off. Then a loud commercial interrupted her nap. She awoke with a start and made her way to bed. Still half dazed, she thought about the shoe sales for the following day. Anything to keep her mind off John. The diversion didn't work. Now wide-awake, her heart thumped wildly in her chest. What if John were purposely avoiding or rejecting her? Her heart slowed as she reminded herself that God would never reject her. He had the best plan for her life.

She stared at the ceiling. Prayer rose from her lips as she asked God to deliver her from this anxiety. God's peace washed through her as she mediated on Him. As she dwelt on God's acceptance, her fears of rejection slowly took a back seat. Hot tears stung her cheeks, and she whispered, "Thank You, sweet Lord."

CHAPTER FORTY-THREE

Shop Until You Drop

Laura might not be cut out for the dating game, but shopping fit her to a tee, as they say. Even at her age, she could shop all day, at least most of the day. Today was no different. She left the house at ten, shopped until noon at Dillard's, and stopped to eat lunch at Luby's.

After lunch, she walked into Foley's and dug in for an afternoon of bargain hunting. She found a pair of shoes on the seventy-five percent off rack and some dresses for the same type of savings. She loved getting bargains she could use. And these items she could wear at church.

She rejoiced and believed the Lord had delivered her from overspending. She made selective purchases now.

The summer clearance racks spilled over with bargains. However, she selected only a few items. She didn't need more summer clothes, so she resisted the urge to buy just because something was on sale. She wanted to save the money for Christina to come home for the holidays.

She also needed to think about money for holiday gifts. A few bargains she bought to stow away as Christmas presents. Around three o'clock, she tired. She didn't want to literally shop until she dropped. So, she loaded all her bargains in the car and drove toward home.

Upon arriving, she collapsed into her lounge chair and caught her breath. She rested for a few minutes. But soon the phone rang. Thinking it might be John, she ran to grab it, but noticed the Caller ID registered a call from the church, probably Pastor Anthony.

She pushed the talk button. "Hello." She didn't have the nerve to say Pastor Anthony. Betty would have, but she needed to get to know the pastor a little better before she could.

"Hello, Laura. I wanted to apologize for breaking our date, and to let you know we probably won't get to have a rain check."

"Oh?"

"Yes, the board and I don't seem to be in agreement about the vision for this church, so I will be moving on. It's been nice knowing you, even for this short period of time." His voice didn't have its usual perky sound.

She pulled herself upright. “What are your plans?”

“For now, I’ll probably go back to New Mexico where my children live, but I’ll look around for another position. I’m not ready to retire just yet.”

“From the sermons you’ve preached, I don’t think the Lord wants you to retire either.” She couldn’t imagine the differences the board found with him. “I’m sorry you’ll not be staying here. I know the church would benefit.”

“Thank you for the kind words, but I think the Lord has other plans for me. May He bless you until we meet again. If not here on earth, I will look forward to seeing you in heaven.”

“Bless you, too, Pastor Anthony.” To her surprise, a few tears clouded her eyes, for her personal loss or for the churches? Maybe both.

She hung up and recognized the Lord’s plan, or His lack of a plan for Pastor Anthony in her life. At least, she thought she did. He had been there long enough for John to dedicate his life to the Lord. But, he wasn’t God’s choice for her. W*ow, the Lord has closed another door really fast. How much clearer could it be? What about*

John? Will the Lord close that door too? At least, so far, no one has gotten hurt. Thank You for that, Lord!

She took out her Bible for more study, and the comfort the Word always brought her. Today she found herself going to her standby Scripture. *And we know that in all things God works for the good of those who love him, who have been called according to his purpose.* Romans 8:28 *(NIV)*

She knew she loved God and He had called her, so she felt confident He would work everything for her good. She read on in the passage and found further comfort, especially when she read verses thirty-eight and thirty-nine: *For I am convinced that neither death nor life, neither angels nor demons, neither the present nor the future, nor any powers, neither height nor depth, nor anything else in all creation, will be able to separate us from the love of God that is in Christ Jesus our Lord.*

She could count on His love forever and always. He would be there for her, no matter if anyone else remained or not. He had only the best prepared for her. He would give her exactly who and what she needed in her life.

That night she went to bed comforted by the mighty Word and love of the Lord. Peace flooded in, even when anxious thoughts about John wormed their way into her thoughts. God loved John more than she did, and He would bless John with what he needed as well. She wanted to be part of that plan, but time and God would tell.

Saturday, Laura looked forward to her trip to the beauty salon. She lounged around, read her Bible, ate her usual light breakfast, dressed, and went to have her hair and nails done. She, also, looked forward to Tom's visit, but still felt guilty.

She regretted not telling John, and now she felt bad about taking him away from Carol for the evening. When she returned home, she rearranged some things in her closet to make room for the new additions she had purchased yesterday. Before she knew it, time sped away and Tom's arrival grew eminent.

The doorbell rang right at seven. Tom stood there with flowers in hand. I*s this a courting gesture, or a peace offering before he brings the news about him and Carol?*

"These are for you." He smiled and handed her the bouquet. "You have been a good friend to me, and I want to thank you."

"Come in." She motioned to the den, and he took a seat in the recliner. I will put these in some water. She walked into the kitchen found a vase and arranged the beautiful array of flowers. When she returned to the den, she sat on the couch opposite him.

She could tell he had something on his mind and decided to make the conversation easier for him. "Carol came over for lunch the other day. I understand you two are seeing each other now."

"Well, yes," he mumbled.

"I think that's just great!" She shook her head in agreement with her statement. "You two will probably fit together perfectly."

He studied her as if trying to see if she were upset or sincere. He looked directly into her eyes and careened his neck closer. "Do you really think so?"

"Yes, I think that's lovely." She repeated her affirmation.

"I'm so glad you understand. The other day when I came here I thought maybe you and I should get back together. I really like you. The way you love the Lord inspires me. Then, I met Carol. We hit it off. I don't really know where it's taking us, but it seems something, or someone beyond us, has control of our relationship."

"Yes, Tom. I think the Lord orchestrates our steps. I believe, He orders yours and Carol's in this."

"Me, too." A huge grin spread over his face. "I do want us to always be friends, Laura. You have been more of an influence in my life than you know." He leaned forward. "Because of your walk with the Lord, I found myself drawing closer to Him. I've watched your life and because of the stands you take, I want to stand, instead of fluctuate."

"Thank you, Tom. You flatter me." Laura didn't blush this time. But she felt warm fuzzes go up her spine and her heart wanted to burst with gladness.

"No. Thank *you*, Laura." He jumped up from the recliner and gave her a hug.

"Are you ready to order pizza now?" He asked as he let her go.

"Not quite. One thing I think we should do first. Let's call Carol and make this a threesome? I'd like that, and I know you and she would, too. I'd like having two of my closest friends here tonight."

"That'd be super." His face lit up at the mention of Carol's name.

Laura picked up the phone and dialed Carol's number.

Yes, the Lord had closed some doors today but opened other doors of friendship and fellowship.

CHAPTER FORTY-FOUR

Open or Closed

The evening turned into great fun for the threesome. Laura enjoyed seeing both Carol and Tom so happy. The three of them played a card game called 'Hand and Foot.' Laura won, but she could tell Carol and Tom felt like winners too. It would be interesting, to say the least, to see what the Lord had planned for the two of them.

They left around ten-thirty. Laura had choir practice early the next morning. And Tom and Carol attended church service around the corner from Laura's church. However, they didn't arrive until nine-thirty for Sunday school. Laura started her choir practice at nine. A thought crossed her mind. *I wonder who will preach in the morning.*

She didn't tell Tom and Carol about their new pastor leaving. She didn't want to start any rumors, and she didn't know all the facts. As much as she loved Carol, she knew how she could spread a story. Laura only knew God closed a door and Pastor Anthony planned to leave.

The rumor mill would start soon enough. A few gossips and busybodies occupied the pews of any church. No perfect churches existed, because they were filled with imperfect people. However, she did hate the damage busybodies, talebearers, and gossips caused.

She woke early the next morning, and wondered if John might call or meet her at church. She dressed in one of the new outfits, along with the new shoes. The stiletto heel, a little higher than she usually wore, but she thought she could stand them, and they were the latest style.

Besides the taupe accented her turquoise dress. She fished in her closet to find a matching purse. She found two and opted for the clutch rather than the shoulder bag. Rummaging through her jewelry box, she found just the right turquoise jewelry to highlight the outfit.

When she looked into the mirror, her reflection pleased her. *Am I becoming too vain?* But didn't the Lord want her best in His house on His day? *Not to mention if John's there. No harm in looking good just in case. I am smitten with this guy, and acting like a teenager.* The wrinkles in her forehead and around her eyes told her differently, but she still felt young inside.

She started to walk out the door and the phone rang. She checked the Caller ID and held her breath. She saw John's number. Excitement overtook her and she almost dropped the phone. She heard John's voice saying, "Hello, hello, hello."

She finally managed to get the receiver to her ear. "Hello."

"Laura, I'm sorry I haven't called you this week, but I've wanted to get some things sorted out." Her hand gripped the receiver tighter. "Then, I went to the Promise Keeper's conference. But I'd like to invite you to lunch at my house today, so we can talk."

"That sounds nice. I want to talk with you too. I've missed you very much. Will you be coming to church?"

"Certainly, I'll be there."

What could John want to talk about? Was he leaving, or had he found someone else? Was God shutting another door on her? Whatever. She knew she and God could handle it. Her heart cried out for John to care for her as she did for him. She sat in the car ready to go and discovered her purse and keys missing. *Well, I won't get very far like this.* Luckily, a spare house key lay under the front door mat.

Her mind drifted in and out on the way to church. She almost ran a red light. Thankfully, she snapped to in time to stop. At the next light, the impatient honk from the car behind her reminded her the light changed. She waved to the driver. *Could be someone who knows me, but I doubt that's why he honked.*

She finally pulled into the church parking lot and went into the choir room. Relieved she didn't run into the pastor this morning. She wondered if he left already, or if he would preach. Laura stared into space more than once during practice. Her mind whirled, and she shook her head. Would she be able to concentrate by church time?

She hoped she wouldn't forget the words to the solo scheduled for her this morning. She practiced some self-talk and prayed. And managed to sing without a hitch. She looked back and John sat in their usual spot, saving a place for her. He didn't look upset or sad. As a matter of fact, he wore a huge grin on his face. However, at times she saw him stare off to no place in particular, just as she had earlier.

When the choir went down into the auditorium, Laura sat beside him. He seemed happy to see her, and took her hand in his immediately. She wanted to shout and hug him, but restrained herself. The love in her heart for him overflowed. His absence did make her know how much she cared for him, and the checklist helped her realize how much she wanted to see him. She now knew how much she valued and appreciated him. He meant a great deal to her. She prayed the feelings were mutual.

One of the deacons came to the pulpit. “Pastor Anthony decided not to stay. He plans to go back to New Mexico. Things didn’t work out for him here. So, this morning we will have a visiting preacher. One I know you all will enjoy. Let’s make welcome, Pastor Stan Wilder.”

Pastor Wilder preached a good sermon. Laura wondered if the whole truth about Pastor Blake would come out within the next few weeks. She knew a lot of stories would go around. Perhaps, Pastor Wilder would be God’s choice for the congregation. Only time and God would tell.

“Why don’t you go home and get into something more comfortable.” John remarked after the service. “You look beautiful, but put on your jeans or slacks.” He knew she liked to wear pants. He probably noted she struggled to walk in the higher heels. “In the meantime, I’ll get lunch on the table.”

"What are we having?" Her curiosity reminded her of Betty's.

"I'm making one of my secret recipe roasts today." He grinned like a sheepish little boy proud of his endeavors.

"I love roast, but I'm the one who usually cooks them." The flashback of the time Laura gave her roast to Betty because Frank hadn't come home wanted to intrude in Laura's thinking but she wisped it away. She had moved on with her life. Laura grinned at John's obvious pride in his cooking.

"This time you get to sit back and let someone else do the labor. Enjoy yourself!"

"I sure plan to." She crossed her arms in front of her body and tilted her head from one side to the other, enjoying the exchange.

At her house, she changed into her jeans and a quarter length sleeve pullover blouse. John kept his house a little cooler than she did, so she wanted to be comfortable. She smiled as she remembered he told her she looked beautiful.

Sure enough, when she arrived, lunch sat on the table. Roast, salad, mashed potatoes, glazed carrots and hot rolls. He ushered her to the table and said the grace. *My, what great things God has done.*

The tender succulent roast separated easily with a fork. The creamy potatoes made just the way she liked them. The glazed carrots tasted of honey and cinnamon. She wanted to find out what type of rolls. For store bought, they tasted marvelous. John must have made his own salad dressing for she didn't recognize the flavor. It tasted of honey and lime. Yes, lime.

Laura complimented John on the meal numerous times. She forgot about the butterflies in her stomach in face of the delicious meal and stuffed herself.

When they finished the main course, John said, "We'll have dessert later."

They sat at the table and the story poured forth. "Laura, I've been doing a lot of thinking, praying, and deciding in the last week."

"Me, too." She searched his blue eyes.

"When I heard you make a date with the new pastor, jealousy almost overtook me, and I wanted to confront you. But, I thought better of it. I've known about your seeing Tom Lockhart, but that stopped. I'd hoped because of me. Then, I found out, his ex-wife appeared back on the scene. You see Laura, in a small church, town, and community everyone knows what's going on."

"I'm sorry, John, I just wanted to be friends with them, and I didn't know what God's plan entailed for me. She looked away. "I think most people come into my life for a reason, a season, or a lifetime. I wanted God to use me in each life, however he saw fit. I should've told you." She looked back at his handsome face.

"You didn't really owe me any explanation, but I didn't want to make a fool of myself. If you were interested in one of them, I figured I'd bow out. Then, I thought, why should I bow out? I love you, Laura, and I'm willing to fight for you, if that's what it takes."

He said he loved me!

Laura couldn't say a word for a minute for the lump in her throat and tears stung her eyes, so John continued, "I've been praying and seeking the Lord at this Promise Keeper's, and even before I went. I've been asking Him to open or close the door, whatever's best for all of us."

Laura started to laugh almost uncontrollably. John's eyebrows shot up; he looked at her and said, "What's so funny?"

"I've been praying the same way and God answered."

"What do you mean?"

"God closed and opened doors for us. After I realized my true feelings for you, Tom found his true love. At least we think so. Pastor Anthony plans to move back to New Mexico. God showed us our love for each other. He made it plain to me that you were His choice. I love you too, John, very much."

At those words, John got up from the table, took Laura's hand, pulled her to himself and kissed her passionately. She fit into his arms like a comfortable old shoe, but one that glowed new and shiny.

Laura snuggled in John's arms and prayed their relationship would last forever. God put it together. She had learned so much this past year. The strength she gained through the process would help her minister to others. She knew love must be something you do. She would love John with all her might.

The possibility of rejection in the future entered her mind, but she knew with her God she could handle anything, for the Beloved held her in His palm. The plans He had for her were good. With Him, she had hope and a future. He would be there for her no matter what the circumstances. He would never leave or forsake her. She need not worry or be anxious for anything. Finding love with John would be worth the risk.

She had truly traded old shoes and habits for new.

#

About the Author

Charlotte holds a Bachelor's degree in English and a Master's in Special Education. After teaching public school for 30 years, she retired to teach and write for Him. Upon retirement, she taught a women's Bible study for five years, using Kay Arthur's *Precept Upon Precept* studies. Then the Lord prompted her to write full time. She loves the Lord with all her heart and wants to share that love with others. For a number of years, Charlotte gave books to others to read of God's love; finally, she decided to write some of my own. Her main passion is to spread the gospel message. She believes through writing she can reach more people than by any other method. She enjoys the process of writing and feels the Master's pleasure when she writes. Her purpose in life is to please Him. Like Jeremiah, His word and message is like fire in her bones. She cannot be silent. She likes to write across the genres: nonfiction, fiction, poetry, devotionals, articles, short stories, and songs. Recently, she went back to leading Bible study as well. She also loves to speak, especially to groups of women. She lives in northwest Houston with her husband of 32 years. Charles owns and operates North Houston Exterminators.

AFFILIATIONS/ORGANIZATIONS:

ACFW (American Christian Fiction Writers)

CWGI (Christian Writers Group International)

IWA! (Inspirational Writers Alive!)

WOTS (Writers On the Storm) local ACFW

Humble Retired Teachers Association

Glorieta Christian Writers Conference Alumni

Mount Hermon Writers Conference Alumni

Delaware Christian Writers Conference Alumni

Colorado Christian Writers Conference Alumni

Greater Philadelphia Christian Writers Conference Alumni

Sandy Cove Christian Writers Conference Alumni

ACFW Conference Alumni

Blue Ridge Christian Writers Conference Alumni

A Sample of published works with release dates

NON-FICTION BOOKS

Praise the Lord for Roaches! (Publish America/December 2002)

Inspirations Book of Anthology (Hurley House Publishing/Dec. 2004)

Charlotte Holt

Contributor for *I Must Decrease* by Janice Thompson (Barbour 2005)

Contributor for *Memories of Mothers (Xulon Press 2007) Multi-Colored Love*

Contributor for *Miracles and Rescues* (Guideposts Books 2007) *God Comforts the Broken Heart*

Contributor for *Miracles and Nature* (Guideposts Books 2008) *Asleep in the Boat*

Contributor for *A Scrapbook of Christmas First* (Leafwood Publishers 2008) *Waffle House*

Contributor for *Secrets to Parenting your Adult Child* (Bethany House 2011) *Handle Disappoints with Care*

Contributor for *Hurray God!* (Wine Press Publishing 2011) *Prayer Confirmation*

ARTICLES:

A Model for Sunday School **(http://sundayschool.ag.org/ 2004)**

Dreams Come True: 7 Keys to Publication **(http://spiritledwriter.com. /June 2004)**

Come Home, It's Suppertime **(Nostalgia Magazine /August 2004)**

Mistletoe Madness **(**www.americanchristianfictionwriters.com **/December 2005)**

Hawaii in Texas (www.bestplaceshawaii.com **/February 2006)**

Turn a Frog into a Prince (Living Magazine /**Spring 2007)**

Ten Essential 'E's for Writers (http://spiritledwriter.com /**March 2007)**

Easter Celebration **(http://www.humblewms.blogspot.com/ April 2009)**

The Exchange (Teachers of Vision Magazine/ **Winter 2012)**